BOOK 1 OF
THE ODYSSEY OF JON SINCLAIR

BlackHeart's Legacy

Sally Copus

ISBN: 1450534422
ISBN-13: 9781450534420
LCCN: 2010900617

For my grandchildren:

Caleb, Peter, Sarah and Zachary

Spanish Main

Atlantic Ocean

ds

San Juan

St. Martin
Barbuda
Antigua

Port au Prince

Santo Domingo

Puerto Rico

St. Kitts

Montserrat

Guadeloupe

paniola

Dominica

Martinique

Sea

St. Lucia

Barbados

St. Vincent

Curacao

Grenada

Tobago

Tortuga Margarita

Coro

Trinidad

Gibraltar

Puerto Cabello Borburata Caracas

Cumana

TABLE OF CONTENTS

ILLUSTRATIONS

CHAPTER 1

TIME-TRAVEL

Midwestern United States, May 1, 2010 AD

The long nails of Trek's feet clicked loudly on the floor tiles as he snorted and sniffed around the back door. Suddenly, he barked and yipped anxiously, turning round and round as the door burst open and Jon stuck his head through the opening.

"Sit, Trek!" Jon commanded. The silver Siberian husky immediately sat down, his tail wagging and whacking the floor. The dog's blue-gray eyes were fixed adoringly on the brown-haired youth.

"We're ready to go, Pappy," Jon said. "I stowed my trunk aboard the *Carousel*." Jon had been studying American history and wanted to travel back in time to Philadelphia, July 4, 1776, to watch the forty-two men sign their names approving the Declaration of Independence. Time travel was not new to the Sinclairs, but only recently had Jon and his grandmother travelled without Alistair, and then only into time periods that Alistair considered safe.

Alistair Sinclair had planned to go on this trip with his wife and grandson, but some urgent matters had come up at NASA that needed his particular expertise. *The two weeks they'll be away will give me the perfect opportunity to work here at the house undisturbed*, he thought. Even though Alistair had retired from NASA recently, they still had need of the astro-scientist's vast knowledge and experience on occasion. This was one of those times.

Jon appeared in the doorway with a grimace on his face. "Grammy's still upstairs grumbling about the stiff, uncomfortable clothes she'll have to wear to look the part of an eighteenth-century lady. Could you get her to hurry up, Pappy?" Jon asked.

"Me? You want me to go up there and tell your grandmother to hurry? You don't like having me around, do you?" Alistair asked, raising one eyebrow with a smirk. Jon broke into a giggle, and Alistair was chuckling with him as Kathryn entered the kitchen. She eyed them both suspiciously.

Alistair smiled at his wife. She was a tall, slender woman who looked too young to be a grandmother. In fact, most of her tennis buddies enviously said she looked like she was nineteen or twenty years old. She prided herself that her short brown hair was virtually without gray—at least, for now.

Alistair was very confident that Kathryn could handle the *Carousel* without him, particularly with the most recent computer hardware he had built and installed.

"Let's go!" she said curtly, smoothing her hair back behind her ears. She was wearing her favorite work clothes: white cotton pants cropped just below the knees, athletic shoes, and one of Alistair's long-sleeved, white dress shirts.

"Uh … did you forget to change your clothes, Kathryn?" Alistair asked quietly, covering his grin. Jon pretended not to hear.

"Yes. On purpose!" she replied. "I'll put on those uncomfortable clothes and the white wig I bought when we're ready to leave the *Carousel* in Philadelphia, but not a minute sooner." Turning to Jon, she said, "Ready to go?"

Jon nodded and was out the door. He waved the dog away as he ran toward the barn. He didn't want Trek to tear the knickers and blousy shirt that Kathryn had made for him. With the old-looking shoes and white cotton knit stockings to complete his outfit, twelve-year-old Jon looked just like the boys of 1776. He had complained about wearing the white stockings until Kathryn showed him pictures of boys of that time. Gradually he accepted the idea, and the clothes.

"Trek, you're staying here at Three Forks with Pappy to keep him company. There won't be a place for you to stay on this trip," Jon said, rubbing Trek's ears and jowls. He was rewarded with big slurpy kisses on his neck and chin.

While Alistair and Jon put Kathryn's trunk in a storage closet of the *Carousel*, she sat down in the red leather seat of the great white swan, facing the computer console. She keyed in a few codes, and several lights blinked on the console. There was a slight vibration as the hydrogen- and solar-powered engines of the *Carousel* began to whirr. The "Power Source Ready" icon blinked brightly on the computer screen.

"Remember our rule, Kathryn," Alistair cautioned. "Stay no longer than two weeks. We're not ready to test the time window beyond that."

"Don't worry; we should be back well before then. I'll be ready to throw out those pointy-toed boots and put on these sneakers," she said, looking down at her comfortable, slightly worn black athletic shoes.

Alistair gave them a hug and a kiss and stepped off the platform. He and Trek had reached the house by the time the roof of the barn slid open and the old relic carousel grew to its three-story height. Gone was the brightly colored antique carousel; in its place stood the majestic, silver time-travel capsule: *Carousel*.

A misty blue gas filtered off the pointed, cylinder shape of the ship, down its sides, and through the open barn door. Staying close to the ground, the blue mist flowed outward, confirming the ship's origination point in time. The mist pulsed up tree trunks, the farm house, the barn walls and fences. Every blade of grass, the rock layers of a nearby bluff, and even the layers of soil were identified as the mist rapidly mapped Three Forks, which was home to the three Sinclairs. This molecular mapping was essential to the *Carousel*'s return to this exact place and time. Should the path deteriorate or become compromised, Jon and Kathryn could be lost forever.

All at once, the mist was sucked back up into the ship, and Alistair knew that Kathryn had initiated the launch sequence; there was no turning back now, just as there had been no turning back for Jon's parents on the morning of their mysterious, fatal plane crash. The events of that morning long ago weighed heavily on his mind as

Alistair watched the metallic *Carousel* slowly disappear, carrying with it the two people on earth he most loved.

The computer monitor inside the ship displayed the view outside the *Carousel* as Jon and Kathryn watched the objects on the ground grow smaller. And then, with a loud *poof*, they were gone!

Inside the *Carousel*, Jon sat strapped in his seat next to Kathryn at the console as the ship swirled slowly in the familiar time vortex.

Suddenly, there was a hard jolt! The *Carousel* began to vibrate and rock side to side with great force. Jon grabbed Kathryn's arm and held onto her as she began clicking all the levers on the console to no avail. Jon could feel gravity pulling at him. His back ached immensely, as if he were being molded into his seat. Everything swirled above him as the ship vibrated and rolled until Jon thought his teeth would shatter out!

There was a terrible knocking noise and a loud sucking sound. Jon felt as if he were in some kind of vacuum, being pulled rapidly down, down, down. And then a jolting thud—and the ship stopped moving!

CHAPTER 2

DISHONEST DEALINGS

Port Royal, Jamaica, May 1, 1692 AD

Sitting at the end of a long pier that stretched out into the turquoise waters of the Caribbean Sea was a tall, stately black ship. Two men walked together on the deck when, very abruptly, an argument and struggle erupted between them. One of the men pulled his sword and shoved the other man high against the ship's side rail.

"*BlackHeart*, ye sleazy bilge rat! There was *no* treasure on that island, like ye *swore* there would be!" shouted the man holding his sword tip to the throat of the taller man in a captain's coat. A crowd of crewmen immediately encircled the two quarrelling men.

"A *minor* detail, Sleg!" Captain BlackHeart spit out as he stared down the long, shiny blade of Sleg's sword and straight into Sleg's beady black eyes.

The crewmen immediately pulled Sleg off BlackHeart and helped their captain off the side railing of his ship and into a standing position.

"Minor detail? Avast! Ye always sez that, ye do. It is not *minor*. And it is not a *detail*!" shouted Captain Sleg.

"You're worse than a thief o' thieves. You're a scourge straight from Davy Jones hisself!"

BlackHeart rolled his eyes and twisted his mouth into a disbelieving smirk, which caused his pointed black moustache to quiver on the ends as he looked at the pathetic excuse for a pirate captain.

Captain Sleg and three of his men had come aboard BlackHeart's ship acting friendly enough, but now Sleg's temper had him in a snit. It would not pay to let Sleg think he had the upper hand on BlackHeart's own ship. BlackHeart punched his long finger forcefully into the dirty, wrinkled ruffles of Sleg's once white shirt, thus shoving him backward a step or two. Sleg's peg leg slipped, and he almost fell on the clean, wet deck of the *Black Opal*.

"You, me misled miscreant, do not trust the honor of any man! I sticks to me code," snarled BlackHeart, lifting his chin in defiance and self-assurance.

"And what exactly *is* your code?" snapped Captain Sleg, squinting his eyes in distrust at Captain BlackHeart.

"Well-ll, I keeps me code secret from the likes of you," BlackHeart said smugly. Sleg swiftly brought his sword back up to BlackHeart's throat, pressing it close under his chin and forcing him backward against the railing. Again, BlackHeart's men pulled Sleg away from their captain.

"Curly, me thinks we may have to remove the fine captain's sword, so's we can get on with this dispute," BlackHeart said to his boatswain.

When Curly placed his hand on Sleg's sword to take it, three of Sleg's men grabbed at their swords. But they thought better of the idea and stepped back when several of BlackHeart's men moved forward, cutlasses in hand. Without any more fuss, Curly removed Sleg's sword from his hand.

"Now, as I was saying," BlackHeart went on, "the trade we made was one of great value for you, Sleg. Your three thousand gold Spanish doubloons for me prized, pure gold Aztec eagle warrior, which just happens to be buried on me island, near Pirates Cay. And, just to assist you in your digging, I might add, I already gave you the map!"

"You're forgetting one thing: it was *not there*!" yelled Sleg.

"You didn't dig deep enough," BlackHeart said slyly as a new strategy to outsmart Sleg came into his mind. "How deep did you dig?"

"Twenty feet!" roared Sleg, his bloodshot eyes glaring.

"Oh, well ... hardly deep enough," BlackHeart drawled as he gave Sleg a sideways glance. "No wonder ye found nothing. I wouldn't bury any treasure that shallow for fear that even a stupid pirate could find it. That's why I buried the Aztec gold statue *thirty* feet down in that hole. A *minor detail* I must have failed to mention to ye, Cap'n."

Then BlackHeart came closer, almost nose-to-nose with Sleg, his cool green, penetrating eyes looking straight into Sleg's black, beady ones.

"I have other of me treasures buried there, as well. Leave 'em be. They're not part of our deal," BlackHeart said.

"Give the good captain's sword back, Curly," BlackHeart went on. "He's waited long enough to receive his part of our bargain. A long trip awaits him and his crew, back to me island to get the Aztec statue before another pirate finds it—now that Sleg's left the sand showing that somebody's been *diggin'* in it."

"Ye better be telling the truth!" Captain Sleg said spitefully. He eyed BlackHeart suspiciously as he shoved his sword into its sheath.

"Mr. Token!" BlackHeart called out to his quartermaster, who was standing on the poop deck. "Take Spider with ye! Bring up me chest o' solid silver goblets, and I'll be asking the fine cap'n here to bury 'em in the hole with me other treasures there, when he digs up the Aztec statue. Eh, cap'n? Saves me having to go there, meself."

BlackHeart knew that Sleg would bury them, all right ... but not on his island.

Spider moved closer to Captain BlackHeart and Mr. Token, and watched Sleg, dragging his peg leg, scurry across the dock below to his ship, the *Scorpion*. His grumbling men struggled along behind with the heavy chest of silver goblets.

"Why did ye give 'em your fine silver goblets, Cappin? He's no real threat to us, eh, Curly?" said the tall, dark Jamaican as Curly joined the men and nodded his bald head in agreement.

"A cheap enough price to pay, Spider," answered BlackHeart in *perfect* English. Gone was his mock pirate's brogue. "We need to get Sleg off this island before the Chinese junk, *Red Dragon*, sails into port. She's laden with gold from their new discovery, a sunken Spanish galleon."

"Galleon, eh?" said Spider with a broad grin.

"Yes," BlackHeart said. "The sunken ship lies in the shallow waters off the string of keys in the Caribbean, according to the drunken sailor they threw off the *Red Dragon* near an island. He was their sailing master; I have no doubt about it. The merchant captain who picked up the sailor from the island was glad to be rid of him because of his constant nervous ranting aboard their ship.

"The sailor has spoken to no one here in Port Royal, save me," BlackHeart continued. "He's been resting quietly for the past few nights in a very private room purchased by me, along with fresh bottles of rum. Skull is sitting with him to be sure he has no intruders.

"According to the sailor, the galleon is overloaded with golden Aztec treasures, thousands of gold Spanish doubloons, and a king's ransom in gold bars from the mines—among other things. She was headed for Spain over a hundred years ago—must have been brought down by a storm because of her weight.

"The *Dragon*'s crew will stay in Port Royal for a week or two, carousing and spending their gold. Their captain, Chum Lee, is a barbarian, but he's a smart tradesman. He'll be here to trade with worldwide merchants," BlackHeart said.

"Plot a course for the keys, Spider," commanded Captain BlackHeart. "Ready the crew and ship to sail, Curly. The *Black Opal* sails as soon as the *Red Dragon* anchors here in Port Royal. The sailor, if one is kind of mind to call him that, will sail with us, willingly or not.

"Chum Lee will also be looking for more diving gear, all of which will be aboard the *Black Opal*." To make his point clear, BlackHeart added, "Mr. Token, disguise a few men and quickly buy up all of the diving equipment in Port Royal, whether we need it or not. That will force Chum Lee to make an unscheduled trip to the island of Tortuga to buy the *Red Dragon*'s diving equipment, giving us plenty of time at the site of the sunken galleon. And, Mr. Token, bring aboard plenty of food and fresh water," BlackHeart said finally. "We'll be gone for quite some time!"

CHAPTER 3

AN UNTIMELY ARRIVAL

Somewhere in Time

Jon struggled to pull himself upright in his seat and stared at the computer screen, which was still set to the outside view. The *Carousel* was definitely on the ground. Green leaves obstructed the monitor's view.

"What happened?" Jon asked Grammy frantically.

"I don't know," she replied shakily, "but it's the same kind of problem you and I had once before, remember? I'll need a few minutes on the computer, checking data to see what's wrong. Why don't you go to a porthole and tell me what you see."

Jon unfastened his seat harness and went to the porthole nearest him. "There's big green plants and tall red and orange flowers and ... *parrots,* Grammy! Parrots! They're flying all around us!"

Kathryn got up from the console and joined Jon at the porthole. The *Carousel* stood in the center of a large clearing of some very tall trees that seemed to form a canopy of sorts over shorter trees. There were patches of thin knee-high grass intermingled with white sand.

"This most definitely is not Philadelphia! We're somewhere in the tropics," Grammy said. *But where, and more important, what year? And what went wrong with the Carousel?* she wondered. She went back to the computer to look for answers.

"Can I go outside and look around?" Jon asked.

"No! Not yet, Jon." Grammy said sharply. "Anything could be out there. We've crashed in the tropics somewhere in time, but I don't know which year. For all we know, there could be dinosaurs out there!"

She keyed in a command, and the monitor displayed line after line of rapidly moving numbers, symbols, bars, and meaningless words as the computer sorted through the mountains of data. Suddenly it stopped. There was a single line displayed in large print on the computer screen:

"Port Royal, Jamaica–Caribbean Sea–May 1, 1692 AD"

CHAPTER 4

DON'T GET LOST

Port Royal, Jamaica, May 1, 1692

"I don't know what has gone wrong with this computer, but I certainly don't trust it now. I'll have to change over to the auxiliary computer we have onboard. It's the quickest and safest way for us to get back on track and proceed to Philadelphia and the correct year. Why don't you read a book quietly while I work?"

"Boring, Grammy, boring!" Jon said impatiently.

"Patience, Jon, patience," Grammy said, and they both laughed.

"Aw, come on, Grammy! I'll just be right outside," Jon pleaded. "Last year on our vacation we were here in Jamaica and it was safe. I'll stay close to the *Carousel*," Jon promised. "Grammy?" No response. Her mind was concentrated on the computer problems. "Grammy?"

"Oh, all right! Here, take the Transformer with you," she said as she flipped open the lid of the handheld computer and keyed in some codes.

"I already know how to use the Transformer," Jon whined. "Pappy taught me, and we practiced over and over." But Grammy wanted to check it to be sure that its coordinates were in sync with the *Carousel*'s and the year in which they had landed.

"Good, the computer mapped this entire area before it broke down. The map in the Transformer will guide you back here if you get lost ... but don't get lost! Okay?" she said sternly as she sat back down at the computer, her mind already focused on her work.

"Okay, Grammy," Jon said and rolled his eyes. *Grammy makes me nuts worrying about me all the time. She treats me like a little kid, like I can't take care of myself!* Jon thought as he walked down the ramp from the ship.

Parrots were flying all around the *Carousel*. Some flew back into the forest while new ones came out as if to inspect this strange new object in their forest. Jon delighted in all the parrots: colorful macaws, white cockatoos, and black toucans with big orange and yellow beaks.

Slowly the parrots migrated deeper into the dense forest, with Jon following their flight.

As he continued to explore, Jon was wandering farther away from the *Carousel* and farther into the green foliage of the forest. He lifted some large palm fronds and walked through to the other side, where he stopped abruptly. Straight ahead of him was a bright green snake with a yellow underbelly. The snake was devouring what looked like a rat. All but the feet and long tail of the rat were already down the throat of the snake. Then with one big gulp, the snake shut its mouth over the remains. Since the snake seemed to be ignoring Jon, he continued to watch as the snake moved ahead.

A small rodent, similar to a chipmunk, sat in front of the snake. Without warning, the large snake sprang at the chipmunk, sinking its fangs into the little creature. The chipmunk wiggled a few seconds and then was still as the snake began to devour the chipmunk, its long body constricting and relaxing as the second ball appeared in its long length. Having seen enough, Jon walked in another direction.

There were so many new and interesting things to see in this tropical paradise that Jon did not realize how long he had been gone, or how far he had walked. A full hour had passed when he came upon an open area under the tall trees. In front of him stood a black withered tree with a limb split and hanging down to the ground. He moved closer. It looked like a bazillion big black ants crawling in and out of a hole in the trunk of the large dead tree. *Those ants must be an inch long!* he thought as he quickly turned and hurried away before any of them could get on him.

Jon swatted at a bee buzzing near his head and turned to see a huge beehive hanging from the lower branch of a tree nearby. The honeycomb was exposed on one side of the hive, and bees crawled in and out of the comb, leaving their deposits of nectar. Jon shied away. He knew better than to mess with bees at their hive.

The crack of a twig behind him aroused Jon's awareness to his surroundings. The forest had grown quieter, and darker than it seemed before. *Where did the parrots go?* he wondered. Looking up, he could see nothing but leaves. The towering trees closed out all but an occasional glint of sunlight. He walked one way, then another way. Nothing looked familiar. He was lost!

"Gram-m-my!" Jon called out several times. No answer, only the soft sounds of the birds chirping and the cicadas buzzing. He tried to backtrack, but the brush and foliage were so thick, he couldn't see any of his foot imprints.

He became increasingly afraid of being alone in this strange place. The forest all looked the same. "Don't panic," he said to himself. Tears were stinging the backs of his eyes, and he was about to let them fall, when he saw a clearing ahead. Running into the opening where the sun shone in, he saw two paths that led away from the clearing. There was only one answer: *follow the path.* At least enough people had been walking here to make a path, but which path should he follow? In frustration, he jammed his hands into his pockets. His right hand felt a familiar metal object.

"The Transformer!" Jon sang out as he pulled the small silver object from his pocket. "I forgot I had it. Grammy said the area around the *Carousel* was mapped. I can follow the map back to the *Carousel*!"

He quickly flipped open the lid of the Transformer and keyed in his code. The words "Computer Off" came up on the screen. He pushed the Reset button and a red light flashed as the Transformer screen cleared. He input his code again, the red light flashed once, and the screen went black. There was no connection to the *Carousel's* computer.

Jon had no way of knowing that Grammy had briefly turned off the power to the *Carousel's* computer while she transferred the cables to the auxiliary computer.

Jon let out a heavy sigh, put the small silver Transformer back into his pocket, and stood looking at the two paths, one narrow, one wide.

Which path?

CHAPTER 5

KIDNAPPED

I'll take the narrow path, Jon thought. *It might lead back to Grammy and the* Carousel.

J on had started down the narrow path when he heard voices behind him. He turned just as a big hairy hand grabbed him by the shirt collar and spun him around. Standing before him were two of the meanest-looking men he'd ever seen!

"Avast ye! What hast we here. A little lamb a' wandering from the fold, as it were," slurred the first man, who was shorter than the other man.

"Shouldn't do that, laddie," said the taller man. "Don't ye know thar be pirates about?" They both laughed coarsely as the first man held Jon's shirt by the front of the collar, pulling him closer to his sweaty, greasy face and foul-smelling breath.

"Beings that ye found the two most fearsome pirates about, that being me and Gallows here, me thinks ye should be quiet-like whilst we decides exactly what to do with ye. Or else Gallows might try to do what he be famous for. Hanging ye!" snarled the shorter pirate. The taller one named Gallows patted the rolled hemp rope attached to his belt.

Both men wore dirty pants and shirts, with cutlasses strapped to their belts. No shoes or patches over the eye, no gold teeth, no bandana skull caps over their heads, no big belt buckles, no hooks, no peg legs— none of the things Jon would expect to see on a pirate. And they smelled of vomit, feces, and worse, if there could be worse. *They must have never bathed in their lives,* thought Jon.

"What ye gonna do with the little lamb, Starkey?" asked Gallows. "Ye gonna cut him? Look good with scars, he would. Boys likes scars, they does."

"Not yet," said Starkey. "Mayhap we ransom the boy. Wouldn't get as much booty if he was scarred up already and might get meself hung, to boot! We may get a treasure trove for this one. Look at his clothes. Wealthy, this one be! We'll take him to Sleg ... have to share with Sleg, but he knows how to ransom peoples."

"Nope," said Gallows. "Too late. Captain Sleg sailed with the morning tides. Have to think of somethin' else."

"We takes him to our hideout and waits for the slave ship. The *Royal Sphinx* comes in next week. If we gets a ransom afore then, we takes the gold! If we don't, we sells him to the slave master, Captain Bruha, we will!" said Starkey. "Ye can cut him then. Bruha don't care if he has scars. Proves he been disciplined already and learnt somethin' from it. Scars brings *more* gold from Bruha."

Jon was scared stiff inside, but he couldn't let these wicked men see his fear or they might hang him from the nearest tree, like Starkey had said, and forget about the ransom! He walked along with them willingly for a while, thinking. Eventually they let him walk freely, deciding he was safely in their control.

Jon's eyes darted from side to side, anxiously looking for the *Carousel*. Then he saw the black withered tree with the broken branch leaning to the ground that he had passed earlier. Now was his chance!

Jon broke from the pirates and ran toward the tree— the tree with all the ants!

"Wha-a? You let him get away!" shouted Gallows. Both pirates chased him through the thick foliage and underbrush.

Jon reached the tree, breathless. Lying near the tree was a big stick, which Jon picked up, hiding it close behind his back as the pirates closed in.

Starkey reached him first, and Jon whopped him hard with the stick, catching him off guard and knocking him off balance. Starkey fell into the trunk of the rotting tree. Immediately, the inch-long black ants were all over Starkey. He screamed in agony, slapping at the ants, which rapidly covered his head and face as if looking for a way inside. Jon ran to the nearby tree where the beehive was hanging, just as Gallows caught up to him.

"Why, ye puny scallywag! I'll put a hempen halter round your neck and hang ye from the highest tree!" Gallows snarled as he crept toward Jon, who was backing up. Jon looked over his shoulder, holding the stick out behind him. He was almost close enough.

"Arr-rrgh!" yelled Gallows as he lunged at Jon. Jon hit the back of the beehive hanging from the tree, flinging the hive right on top of Gallows as the bees went wild, flying everywhere. Jon ran. The angry bees took over as Gallows screamed and cursed loudly, using words that would shock even Pappy's ears.

Jon crossed the clearing quickly and lay down under a fallen tree trunk amongst thick foliage, rubbing his arm where two bees had stung him. He heard them coming. He lifted his head ever so slightly and saw them slashing through the brush and foliage with their razor sharp cutlasses. He rolled to his back and slid farther into the crevice under the big log.

"Where's that maggot? Put them stings on me, will he!" snarled Gallows as Starkey continued to whine, cursing profusely and slapping at the ants under his clothes. The pirates continued slashing their way through the tall brush.

Lying as still as death under the log, Jon heard a faint rustling in the leaves near his head. His heart skipped a beat as he felt the tickling on his neck and cheek of a giant brown spider, just as Gallows and Starkey paused nearby. If he jumped up, they would cut him to shreds and forget about the ransom. *No,* he thought, *I'll have to lie perfectly still and pray this spider won't bite me ... and those pirates won't see me!*

The moldy-smelling spider was now completely on top of Jon's eyes, moving one step at a time with its eight legs spread across his entire face. He had his eyes shut and was afraid to breathe as the spider continued, one foot on his ear, another on his scalp, and one on the other side of his head. He heard the men cursing, yelling threats and then slashing through the foliage again.

When the spider stepped its last leg off Jon's head, he jerked aside and rolled to a sitting position as the giant

spider, the size of a man's open hand, crept farther under the log where Jon had hidden. He looked quickly
through the thicket for the men but couldn't see them.
He got to his feet, crouching low. He could see them
now, moving toward the narrow path where they had
first seen him, cursing each other for losing their "golden
treasure," as they called him.

Jon waited until the men were far enough down the
narrow path before he stood up. Then he cautiously crept
back to the clearing, and still carrying his big stick, he
took the wider path that went in the opposite direction.
He was thankful he had gotten away—this time. From
now on, he would be more careful!

The wide path he had chosen eventually led to a
clearing. Leaving the forest, Jon faced the emerald green
waters of the Caribbean Sea. He could see a road below
that stretched out like a long finger into the sea, ending
at a town. He needed to find Grammy; but finding her
in this forest was hopeless for him, he reasoned. And he
couldn't stay here, because more men like Starkey and
Gallows might try to capture him again.

Going to the town will be safer, he thought. *Eventually
Grammy will go there looking for me.* His decision made, he
hurried down the hill to the road.

A light sea breeze blew through Jon's damp hair as he
jogged toward the town and away from that dreadful forest. He had no idea that being alone in a strange city in
the seventeenth century could be even more dangerous,
especially when that city was known as the wickedest
city in the world.

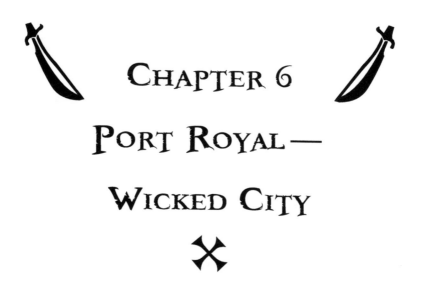

CHAPTER 6

PORT ROYAL—

WICKED CITY

It was afternoon when Jon got into Port Royal. He passed small shops that had various ship devices, like compasses, sextants, spyglasses, and such.

His eyes brightened when he saw four men in bright red military coats, wearing black hats with brims turned straight up in the front and back, forming points on either side. The huddled men were sharing a story and laughing jovially. All wore swords and had muskets hanging from leather straps over their shoulders. From books Jon had read, he recognized the men in red coats: British soldiers.

He started to run to them, to tell them he was lost and ask if they would help him find his way to Grammy and the ... *Carousel*.

He stopped abruptly, thinking through his situation. How could he explain the *Carousel* and how he came to be in Port Royal to the British Red Coats? Likely as not, they would think him loony. Or worse, they might take him to the *Carousel* and then lock him and Grammy both in a jail cell!

No! he thought. *I'll have to figure this out for myself. I know Grammy will come looking for me, or I'll learn enough about the forest to find her.* He backed away from the soldiers and walked down another street.

The streets of Port Royal were crowded with men bustling about. Some wore pants cut below the knees and long coats. Others wore loose-fitting shirts with blousy sleeves, knee britches, and leather boots or shoes. Most wore guns, knives, or swords—or all three. There were also sailors with striped T-shirts, daggers in waist belts, or cutlasses hanging. Some sailors wore rope sandals; some were barefoot.

Regardless how the men were dressed, they all seemed to be carrying a weapon of some sort: a dagger, a pistol, or such tucked in their waistband. There was no doubt about it. There were no gun or weapons laws here! And obviously, people had need of protecting themselves.

Farther into town, three men cursed and shoved at each other as they came out of a tavern. The plaque over the entrance read *The Catt & Fiddle Tavern.* Peddlers with carts of all kinds were trying to move down the crowded street, hawking their goods at those passing by. Then Jon saw them: the peddlers with food!

CHAPTER 7

CAPTAIN BLACKHEART

Suddenly, Jon was very hungry. He walked over to a cart stacked high with red and orange mangos. They looked delicious. He picked one up, and a skinny barefoot peddler wearing a ragged shirt pounced at him.

"That'll be three pieces of eight, mate!" he exclaimed in a heavy English brogue as he stuck out his gnarled, dirty hand.

"Pieces of eight? I … I, uh," Jon stammered as he stuck his hand into his pocket. "I don't have the correct money," he said, pulling his hand from his pocket, holding two quarters and some pennies in his open palm. The peddler's eyes glared wider as he stared at the two silver quarters. Then he grinned, exposing two front teeth that stuck almost straight out, flanked on both sides by brown, rotting teeth.

"Take 'em both, I will!" he declared, grabbing them from Jon's open hand. He put one between his teeth and bit down on it to see if it was real or if it would bend. Deciding it was the real thing, he grinned broadly.

"*Silver!*" the peddler exclaimed loudly, causing several men to turn around and look at the peddler and his young customer. Realizing he now had an audience, the peddler quickly stuck the quarters in his pocket. But not before a certain captain, who stood in front of a gentry's tavern with one foot propped atop a large rock, saw the happening. The peddler looked fearful as the tall, finely dressed captain strode forward from the group of gentlemen standing in front of the Three Crowns tavern.

The black-haired captain had a moustache and a small, well-trimmed black goatee. His hair was pulled back into a braid under his tricorn hat. The gold loop that hung from his left ear shined in the sunlight. He wore a dark blue coat, with gold epaulets atop both shoulders and gold buttons down the front. The point of a sword showed at the bottom of his thigh-length coat. His black leather boots came all the way to his knees, with cuffs that folded down. He glanced briefly at Jon and then focused his attention on the peddler.

"Me thinks ye have cheated the boy," he said as his piercing eyes narrowed and looked straight into the peddler's eyes.

The peddler squirmed backward, his shoulders quivering slightly. His eyes darted back and forth between the captain and the boy. Finally, he pulled out the two quarters, which the captain took roughly. The captain reached into his own coat pocket and pulled out one piece of eight.

"More than enough for one mango," he said as he handed the coin to the peddler. "Give 'em another," demanded the captain, and the peddler quickly handed Jon another mango.

"Now, be off with you!" shouted the captain as he rested his hand on Jon's shoulder. The peddler turned his cart and scurried down the brick-laid street.

The captain tipped his black tricorn hat toward Jon and said, "Captain BlackHeart is me name. What be your name, lad?"

"Jonathan Alistair Weston Sinclair," he replied curtly, biting down into one of the mangos.

Captain BlackHeart tossed the two quarters in his hand as he eyed Jon, who was ravenously eating his mango, juice dripping from his hand and onto the street.

The boy's stockings are as white as the wind-driven English snow. From the way he's dressed, he comes from a well-respected and probably wealthy family. Well cared-for, he is—and manners, thought BlackHeart. *And this silver coin, I've never seen coin like it. A nice little treasure for a boy to be carrying. Mayhap I could ransom the boy for a small bounty before we set sail for the sunken Spanish galleon.*

"Where ye be headed, Jon?" inquired Captain BlackHeart.

"I'm trying to find my way back to the *Carousel*, sir," replied Jon as he looked up at the captain. The captain had the greenest eyes Jon had ever seen, almost the emerald color of the Caribbean waters. He was holding Jon's two quarters in his left hand and picked one up with his right hand. At that moment, Jon's eyes fell upon the ring on the captain's right hand. The large black stone in the ring held his attention. A sly smile came across

BlackHeart's face as he stopped the motion of his hand so Jon could look into the stone in his ring.

"Ever seen a black opal before, lad?" asked the captain.

"No," replied Jon as he gazed down into the black and green stone. There were so many colors of green, just like the sea, and deeper in the center of the black opal were many flecks of brilliant aqua, emerald green, turquoise, pink, and even crimson. Jon was mesmerized. "It ... it looks like a city, in the middle of the sea," said Jon mistily.

"Atlantis?" BlackHeart remarked.

"No one knows where the lost city, Atlantis, is, or if there ever was one," Jon said flatly, breaking the spell. He looked up at the captain, who was smiling broadly.

"No?" questioned the captain with a sly grin as he raised an eyebrow and looked straight into Jon's eyes. He gave Jon's two quarters a final toss, caught them, and handed them back to Jon.

"Perhaps you are right," BlackHeart laughed. And then very smoothly, he said, "Or perhaps, Jon, it hides beneath the sea only to resurface slightly when the tides are right." Then his smile faded and he abruptly changed the subject. "At any rate, where did you say you were going? And what is the *Carousel*?"

"It's our ship," Jon replied as he bit into the second mango, the juice still dripping from his hand. He was struggling now to keep the juice from his clothes. BlackHeart grinned.

"My grandmother is waiting there for me. I wandered away and couldn't find my way back. I wasn't scared, though," Jon fibbed. The captain grinned knowingly.

The captain turned a corner, and they were now walking toward the docks. The closer they got to the harbor, the more putrid the smell became. It was a mix of stale fried food, vomit, trash, and rotting fish. A seagull flew over, dropping a large deposit of poop, which barely missed Jon. It splattered on the street right next to him and onto his shoe. He wiped his foot on the back of his other leg, smearing the smelly poop on his white stocking. The captain grinned again.

As they passed a peddler, the captain grabbed a towel from his cart and handed it to Jon, who struggled to no avail to rid himself of mango juice and poop.

There were lots of taverns like The Catt & Fiddle and lots of drunken sailors. Many of them would glare or sneer at Jon, some even taking a step or two toward him. But when BlackHeart turned his attention toward them, they acted agitated and backed away. Jon was glad the captain had befriended him, and turned to look at him. That's when he noticed, for the first time, the two pistols that rested under BlackHeart's unbuttoned coat, one in the holster of a sling that went across BlackHeart's chest. The captain's blue coat quietly hid the other pistol, a flintlock with two hammers, which was tucked into his black waistband. Jon had seen flintlocks at antique gun shows with Pappy.

"What be your ship's colors, lad?" asked BlackHeart as he gazed down the piers toward all the ships docked there.

"Silver," replied Jon. "It's not the kind of ship like you think, sir. It's not here at the pier. You see ..."

"Silver, eh?" The captain cut Jon off midsentence, thinking, *A ship adorned with silver? It would be a grand ship, that's for sure. And not anchored here for the likes of Port Royal to witness? It's a reasonable plan. They might hide such a ship in a cove near the forest. Or mayhap the boy's lying. I plan to learn the truth of this matter. The prospect of holding the boy for ransom is looking more promising by the minute!*

CHAPTER 8

THE *BLACK OPAL*

At the coaxing of BlackHeart, Jon was chattering about his experience in the forest and paying no attention as the captain turned him away from the main dock. They walked out toward the end of a long pier where a tall, imposing black ship was docked.

Jon eyed the ship with admiration. The two tall masts had a crow's nest atop each of them. Rolled white canvas sails, which were tied up at the yards on both masts, and the white sail tied at the bow stood in stark contrast to the rest of the ship, which was tar black. Gold swirls that looked like waves decorated the top of the ship's wooden side rails and polished brass could be seen shining here and there. The only other color on the ship was the sea green mermaid, with long golden hair to the waist, which was fitted on the underside of the bow. In her outstretched hands, the mermaid held a giant black shiny stone similar to the black opal in the captain's ring.

A British flag flew at the ship's stern. Flying off the foremast of the ship was a white flag with a big black heart in the center. The name on the side of the bow in large gold lettering read, *Black Opal*.

"Where's your ship docked?" BlackHeart inquired.

"Docked? Uh, inland, I guess," replied Jon.

"Which way?" asked the captain

"That way—maybe," Jon said, pointing toward some hills dense with trees off in the distance. "You see, it's like I was telling you before. I got lost in the forest, and ..."

"Yes, I remember," the captain said impatiently, his mind focused on exactly how to lure the boy aboard the ship. Then, gesturing grandly, he said, "Come aboard me ship, the *Black Opal*, Jon."

"This is *your* ship?" Jon asked excitedly, because this was the most beautiful sailing ship he had ever seen. Even pictures in the books he had read could not equal it.

"Yes, my ship. She's a beauty, eh, lad? A brigantine, she's called, with ten cannon in her ports," replied BlackHeart, smiling, as Jon stood gawking at the tall black ship, which rocked gently in the breeze.

"We just outfitted her with four more small cannon on the top decks—'small guns' we calls them." BlackHeart was pleased that the boy admired his ship, just as he did. That would make it easier for the captain to coax him aboard. "She's a new ship, lad—British-made. First ship built of her kind. There's not another like her on the high seas!" BlackHeart said proudly.

"Come aboard, Jon, and we'll sail the coves and look for your ship. Nightfall will come soon, and your grandmother will be frantic with worry, she will," BlackHeart said with mock comfort in his silky, smooth voice.

Oh, yes! She'll be worried, all right, Jon thought as he remembered his disrespectful attitude when he'd left the *Carousel.* Grammy had tried to keep him safe, even from himself and his own stubborn independence.

As they walked up the wooden ramp and boarded the ship, the crew on deck and in the riggings stopped their work and gawked at Jon.

"No women and children aboard the *Opal*—pirates' code," remarked one of the crewman under his breath, but loud enough for the captain to hear and rebuke himself for breaking his own rule.

A red parrot with blue wings flew to the captain's shoulder.

"This be me parrot, Jon. I calls 'em Pyrate," BlackHeart laughed.

"Squa-awk! Put him in chains! Put his gold in me chest below!" recited Pyrate. Jon grinned and reached up to rub the soft, silky feathers of the parrot's red breast with the back of his forefinger.

"Hush, Pyrate! Ye talks too much," scolded the captain as he took the bird on his hand and threw it upward. The parrot immediately flew to a perch on one of the masts of the ship.

"Squa-awk! Talk too much!" squawked Pyrate.

Captain BlackHeart walked toward a tall, thin black crewman with long black hair, some of it braided, some not. The crewman, whom the captain called Spider, had a bushy black beard and mustache, and long, thin fingers. They spoke briefly in low tones, after which the crewman nodded and immediately walked down the ship's ramp.

Jon's attention was drawn to the parrot as it landed on his shoulder, almost knocking him down. Pyrate was a heavy macaw with thin black and white stripes surrounding its eyes. Jon held up his arm, and the parrot inched along his arm past his elbow, its sharp talons almost piercing Jon's flesh. He watched the captain remove his tricorn hat, and for a brief second, Jon saw a long scar across Captain BlackHeart's forehead and temple; his black hair flopped down to cover it.

The captain then removed a small dagger from the top of one boot and a very small pistol from the other. He placed his weapons inside the crown of his hat and handed it to a short gray-haired man in a knee-length black coat and top hat, whom he referred to as Mr. Token.

Jon looked around in time to see Spider come back onboard the ship. With him was a tall, baldheaded man with only a small patch of braided blond hair on one side of his head. The crewmen addressed the man as Skull. The two men carried a groggy sailor between them.

BlackHeart gave a nod to Spider and Skull as the two men, sailor in tow, headed down to a deck below. Then the captain walked up the steps to the quarterdeck, where the ship's helm with the big wheel stood.

"Curly! Standby to cast off!" the captain shouted.

"Standby to cast off!" echoed Curly. Immediately, dozens of men quickly moved about the ship and up the ropes leading to the tall masts.

"Guidry! Drop top sails!" shouted the captain.

"Drop tops'ls!" shouted Guidry, the first mate, to the eight crewmen at the very top of the two masts. The crewmen immediately began dropping the short, wide sails at the tops of the masts and securing them to the yards, which were the crossbeams attached to the tall masts.

"We're sailing the coves to help Jon, here, find the *Carousel*," BlackHeart shouted, "his ship o' silver!"

As the *Black Opal* pulled away from the dock at Port Royal, a murmur of *"Ship o' silver"* spread through the crew and ended with Pyrate announcing the results for all to hear.

"Squa-a-awk! Ship 'o silver! Ship 'o silver!" echoed Pyrate. "Find the silver ship. Ransom. Pots with silver. All mine! Pirates' code!"

CHAPTER 9

BACK IN THE FOREST

From the moment Jon had left the *Carousel*, Kathryn had worked diligently moving all the data files from the broken computer to the *Carousel*'s back-up computer onboard.

She had not seen Jon for quite some time but didn't know how long. Her watch, along with the clock of the computer, had stopped when they passed through the window in time. She had stepped outside and called out to Jon several times but with no answer. Trying to find him in the dense forest would be impossible, and she might get lost herself. Once the auxiliary computer was running, she would be able to contact him through the Transformer he carried.

The last diagnostics were processing now, and if all went well, the computer would soon be running. She stood waiting at the monitor.

"There! The transfer's finished. The computer's running," she said happily. She sat down at the console and keyed in commands to the Transformer. The signal to the Transformer was strong. She watched and waited, but there was no signal coming back from Jon.

That's strange, she thought, looking at the monitor. *The locator map shows the Transformer to be in the Caribbean Sea, south and just a little east of the bay to Port Royal. But that's impossible. There must be some mistake. The Transformer couldn't possibly be in the sea!* She keyed in the commands again. And again the same map came up, showing the Transformer, marked by a red X, to be in the Caribbean Sea.

Maybe there's a glitch in the new computer system. I'll go outside and walk in a wide circle around the Carousel. *Perhaps Jon's nearby in the forest. Yes, there must be an error,* she thought.

She clicked the print icon to print off a copy of the map. Nothing happened. Impatiently, she clicked it again and several times more before she realized the printer was jammed.

"Drat the luck!" she said angrily. "That thing always jams when I need it! Well, I don't have time to fix it now!" She looked back at the computer monitor, memorizing the coordinates on the map. Then she grabbed a digital compass and a small LED flashlight. Cramming them into her jeans pocket, she left the *Carousel*.

CHAPTER 10

SHIP O' SILVER

The crew was in high spirits at the idea of adding silver to their treasures, in addition to more gold from the ransom they would get for the boy. They'd never heard of a silver ship sailing on any sea, and any man among them would love to take command of such an exquisite vessel!

But after lacing the coastline from the west to the east without any sighting of the splendid silver ship, they began to question the truth of the story they had heard.

Even the captain had concerns that he was being made to look the fool in front of his crew by this young boy. On a pirate ship, being courageous, crafty, and the one most respected by the crew were essential to remaining captain, and to staying alive.

One at a time, with looks of hostility and anger, the men moved closer to Jon, making snide comments. Their tempers were beginning to boil and flare, and when a crew took on tempers, they were hard to calm.

Jon had thought that anything as tall as the *Carousel* could be seen from the water, but the tall trees were hiding it well. There was no sign of it anywhere.

And worse than that, thought Jon fearfully, *none of these men believe me—just like the Red Coats wouldn't have believed me. What'll they do to me?* Jon fretted and watched as the crew became more aggressive, moving closer, one putting a dagger just inches from his nose.

"Avast, boy! Why did ye lead us on this wild goose chase?" asked Spider, the tall sailing master. He stuck his face down close to Jon's, his menacing black eyes clearly threatening. Jon recoiled as far back as he could before he bumped into Curly, who grabbed him by the shoulder, jerking him around forcefully, causing him to stumble.

"Because he's daft!" Curly spit out, leaving some of his spittle on Jon's cheek. Jon wiped it away with the back of his hand. Curly spat again, next to Jon's foot, and shoved him to the deck in disgust.

"Mayhap he's sick with the heat!" suggested Gituku, the short, stout, Swahili second mate.

"If he had a fever, he'd be hot, now wouldn't he be?" shouted Spider as he grabbed Jon, lifting him forcefully off the deck with one hand. He stuck his long fingers to Jon's forehead. "Look! He's cool as a wet frog in a waterfall!" Then, holding Jon by his shoulders, he gave him a shaking. "He be bamboozling us, he is!"

They taunted Jon, shoving him roughly back and forth between them as though he were a ball. Spider grabbed him again and held him tightly. "Let's see what he be hiding," he shouted as Curly rammed his hand into Jon's pocket. Curly pulled out the Transformer and held it up. The small, silver, handheld computer with the red light flashing on top sparkled in the afternoon sun.

The red light's flashing! Grammy's trying to reach me, Jon thought frantically. He squirmed loose from Spider's grip and grabbed at Curly and the Transformer.

"What's this?" Curly drawled, looking at the silver object and holding it up high, out of Jon's reach. The group of crewmen quickly gathered around Curly, shoving Jon aside. Curly opened the flip-lid of the Transformer. The tiny screen and the various buttons with numbers and symbols on them lit up as a murmur of awe passed through crew.

"Let *me* see!" shouted one of the crew, grabbing at the Transformer.

"No, me!" shouted another, and another. It was a free-for-all as they grabbed and shoved at one another, each trying to get hold of the Transformer.

"No! Stop!" yelled Jon, to no avail. "You don't know what you're doing! You'll cause a disaster. *Stop!*"

"Stop! Stop!" mocked members of the crew as they all jeered and taunted Jon. They took turns punching all the buttons on the Transformer, laughing and cheering when another colored light flashed, signaling that they had accomplished some unknown feat. They had never seen a device with bright lights. In fact, they had never seen brightly colored lights, only lanterns with candles or oil burning in them for reading or showing the way in the dark.

"The boy wants his sil-ver toy!" one of them yelled as he tossed the Transformer over Jon's head to another sailor. They all laughed coarsely and began playing a game of keep-away with Jon. They tossed it back and forth high over his head as Jon, now crying, grabbed into the empty air above him for the Transformer.

"Stop! Please, oh please. Stop!" Jon pleaded. But there was no stopping them. They now had a mob mentality and nothing short of ...

Bam! Bam! The sound of gunfire echoed against the deck of the ship.

"Avast! Enough! *Stand down!*" Shoving his now empty double-barreled flintlock back into his waistband, Captain BlackHeart moved fearlessly into the crowd of men, parting them roughly like a boat parts the waves of the sea. He grabbed the Transformer. "You've had your fun with the boy! Now! Back to work! All of you swabs!" BlackHeart snapped as he eyed Curly and Spider. He had expected more of them. After all, they were more than just crewmen; they were his trusted officers: Curly, the boatswain, and Spider, the master sailor and navigator.

The men grudgingly moved back to their tasks, eyeing Jon angrily, some cursing, others vowing to get even. Captain BlackHeart took Jon and the Transformer to his quarters.

As Jon sat in the quiet of the captain's cabin, awaiting his fate, he had no idea of the damage the crew had inflicted. While pushing the buttons and playing with the Transformer, they had somehow managed to push the command buttons in the proper sequence to cause the *Carousel* to disappear. Jon—and Grammy—was now stranded in the seventeenth century!

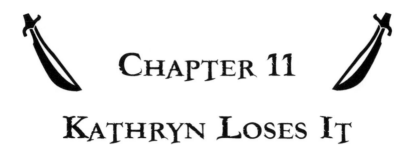

CHAPTER 11

KATHRYN LOSES IT

Kathryn now sat staring at the empty space in the forest where the *Carousel* had stood.

She had been looking for Jon in the forest a short distance from the *Carousel* when she saw the familiar light flash brightly and heard the loud *poof*, like that of a flashbulb exploding. She watched the bright light of the *Carousel* hover in the air as it grew smaller and dimmer, and then it was gone.

She had come back to the place where the *Carousel* had stood. The only thing left was the round impression in the wild sawgrass where the ship had been.

She didn't know who had made the *Carousel* disappear, or how, only that it was gone, and with it their link to the world they knew. Just like that!

She sat thinking through the recent events, trying to make sense of all that had happened. Jon had the only Transformer, but he knew not to mess with the command buttons. Alistair had instructed him well regarding the dangers and consequences of playing with the buttons on the Transformer, particularly the command buttons.

So, what has happened? Is the Carousel *still here? Is it just invisible or is it gone?* She didn't know, and without the Transformer, she could not find out.

"No, no!" she had yelled when it disappeared. And then she had cried an ocean of tears, it seemed, as she sat there thinking and waiting to see if the *Carousel* would reappear. It did not.

I'm all alone, thought Kathryn, *and Jon is out there somewhere all alone for the first time in his life.* Since the death of Jon's parents, which left him an orphan and their ward, she and Alistair had loved and protected their only grandchild. Jon's father, Weston, had been their only son, and the circumstances surrounding his death had left them devastated. They had turned all their love and attention to his son. And now, Jon was lost and the *Carousel* was gone; and Alistair was not here to help her. It was up to her … and only her … to find him.

She took a deep breath and straightened her shoulders. She was resolved. She must find Jon and the Transformer, and quickly. It was getting late in the day, and night would catch her in the forest if she didn't hurry.

Taking her flashlight, she looked at her compass and headed toward the last known location of the Transformer and Jon: the Caribbean waters, offshore from Port Royal, Jamaica.

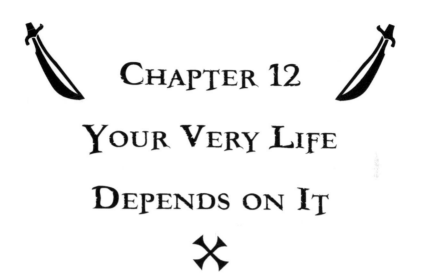

CHAPTER 12

YOUR VERY LIFE

DEPENDS ON IT

Inside the quiet of Captain BlackHeart's cabin, Jon turned his back to the captain as he wiped away the tears and blood from a gash on his cheek. He was still shaking from his clash with the ship's crew. The captain handed him a cloth to wipe the blood.

"It'll heal; it's a small cut. Unload your pockets, Jon!" demanded the captain. Gone was the pirate's brogue. He spoke in perfect English with a British accent. "Let's see what else you have that could cause a crew to mutiny."

Jon took out his small Swiss army knife, the two quarters, and three pennies, and laid them on the captain's desk. BlackHeart laid down the Transformer and picked up the Swiss knife. He pulled out all the small knives, bottle opener, nail file, scissors, and clippers. He turned the device side to side, looking at the large cache of small weapons contained in the slender, silver, three-inch-long device.

"Impressive," he said quietly, laying it aside with the other items from Jon's pockets. He picked up the

Transformer with all its lights flashing on the top and turned to Jon. "Now, talk, Jon ... and don't leave out any *minor details*. Your very life depends on it!" The captain sat down in the chair behind his desk. He leaned over his desk and looked straight into Jon's eyes, his hand with the big black opal ring rolled into a fist.

"Tell me about the *Carousel*, your ship of silver," he said in a snide voice, "which is *not* to be found on any waters of this entire coast!" he fairly shouted as he slammed his fist down on the desk. Jon jumped backward fearfully.

"The *Carousel* is n-not a sailing ship, sir. I-it's a time-travel ship," Jon answered shakily. *How will I ever explain this to the captain, especially now that my very life depends on it?* he wondered.

"A what?!" snapped BlackHeart.

"T-Time-travel ship, sir. I've been trying to tell you, but you won't listen! I came here in the *Carousel* from a time in the future with my grandmother, Kathryn," explained Jon. "I call her Grammy."

"And where is your Grammy now?" BlackHeart inquired sarcastically.

"In the forest," replied Jon shakily.

"You said she was aboard the ship of silver!" BlackHeart spit out.

"She is, sir. You see ..." Jon stammered, almost tongue-tied, as he searched frantically for proper words to explain.

"Don't try to confuse me, boy!" BlackHeart yelled and pounded his desk again. "How can a ship be in the forest?"

Jon let out a heavy sigh, and worry lines etched his brow as he shakily replied, "It's not an ordinary ship."

"Obviously not! And you are not an ordinary boy. And I am not an ordinary captain! A minor detail you have overlooked. I'm an angry one! Do you understand!" he yelled as he reached his long arms over the desk, grabbed Jon by the shoulders, and shook him until his teeth rattled. He was so close that Jon could see that the captain's green eyes had turned almost black—and chilling.

"You ... you see, Captain, sir," Jon stuttered, "I-I had wandered away from the *Carousel*, Captain, sir, and I got lost in the forest." Looking into the captain's disbelieving eyes, he quickly added, "I can talk to my grandmother with the Transformer you're holding in your hand."

BlackHeart looked down at the Transformer with the blinking, colored lights. "Show me!" he demanded as he slammed the Transformer down hard on his desk and shoved it at Jon. *"Now!"*

Jon picked up the Transformer in his shaky hands and quickly looked up at the captain. *His eyes have turned back to green again. That's a good sign ... maybe,* Jon thought.

With the captain now standing over him and watching every move, Jon keyed in his code. The device flashed twice. The screen and all the lights went dark. Jon pressed the Reset button and the red light flashed once, signaling that it had reset the handheld computer. He keyed in his code again, and again. Each time, the same thing happened. No screen, no brightly colored lights. The red light would flash once and the screen would go black.

"The crew, they ... broke it, sir," Jon said in a whisper as he looked up at the captain with the saddest, most fearful eyes the captain had ever seen.

There was a loud knock at the door. "Cap'n! Cap'n?" shouted Curly.

"Enter!" shouted BlackHeart, and Curly opened the door. "What now?" roared the captain, and Curly recoiled instantly.

"Ship ahoy? Captain, sir?" Curly said in a meek voice, pointing a shaking finger toward a ship off in the distance. "It be the *Red Dragon*, cap'n sir! Chinese writtin' on her bow. I can see it through me glass." He patted his spyglass. "Mr. Token said so, too! She's fast making way to port, Cap'n!"

BlackHeart moved to the door and grabbed Curly's spyglass. Peering at the ship through the glass, the captain could see that the *Red Dragon* was indeed arriving at Port Royal. "I'll be right out. Tell the crew to make ready to sail!" BlackHeart said.

Turning to Jon, he said, "Looks like I have a minor detail to attend to right now. Tonight, you'll sleep here in my cabin in this niche by the door, so I can keep an eye on you. The niche and bed were built for a cabin boy. Since I don't have a cabin boy, you can sleep there. The crew can be a mean lot when they're all riled up, and they're riled at you, Jon. You might wake up dead, sleeping in the crew's quarters tonight."

With that, the captain removed his coat, tied a black scarf over the top of his head, and was out the door. Looking back over his shoulder, BlackHeart yelled, "Our little talk is not finished, Jon!"

Jon sat motionless, staring at the broken Transformer and wondering what was to become of him now. Through the open door, he heard the captain's command: "Check your plotted course for the Keys, Spider. We sail for the sunken Spanish galleon!"

Jon watched through the door as Gituku unfurled a heap of black cloth. The pure white of the skull and bones struck fear into Jon. *The Jolly Roger! Pirates! I'm on a pirate ship!* he realized for the first time.

A cheer went up from the crew as a tear rolled down Jon's cheek.

The Black Opal at Sea

CHAPTER 13

THE NEW BOY IN TOWN

It was dark when Grammy approached Port Royal. She could smell it before she could see anything with her small LED flashlight. She was near an animal stockyard. The smell of animal excrement was instantly identifiable and very strong. A lot of animals!

She heard low voices behind her and quickly turned her flashlight on two burly figures hastily moving toward her. Both had muskets. The cutlasses fastened at their waists reflected the bright light from her flashlight as they walked briskly toward her. *Guards!* thought Grammy.

The two guards grabbed her by each arm, knocking her flashlight to the ground. The light shined on their boots, which were covered with smelly animal excrement. It made Grammy gag. The short, fat guard snorted as he picked up the flashlight.

"Avast! Hoss, look!" shouted the short, fat guard excitedly to the tall guard. As Hoss held Grammy tightly with one hand, both guards examined the four-inch-long flashlight for the longest time. They flashed it this way and that, oohhing and ahhing, as the light played against the trees, farm animals, brown fences, sheds, and Grammy's face. The short guard yanked the flashlight away from Hoss, flashing it around wildly.

"Don't put that light in me eyes, Bacon, you squatty hunk of ham!" Hoss snarled, shielding his eyes with his free arm.

With his other hand, Hoss yanked Grammy's arm, jerking her to his filthy side. "And what ye be a' doing here in our yards in the dark, like the true thief that ye is, boy?"

Boy? thought Grammy. *Do they think I'm an adolescent or young man?*

Hoss gave her a sound shake, "Answer me, boy!"

"Uh, uh, I'm just g-going into t-town," stammered Grammy.

"Well, ye've come the wrong way tuh do it," snarled Hoss as he gave Grammy's arm another yank.

Grammy's mind was racing. *If they think I'm a teen-ager, it's safer for me if I let them continue to think that,* she thought, not knowing what they might do next.

"Where did ye git this strange light, boy?" Bacon wheezed.

"Uh-h-h," Grammy stammered. She knew the city of Kingston was nearby on the mainland. "Uh, Kingston."

"I'll be keeping the light, boy. Can we go to King'sun soon, Hoss, can we?" Bacon asked longingly as he continued to play with the flashlight, his breath coming in short puffs and snorts

"Harumph! Nope! You already done your shopping right here from the boy," snarled Hoss gruffly. Turning his attention back to Grammy, Hoss said, "Ye knows, boy, that the most val-u-able thing on this here island is meat and such. The colonies ain't sent none down to us fer a long spell now. D'ye think nobody's gonna be a' guarding the lambs and goats and such? Huh? Did ye? Answer me, boy!"

"No, sir!" squealed Grammy as Hoss tightened his grip on her arm.

"Did'ja come a' stealing chickens for your ship?" snorted Bacon as he grabbed Grammy's other arm and gave it a jerk backward.

"No, sir!" yelled Grammy as she jerked her sore arm away from Bacon and looked the guard in the face defiantly.

"Ye know, boy, it be a strange thing that some of our animals always disappears soon as a ship's gone from the bay. And seems the pigs is the first to go!" Hoss said, mulling it over in his mind.

Bacon gave Hoss a sly glance out of the corner of his eyes. Hoss didn't see the crafty look on the portly guard's face when he talked about the disappearing pigs, but Grammy saw it. She was sure Bacon knew exactly where some of those missing pigs were going.

Hoss pulled up on Grammy's shirt collar, pulling her nose-to-nose with his greasy, grimy face. She coughed and turned her head away from the smell of garlic and bad breath being spewed at her. "See to it that ye don't come back here! Understand?" he growled. Grammy nodded.

With that, they dragged Grammy down a sandy slope to the road and shoved her stumbling in the direction of Port Royal.

"Be off with ye, boy. And don't be a' coming back, lessen ye wants the best part o' your belly a' filling up with blood from a musket blast!" Hoss shouted. The guards laughed loudly and walked back up the slope toward the animal yards, their new flashlight showing the way.

Whew! thought Grammy. *I feel like my arms are both out of their sockets.* She hastily ran toward the city lights off in the distance. If those guards thought she was a male, an adolescent, then others might believe it, too. *Maybe it's best to pose as a young man,* she thought. *It'll be safer for me. Then I can look for Jon without so much notice.*

She smoothed down her short brown hair and wiped her hands over her sweaty face. She had always struggled to make her straight, thin figure look feminine. Maybe, for once, having an athletic look would benefit her. She straightened her shoulders, walking toward Port Royal with a new stride. The new *boy* in town. *Gramm, I'll call myself.*

The half moon gave off some light, once her eyes adjusted to the darkness. Her flashlight would have helped, but it would also have attracted unwanted attention. She snickered to herself when she thought about the guards and what would happen to the flashlight when its batteries wore out. Then her face straightened as she thought about her new name, Gramm. Now she had three names to listen for: Kathryn, Grammy, and Gramm. Life in the seventeenth century was sure getting complicated.

Port Royal was quiet when she first entered it, but closer to the harbor area, there was a lot more activity.

The taverns were bustling with seamen coming and going. As she passed The Catt & Fiddle Tavern, two young ruffians darted out from an alley nearby and yanked her into the alley.

Kathryn screamed loudly, but no one came to help.

"Empty your pockets, boy!" the taller one with the knife shouted. Grammy froze in terror. They were only boys! But they were much bigger and tougher than Kathryn, and the stench from them was ghastly.

"But I-I-I have n-nothing," she said, trembling.

"Then, I'll empty 'em for ye!" the smaller one snarled. He reached his hand down into each pocket and pulled out Kathryn's compass.

"Only this compass!" he hissed regretfully.

"I'll take it," the taller one said as he grabbed the compass. "No coin, eh?"

"No coin. Nothing for me," slurred the smaller tramp, the whites of his eyes shining from the light of a nearby lantern. "Me takes his shoes, I will. He won't need 'em where he's a going. Them there shoes will fit me, if I cuts away the toe part. Gimme your knife!"

"No! Stop!" yelled Kathryn as they threw her to the ground and struggled with her to remove her shoes. She hit at them, and they hit back—hard! The more she struggled, the harder they hit. Then, there was a thud as one of them struck Kathryn, and a deep darkness settled over her. Without any further trouble, they removed her shoes—and socks.

A few minutes later, the two ruffians came out of the alley with a smile on their faces. One was playing with a compass. The other was wearing some strange-looking black leather lace-up shoes, with his white sock-covered toes sticking out through the newly cut holes and over the black shoe soles in front.

A limp form clad in white, and sprinkled with red, lay barefoot in the alley ... not moving.

Chapter 14

We're on Fire

Morning was dawning when Jon awoke with a jerk and grabbed the sides of the narrow cot where he was sleeping. *Where am I?* he wondered, and then he remembered all the horrible events of yesterday.

He had spent the rest of the evening in the captain's cabin as the crew worked diligently putting out to sea. A squall had come through, and rain poured down like it was coming out of giant buckets, splattering hard on the decks, and the wind blew in great gusts. The little bell outside the captain's cabin door rang continuously as the ship dipped and dived through the waves.

Gituku, the Swahili second mate, had brought Jon's dinner to him in the captain's cabin and asked in his heavy African brogue if he was okay. Jon had eaten ravenously. The food was a stew of some sort, with meat, vegetables, and bread. No milk, just water. It tasted very good to the twelve-year-old boy who had eaten only two mangos all day. Afterward, he had fallen asleep on the cot in the captain's cabin.

Several times, Jon had awakened and been lulled back to sleep by the low chanting of the men working outside and the rhythmic swaying and creaking of the ship. He had not seen the captain since he angrily left his cabin yesterday. Jon crooked his neck and looked around the archway from his niche at the captain's bed. The covers were rumpled. The captain had slept there, but Jon had not heard him come or go.

He walked out onto the damp deck in his bare feet. A blanket of dense fog covered the water surrounding the ship. Jon stretched his arms upward, and then he saw it. Flying in the mist from the main mast was the Jolly Roger, and beneath it, the smaller white flag with the black heart in the center. The British flag was nowhere to be seen.

They must fly the British flag when docked to fool the people in Port Royal, people like me, thought Jon.

"Guidry! Top sails down! Hoist the stay sails!" shouted Captain BlackHeart as he gave the wheel to Spider and turned toward Jon.

"Tops'ls down! Hoist stay sails!" repeated the red-haired Guidry in his loud Irish brogue. At that, the stay sails started moving up the mainmast.

"Walk thataway, Cap'n. This part of the deck be cleaned already with the holystones, sir. That squall mussed up me decks. It'll take the better part o' the morning to git them clean," groaned Curly, the boatswain, or bo'sun as most of the men called him. Curly was a stout Irish man with a red bushy beard—but not one hair on his head. He stood feet apart, hands on his hips, and barefoot, overseeing his crew scrubbing the quarterdeck.

The Flags atop Black Opal's Mast

"Have us all removing our boots afore coming aboard the *Black Opal* next, he will! Just so's not to muss his clean decks. Have you removing yours, too, Cap'n sir. Best to make him stop this foolery, Cap'n," whined Guidry, the first mate.

Curly jumped up, shaking his fist at Guidry, accidentally kicking over a bucket of water. Dirty water splashed all over several crewmen who were down on the deck, scrubbing. They yelled out, holding their hands and arms up, protecting their faces.

"Ye *can* be replaced, Guidry!" Curly shouted down to the first mate, who was standing on the main deck.

"Carry on, men," the captain said as he crossed the quarterdeck, blatantly ignoring Curly's instructions and walking right through the middle of the clean, wet, newly mopped area. Curly cursed under his breath and gave a dirty look in the captain's direction, and then at Guidry. The captain turned his face away from the crew, but Jon could see his grin.

"Harrumph! You slept well, I noticed! It's nigh unto the end of second watch!" the captain said, his grin turning to a scowl.

Jon said nothing but just looked down at the deck. He didn't know how long the crew's deck watches were or what time it was, only that the captain wasn't pleased about it, not one little bit.

"Every man on a ship pulls his own weight. I left work clothes for you in the cabin. Put them on and go down to the galley and get your breakfast," said the captain briskly. "I'll have work for you when you finish! You'll be my cabin boy. I'll explain to you what I want done every day and what to do when I have guests aboard. Hurry on! The day's wasting!"

In the cabin, Jon put on the two-sizes-too-big clothes and long rope sandals, which flopped around on his feet. Holding his pants up with both hands, he stepped out of the cabin, took two steps, and fell flat on his face, tripped by the floppy deck sandals. The men who witnessed the event burst into laughter.

Feeling sorry for Jon, Gituku stepped forward. "Take this and tie pants to middle," he said, handing Jon a rope. He took Jon's sandals. "Go without shoes. Sailmaker make more tonight. Shoes fit tomorrow."

Jon nodded and hurried down the stairway and through the dimly lit corridor. He passed a wide door that stood ajar. There was no light coming from the room, only strange noises. Jon crept forward and pushed the door slightly, and it creaked open.

A lantern with a candle was fastened high on the wall at the far end of the room, casting a dim, flickering light over what appeared to be the crew's quarters. There were several crude wooden tables with stools and some benches. Jon crept farther into the room. Beyond the tables were many poles with hooks on them. Hammocks were stretched high and low between some of the poles, with snoring, sleeping sailors in them. On other poles, the hammocks were wound tightly for storage.

I wondered where all these men slept, Jon thought as he backed quietly out of the room.

He had no trouble finding the galley; he just followed the smell to a spot in the corridor where light shined through an open doorway. Inside, a man stood at a stove with his back to the door.

Cook was a smallish man with a little potbelly; a long, pencil-thin black mustache that curled upward on each side; and slicked back, shiny black hair. He wore a cook's coat that had once been white but was now covered with spatters of many colors.

"Uh, the captain said I should get breakfast in here," Jon said hesitantly.

"Oui, I shall give it. Seet there," Cook said as he pointed with his spatula to a long wooden-planked table with wooden benches on each side.

French cook, thought Jon, dreaming of a delicious ham and cheese omelet with a flakey croissant.

It took no time at all for Cook to bring over his breakfast: a bowl of hot gruel with a spoon standing straight up in the middle of it as if glued in place. He handed Jon a piece of dry bread and a small cup of milk. No sugar, no butter. Jon looked down at the food and back up at Cook with disappointment in his eyes.

"There iz-zz some pro-blem?" Cook asked as he moved closer to the table, the long wooden spatula still in his hand.

"Uh, no," replied Jon, looking at the spatula.

"You drink cof-fee, meybe?" Cook asked.

"No, thank you," Jon replied.

"Then eat, eat, so that I may be on with the cooking of the midday meal!" Cook demanded.

Jon took a sip of the milk. The sour face he made was noticed by the cook, who scowled.

"You do not like milk of the goat?" inquired the cook, squinting his eyes, the wooden spatula still gripped in his hand. "You would pre-ferh cow's milk, meybe?"

"Yes, thank you," replied Jon.

"And do you think we have room for a herd of cattle on this ship, yes?"

Jon could tell from the way the cook was shaking the spatula that the answer to the question was no, which he said in a low voice.

"Then, drink your goat's milk!" Cook demanded and turned his back to Jon, slamming the pots together and grumbling to himself in French, occasionally holding the spatula high over his head and shaking it as he made a loud exclamation of some sort.

Jon finished his breakfast quickly and walked into the dark corridor. He had turned toward the stairs when he heard gurgling and whimpering sounds coming from behind him. He turned and crept quietly down the dark corridor toward a light at the end. He stopped by a bolted door. The sounds were coming from within. He rattled the door and the sounds stopped. He lifted his hand and was about to unbolt the door when he heard the plopping sounds of someone's feet coming down the corridor.

"And why are you here? The stairs are that way!" shouted Cook angrily as he pointed with his spatula toward the other end of the corridor.

"Y-yes, sir," Jon said shakily.

"Be quick about it!" Cook said, and Jon hurried up the stairs, hoping Cook would forget about the incident and not tell the captain.

As he passed the parrot's perch, Pyrate flew down to Jon's shoulder.

"Squawk! Cabin boy! Cabin boy! Leave 'em be! Captain's orders! Leave 'em be!" gurgled Pyrate. Then he flew back to his perch.

"In here, Jon!" snapped BlackHeart from behind the open door in his cabin. He was writing in his journal, but immediately stood when Jon entered. He opened the doors of the narrow wall cabinet, exposing his fine china, crystal wine goblets, and silver tableware.

"These are what I use for myself and for my guests who come aboard," BlackHeart said. BlackHeart pointed toward the long table and chairs that stood between his desk and the back windows of his cabin. "Every night, this table will be appropriately set by you, using these things. Gituku will bring up a fresh linen cloth and napkins. I rarely eat with the crew. You have heard the clang of the loud ship's bell on the main deck?" Jon nodded.

"The bell is used instead of a clock. The twenty-four hours of each day are divided into six watches, starting at midnight," BlackHeart instructed. Jon looked confused.

"Gituku will teach you about the bells. Soon you'll understand and will count bells in your sleep. Have my breakfast in this cabin at six in the morning, which is two hours into the second watch, and my dinner in the cabin at six in the evening. Every morning, after I've eaten, washed, and dressed myself, you will make my bed and your own bed. Then, you will take your own breakfast. Don't be late! Do I make myself clear?" the captain snapped, looking sternly down at Jon.

"Yes, sir," Jon said quietly, wondering how he would wake up by himself that early in the morning.

"*Aye, Captain!*" corrected BlackHeart.

"Aye, Captain," repeated Jon.

"Do you know how to clean?" asked the captain.

"Yes, uh ... aye, Captain," replied Jon.

"Very well," said the captain. "Gituku will bring anything you need. I'll leave you to your work." With that, he was gone.

Jon was glad Grammy had insisted that he learn to keep his own room clean. He busied himself cleaning the captain's cabin, all the while looking for his Transformer as he cleaned. He didn't find it behind any of the many objects in the cabin and wondered if it might be in some of the cabinets or drawers. He found a key amongst some papers on the captain's desk.

Maybe it belongs to these desk drawers with the keyholes, he thought. *Maybe the Transformer is in one of them.* Grammy had taught him not to meddle with other people's belongings, so he laid the key beside a quill pen on the desk. Later he would ask the captain if he could have his Transformer.

The captain had a grand sextant and magnifying glass on his desk, along with the quill pen, inkwell, and a leather box that held parchment writing papers. The captain's journal lay next to a short, fat candle and a small metal dish with a handle, which held black wax. Jon picked up the stamping seal laying next to it, wiping it with the soft cloth Gituku had brought. On the end of the seal was a big heart. Engraved in the center of the heart was the letter B. *BlackHeart,* thought Jon.

Suddenly there was a thundering *Boom!*

The explosion outside rocked the ship from side to side, causing the crystal goblets to rattle together with a delicate tinkling sound. One goblet fell from an open cabinet and shattered on the wooden floor. The small bell outside the cabin door tinkled urgently.

Jon dropped the seal on the desk and ran out the cabin door and onto the deck.

Then, in the distance, a second blast sounded, followed by a loud whizzing sound as the cannonball crossed the ship's deck and splashed in the water on the other side.

The seawater splash sprayed Jon and the crew on the decks of the *Black Opal*.

"Man the cannon!" shouted BlackHeart as several crewmen ran to the two brass cannon on the ship's quarterdeck.

"Gunners down! Open the ports! Man the cannon below!" shouted Skull as he ran down the stairs. The gunners were scrambling over each other, getting down the stairway to the deck below.

Jon tried to see through the dense fog but could see nothing.

Then, another deafening shot thundered, the sound echoing against the water. Suddenly, the ship sank down into the waves and then sprang forcefully upward, water rolling off the main deck as the shot found its mark. There was loud clattering and banging as split and splintered deck planks crashed back down to the deck. The cannonball exploded in a ball of fire on the deck of the *Black Opal*.

"We're on fire!" yelled Curly sharply. A wild uproar burst out among the frantic crew while the flames blazed higher and rapidly spread to the quarterdeck where Jon stood.

CHAPTER 15

WAKING UP ALIVE

Ouch! My head hurts! thought Kathryn. She grabbed her head and tried to sit up. It was morning now, and foggy.

"Blood!" she said quietly, looking at her hand as she pulled it from her head. She blinked, trying to remember the events leading to the blood. *The ruffians*, she thought as she looked at her bare feet and remembered the mean boys last night pulling at her shoes. *They must have hit me with something.* She looked around her and saw a rum bottle lying nearby. *Guess it was that bottle,* she thought, grimacing as a pain shot through her head. She put her hand to her head near the pain and felt a large swollen place by her eye, and another by her jawbone. Her shoes and socks were gone—the compass, too. A large black bruise almost circled one ankle, and another bruise swelled out near the other ankle. She had been robbed.

She stood up. Her ankles were unsteady; her head hurt, and her muscles ached all over her body. She stumbled out to the street, looking around for help. There was no one to help, only locked-up taverns with dirty doors and filthy bums lying about in the doorways. Some were beat up, maybe mugged like she was, but more likely from drunken brawls. The streets smelled putrid, with odors of trash and worse.

Two blocks down a side street, Kathryn saw a bakery. The fresh bread smelled so good. She went inside the storefront, and the small lady tending the store gasped at the sight of her. "George, come quickly! There's a young man here in front. He's wounded!" she shouted through the open door that led to the back. The man came running out—and then backed away.

"Mayhap he's a hobo, looking to rob us," he said quietly to the woman, but not quietly enough for Kathryn not to hear. At least her ears worked well.

"I won't harm you. I've been harmed myself … and robbed … last night on the street," Kathryn said weakly.

The woman quickly went through the door to the back, brought back a wet towel, and started to clean the wound on Kathryn's head.

"You're always too distrustful," she protested to the man with a grimace. "A body could be bleeding to death and you'd think they was about to rob us!" Turning to Kathryn, she said, "I don't think the wound is too bad, but your head must hurt terribly."

"Throbbing," Kathryn said as she touched the side of her head where the bottle had found its mark, leaving a patch of hair matted with blood.

"Here, sit down and tell us what happened, young man. What's your name?" she asked kindly.

"Grammy, uh … Gramm! Gramm's my name," replied Kathryn. "I was mugged in the alley last night and they took all I had." She looked down at her bare feet as George and Mary looked at each other and then back at her with pity.

"Get him some muffins and milk, Mary," George finally said, and Mary did just that. No food ever tasted as good to Kathryn as those muffins did.

"Where do you come from, Gramm?" asked George.

"The colonies," answered Kathryn. "I need a job. I have no money or home."

George and Mary looked at each other.

"We don't have a cart peddler on the streets," said Mary as she looked at George for help. "What do you think, George? We could bring out the old cart and give him a job."

"Maybe," said George, rubbing his chin, thinking as he paced back and forth in front of the window of the bakery. "He could sleep in the back storage room, if we straighten it up, Mary." Turning to Kathryn, he said, "It wouldn't pay much, Gramm."

"I'll take it!" Kathryn burst out and stuck her hand out to shake on the deal. "I can start today, as soon as we clean up your storage room."

"It's a deal," said George, and he shook Kathryn's hand. Feeling the softness of her hand, he turned it over, examining it briefly and looked back at her. "You runaway boys from the colonies must find roughing it alone down here in Port Royal very difficult, huh, Gramm?"

"Yes," replied Kathryn as she jerked her hand down and wiped her palm on her pants. If he thought she was a runaway as well as a young man, then, from now on, it would be her disguise.

George shoved the cart out of the storage room while Gramm piled the boxes high in the corners, making room for the sleeping cot George brought down for Gramm from their quarters upstairs. By the time they had finished cleaning the storage room, Mary had the cart cleaned and piled high with muffins and fresh bread.

"Looks like I have my work laid out for me," Gramm laughed as he looked at the cart, full of baked goods. "You won't be sorry you trusted me."

George gave Gramm a little change and explained the value of each coin to him. He waved bye to them and was off on his new job.

Two hours later, the cart rolled up in front of the bakery and George went outside to see Gramm—and an empty cart!

"Did you get robbed again?" he asked anxiously.

"Not at all," Gramm grinned as they walked inside. Gramm emptied his pockets and piled the coins up on the counter. "I sold all of it ... to the sailors coming off the ships along the docks!"

"The docks?" asked George.

"Yes," replied Gramm, "and I doubled the prices, too. They expect to pay more for delivery to the docks, and they're all loaded with coins to spend."

George burst into laughter. "Mary, bring out tomorrow's bread and muffins," shouted George with a big grin. "Gramm is a genius!"

They piled the cart high, even higher than before, with fresh muffins, bread, and small chocolate cakes.

Gramm was off again and Mary and George went back into the kitchen to bake. Twice more, Gramm came back for baked goods, and at the end of the day, they all sat down, exhausted.

"Mary, with Gramm's help, we have almost a week's earnings here," said George with a smile, "and in just one day!"

Gramm's feet were blistered and red on the bottom, and they burned like fire. He rubbed them as he sat on the floor of the bakery.

"You'll need shoes, Gramm, and some more clothes, too," said Mary. "George, take Gramm over to MacIver's and get him some shoes and a change of clothes. I'll wash these for him tomorrow."

When Gramm and George returned from MacIver's, Gramm was wearing new shoes, long socks, knickers, a man's blousy linen shirt with long sleeves ... and a smile, for the clothes hid the fact that Gramm was a woman very nicely.

It had been a good day for Gramm. While at the docks all day, he had asked the sailors lots of questions about the ships that had come in and out of the port in the last few days. Not only did it cause the sailors to linger at the cart, buying and eating more cakes and attracting other sailors, but it had enabled him to get helpful information.

One sailor had thought he saw a young boy go aboard a ship named the *Black Opal*. Another told him that he thought the *Black Opal* had sailed yesterday but wasn't sure. Tomorrow he would go back and ask more questions. But for now, he would sleep. It had been a long day, but a good day. He was closer to finding Jon, he thought.

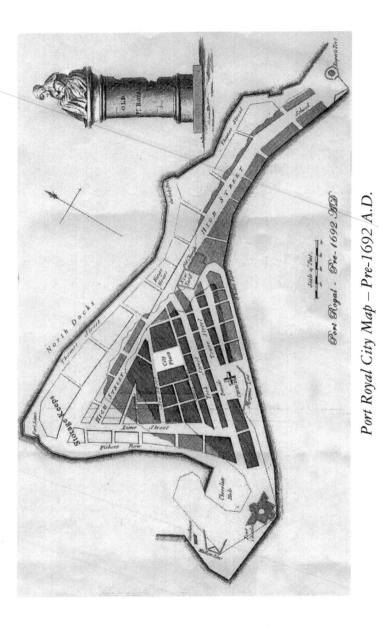

Port Royal City Map – Pre-1692 A.D.

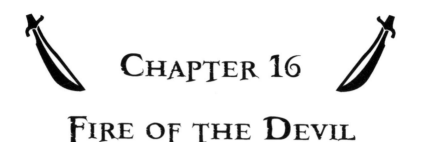

CHAPTER 16

FIRE OF THE DEVIL

"Who is firing on us?" demanded BlackHeart. He strained to see the villainous ship through the fog and smoke.

"Can't see anything out there, Captain," Mr. Token responded.

Curly and his men now had the fire under control, but another shot like the last one could be devastating to them.

"BlackHeart!" sounded a bloodcurdling shout through the misty fog.

BlackHeart froze. He recognized that gravelly, croaky voice. "*Shark Scar!*" he whispered. Captain Shark Scar, it was said, had survived having his head inside a great white shark's mouth, with its four rows of teeth. And, indeed, his face looked as though the tale was true. To detract from his grotesquely scarred face, he dressed in the most flamboyant styles of that day and, unlike most pirates, his clothes were impeccably clean.

"Answer me, BlackHeart! Do I finish you now ... or do we talk?" the weird voice croaked wickedly from within the fog.

"I need to coax him aboard the *Black Opal*," BlackHeart said to Mr. Token, who nodded in agreement.

"Why, Shark Scar, me ole friend, I didn't know ye were in our part of the sea! Come aboard and have a glass of port with me," shouted BlackHeart convincingly.

"Send Mr. Token over in a dinghy first, as me hostage," shouted Shark Scar, "so I'll be knowin' for sure that ye won't fire on me or me ship!"

BlackHeart hadn't planned on that. Shark Scar was smarter than he thought. He knew BlackHeart would not fire on the *Shark* with the elderly quartermaster onboard.

Mr. Token stood on the quarterdeck, his long black coattails flapping in the wind. A black wool top hat covered his frizzy gray-white hair, which blew in the breeze. His stony white face showed no emotion. He moved close to BlackHeart. "I'll go," he said quietly.

"I don't like it," BlackHeart said in a low voice. "It may be a trap of some kind. I won't have anything happening to you on my account."

Mr. Token combed the side of his short white beard with his fingertips. "Nothing will happen. Shark Scar wants something," he said, eyes squinted. "Or else we'd all be dead or treading water. They clearly had us at the disadvantage, Captain. I'll go." BlackHeart nodded.

"Okay," BlackHeart shouted to Shark Scar. "But come with only two oarsmen ... unarmed!"

"Ready the dinghy for Mr. Token! Four oarsmen! Fully armed!" BlackHeart commanded, and it was done.

Mr. Token and the two burly, heavily armed rowers, hatchets in hand, were lowered to the water and then lost in the fog as they rowed to the other ship. Several minutes passed.

"Dinghy ahoy!" shouted Guidry, and Jon ran to the railing to watch as a dinghy came out of the fog. Two oarsmen, their backs to the *Black Opal*, plied the deep waters, escorting their tall passenger: a man wearing a red coat and a large black hat with a white ostrich plume.

Once aboard the ship, the man, clad in the red silk thigh-length coat, a gold vest, and gray striped pants, faced the captain. Jon could not see his face, but the crew seemed to shy away as he passed them and walked haughtily to the foot of the stairs leading to the quarterdeck, where BlackHeart stood waiting. He climbed the stairs.

Captain Shark Scar was a little taller than Captain BlackHeart, considered by Jon to be a very tall man. He stood for a moment, eyeing BlackHeart. The silence was broken by BlackHeart with a grand smile.

"Well, me fine friend, what brings ye to me ship, the *Black Opal*, and why did ye announce yourself in such grand style?" inquired BlackHeart in a silky voice.

"Ye knows exactly why I'm here, ye blackguard!" exclaimed Shark Scar.

"No, I don't," replied BlackHeart, still smiling at Shark Scar. "But sure I am that you'll be telling me soon enough, eh, cap'n? Let's go to me cabin and sit a spell whilst we share stories and a glass o'port."

BlackHeart ushered Shark Scar toward his cabin. Motioning to Jon, he said, "Come attend us, Jon."

Jon went running to the cabin door, opened it, and turned around just in time to see the most hideously scarred face he had ever seen coming toward him. Jon quickly looked away, wishing he could stay outside with the crew. But the captain had made it clear that his job was to attend the captain, and his guests when they were onboard. So he went into the cabin, removed two goblets from the open cabinet, and filled them with port wine. Then he turned to the broken glass on the floor and began picking up the pieces.

"That'll cost ye, Shark Scar, me friend!" BlackHeart said, pointing to the broken crystal wine goblet on the floor.

"Every time I comes nearst ye, it costs me," snarled Shark Scar. "But this time, it could cost *you*, BlackHeart. Your life!"

"Now now, Shark Scar, what has ye in such a snit this time?" asked BlackHeart, as if he didn't know.

"I sailed to the island on the map I traded from ye, you thief! I lost six men to them eatin' fishes whilst my men waded through the pond in front of the waterfall where ye said the Inca treasures was hid. There warn't no cave behind the waterfall in which to hold the Inca treasures!" yelled Shark Scar with a fury that echoed throughout the ship.

"There was eatin' fishes in the pond? Hmmm," BlackHeart said quietly as he rubbed his chin and turned away, hiding his shock. He knew the "eating fishes", as Shark Scar called them, were piranha.

"Ye knew there was eatin' fishes on that island, ye sleazebag! Ye sent me and me men there to be attacked by them fishes!" Shark Scar screamed as he pounded his fist on BlackHeart's desk, his eyes glaring.

"If that be true," BlackHeart said in a soothing voice, trying to settle Shark Scar down a bit, "how did ye get over the water with the eatin' fishes to get to the waterfall?"

"We used sticks to pull the fallen men together and pushed some on top each other whilst the fishes was still hanging on to the dead men's flesh, still a biting. Then we walked across the dead men and under the falls. And there *warn't no cave* there! Just rock!" roared Shark Scar.

"Where's the map? Hand it to me, if ye will," said BlackHeart quietly, covering his shiver with a shrug of his shoulders.

"I ain't got it. I tore it in tiny little pieces, as I thought about tearing *you* into jest as many tiny pieces!" Shark Scar seethed as he sat grumbling under his breath and grinding his teeth in anger. His scarred chin settled into the white lace ruffles of his shirt. "Then," he said dreamily, "I burned the map." He shuddered, shaking his head as if coming out of a trance and jumped to his feet. Glaring down at BlackHeart sitting on the other side of his desk, he shouted, "Just like I burnt your boat today!"

"Oh!" BlackHeart said, recoiling from Shark Scar's enraged face and spewing spit. "Yes, well, a minor detail we shan't tarry on," BlackHeart went on calmly as Shark Scar sat back down. "If there be no cave on the island, well, then, obviously ye didn't follow the map correctly, and therefore, uh, ye been searching on the wrong island. And now, we don't have the map to look at, because ye burned it in a fit o' your temper. Another *minor detail.*

I'll just give ye another map and ye can be on your way," BlackHeart said, like an adult coddling a small child.

"I don't want another map! I want the Inca treasures and my five thousand gold pieces I paid ye ... or, I will see the *Black Opal* with its conniving Cap'n BlackHeart going straight down in this sea, with the rest o' Davy Jones crew," Shark Scar said pointedly. "Today!"

"Well, now," BlackHeart said calmly as he picked up the key laying next to his quill pen on the desk. "If ye had my expert goldfinder, ye might not have had this problem." BlackHeart walked to the door and called out to Spider, who came running.

"Take this key and unlock the hold. Bring up me fine new silver goldfinder with the lights on the top, Spider," instructed BlackHeart, raising his eyebrow. Spider looked confused. "You know ..." BlackHeart winked behind Shark Scar's back as he looked at Spider, "the one Jon brought the day he came aboard, which excited all the crewmen." Spider's eyes brightened, and Jon's eyes widened with shock.

That's why I couldn't find the Transformer. It wasn't here, thought Jon as he moved toward the door to follow Spider. But BlackHeart turned a cold glare at him, and he stayed where he was.

Spider was back in a few minutes, holding the Transformer out to BlackHeart. Jon reached his hand out quickly to grab the Transformer from Spider. The captain grabbed Jon's shoulder, his fingers digging sharply into Jon's flesh. Again the captain gave Jon a look with eyes that had the threat of *death* in them.

Jon dropped his hand and stepped back. It was of no use; he knew he could not battle all of these cruel, wicked men. And for what, a broken Transformer? For all he knew, Grammy might have gone back home in the *Carousel* without him, thinking he was dead. He felt truly alone and defeated.

"Now, ye see, Cap'n Shark Scar," BlackHeart was saying, "ye points the silver goldfinder at the place where ye thinks the gold is at, and if indeed there be gold there, the goldfinder has a red light that flashes." Jon and Spider knew BlackHeart was bluffing, but Shark Scar didn't.

"Lemme see," said Shark Scar as he grabbed the Transformer, looked it over, and pointed it here and there. "It don't work!"

"Well, o'course not," BlackHeart said. "That's because there ain't no gold where ye be pointing, so the goldfinder is saying so by not having a light, ye see! Do ye have any gold on ye, cap'n?" BlackHeart asked with a sparkling glint in his eyes. Shark Scar pulled out five gold doubloons and dropped them clinking onto the desk.

"Jon, show the fine cap'n how the goldfinder shows the red light when gold is present," BlackHeart drawled. The Transformer lay in the palm of his hand as he extended it outward to Jon in a ceremonial manner.

Jon knew what the captain wanted him to do. He input his three-digit code, and the screen of the Transformer and all the numbers lit up with blue. Shark Scar's eyes widened with surprise. He moved closer and watched intently as Jon pointed the Transformer at the 24-karat gold coins laying on the desk and clicked the Off button.

The Transformer flashed its red light once, and the device went dark. Believing the red light was an indicator of pure gold, Shark Scar grinned broadly, showing very red, bleeding gums with a few scraggly teeth.

"Now, let me be sure ye have the correct map!" BlackHeart said hurriedly, rummaging through some papers in his desk drawer. He brought out a tattered and worn folded paper and thrust it toward Shark Scar. "Here 'tis, cap'n. Sure I am that ye wants to be on your way quickly. The island where the Inca treasures be hidden is very near to Port Royal."

"Now," BlackHeart said, "would ye please be yelling to your crew to release Mr. Token. And soon as he arrives back here safe-like, ye can shove off for your own ship."

Ignoring BlackHeart for the moment, Shark Scar opened the folded paper and looked at it. "Is the X marking the Inca treasures behind a waterfall? I don't see markings showing no waterfall here on the map," he said, suspiciously eyeing BlackHeart.

"Maybe, maybe not. But sure I am that ye knows how to find the X on a *true* treasure map, eh, cap'n?" replied BlackHeart as he cocked one eyebrow and grinned slightly.

Shark Scar nodded, put the folded map inside the breast pocket of his coat, and headed for the door. He looked back at BlackHeart with a devious grin.

BlackHeart could see the happy, greedy look in Shark Scar's eyes, and said, "That's right, me old friend, ye take the best of me: ye get the map to the Inca treasures and the goldfinder to find more treasure, all for only five doubloons."

Shark Scar's devious grin turned angry at the mention of doubloons; he'd forgotten about his doubloons.

"Me five gold doubloons I left layin' on your desk, if ye please, ye thieving blackguard," Shark Scar said as he held out his hand.

BlackHeart stuck his hand in his pocket, pulled out one of Shark Scar's gold doubloons, and handed it to him.

"But, I give ye five!" Shark Scar snarled in disgust.

"I'll be keeping the other four to pay for the broken crystal goblet," BlackHeart said, motioning toward the now clean floor where the glass had laid. "And for the damage ye did to me ship when ye sent me your fancy callin' card, the cannonball announcing your arrival, which set me ship afire. Sure I am that ye wants to pay your debts by giving me these four doubloons. Eh, cap'n?"

"Harrumph!" sneered Shark Scar as he turned and walked toward the door, looking down at his new goldfinder. He stopped and turned to BlackHeart. "Me trading partner in Port Royal got real angry when I didn't bring him the Inca treasures like I promised. Sez his buyer in London was real disappointed, and since he buys all of me plunder taken from British ships I raze, I don't want to be making him unhappy again." Then he turned and pointed his finger into Blackheart's chest.

"If ye be lying again, I won't come a' quarreling with ye," Shark Scar said. "Ye'll be dead afore ye knows I'm nearst ye. Then I'll hang your body in a cage in the docks of Tortuga for all to watch the birds pick your bones clean, eyes first!" With that, Shark Scar turned and walked out onto the quarterdeck.

The fog was lifting when Jon stepped outside the cabin behind the two wicked captains. He could see Shark Scar's ship through the light haze, a big green and brown square-rigger with four tall masts. Flying at the top of the mizzenmast was a huge, red flag with the skull and bones. The name *"Shark"* was printed on her bow, and mounted directly under the bowsprit was the skull of a great white shark, with all four rows of teeth. On the starboard side of the ship could be seen twenty gun ports, all open, with cannon muzzles protruding and aimed straight at the *Black Opal*.

A dinghy had arrived from the other ship, and Shark Scar went down the ladder to the boat below.

Jon looked down at the coarse, gaudy man sitting in his dinghy below and wondered if Shark Scar wore such fancy clothes to draw attention away from his gruesome face or to hide the bloodthirsty monster that lived inside the clothes.

Captain Shark Scar yelled in a loud, strong voice for his crew on the *Shark* to release Mr. Token and his oarsmen. As soon as Mr. Token arrived at the *Black Opal*, Shark Scar's dinghy shoved off.

By the time Shark Scar was twenty yards away, Mr. Token and the oarsmen were aboard, the dinghy was stored, the anchor was hoisted, and the *Black Opal* was rapidly underway in the opposite direction, dropping her wide sails as she went.

CHAPTER 17

NO QUARTER GIVEN

"**G**ive us a bearing, Spider," yelled BlackHeart from the helm. "Let's get out of here!"

The square sails of the *Black Opal* had been secured in place within minutes after leaving Shark Scar, and billowed out like big balloons as the wind swiftly carried the *Black Opal* to safety. The *Shark* and its notorious captain were now far off in the distance behind them.

Spider held both hands up in the air, linked his thumbs together and splayed his long fingers apart, looking toward the sun as it shined through the broken clouds. He appeared to be measuring some kind of distance by hand. Then he unrolled a sea chart and laid it atop one of the storage boxes on the main deck. Jon watched as the long, hairy, black fingers of his right hand moved this way and that, using his thumb and little finger as pivots. His fingers worked their way across the map like a giant black spider taking steps. Then he did it again from the beginning, checking himself for accuracy.

"Northeast by north," yelled Spider.

The captain thought for a minute and then yelled, "Our new course is north two degrees by northeast one degree! Check me out, Spider!"

Spider measured from the sun again. Then his hairy fingers performed a new dance across the map. He checked it twice.

"That will put us just northwest of the last key near the Florida Straits, Cappin," he yelled out.

"Perfect!" shouted BlackHeart. "Alter the sails accordingly, Guidry.

Spider didn't even use a sextant, thought Jon, *and the captain calculated the math in his head! Wow!* Jon knew a little about sailing. He and Pappy had a small sailboat for a time on the lake at home.

"Drop the stay sails and secure! Drop the tops'ls. Drop the square sails," yelled Guidry to the sixteen men who rapidly climbed the rigging to the yards that held the big square sails. Jon couldn't help noticing the sailor with the shrunken head dangling from his rope belt as he climbed the riggings, the same shrunken head that had dangled in Jon's face yesterday when they took his Transformer. He shuddered.

"We be making a lot of noise, Cap'n, repairing this here deck from the escapades o' Shark Scar," slurred Curly as the chopping and ripping out of charred wood began.

Jon was watching the men repair the hole made by the cannonball and fire in the main deck when Spider walked by.

"How ye be, Jon?" asked Spider as he quickly passed with his rolled charts.

"Good," answered Jon. *That's the first time a crew member has spoken to me since the fight over the Transformer yesterday,* thought Jon with a slight smile. Moving closer to Curly, who was standing by the main mast, Jon asked, "Is Captain Shark Scar a friend of Captain BlackHeart?"

"Are ye daft, boy?" asked Curly, looking shocked.

"But he called him 'friend' all the time," said Jon.

Curly rolled his eyes. "Can't ye see the cap'n was a trying to make Shark Scar pipe down and be civil-like instead o' the madman that he is?"

Jon thought about that for a minute and then asked, "The skull and bones flag flying on Captain Shark Scar's ship was red, Mr. Curly. Why wasn't it black like the *Black Opal's* flag, sir?"

"Red means 'no quarter given,'" replied Curly, "and don't call me mister!"

"But what does 'no quarter given' mean, Curly?" asked Jon.

"Take no prisoners. Leave no persons alive," replied Curly sharply.

"Would they have killed us all if Captain BlackHeart had not made Captain Shark Scar happy by giving him my Transformer?" asked Jon.

"They would a' tried. Skull would nary let them harm the cap'n, though. Very loyal to the cap'n, he is," said Curly. "Ye has to choose your battles in this world if ye can, boy, when they is the most advantageous to ye." Then he jumped as if jolted by something, and quickly turned toward Jon. "Why, the *Shark's* a four-mast square-rigger! Don't ye know nothing 'bout ships? They had twenty-two loaded cannon aimed directly at us—twenty in the ports and two more on the foredeck. Didn't ye see 'em, lad?" asked Curly, clearly annoyed.

Curly pointed toward a spot on the deck for two men to place another pile of new deck planks and then turned back to Jon. "Look at the damage from jest one o' them cannonballs! What advantage be there for two ships to blow each other outta the water in the middle o' the sea? Ye has to negotiate your way outta these situations, and BlackHeart's the best! Where do ye get all these questions from, lad?" he asked with his hands on his hips.

"Oh, just wondering," Jon answered quietly as he walked away, his mind already working on his next curiosity. *Skull must be the man with all the scars and that little patch of braided blond hair hanging from his head. Wonder how that happened to him? And why he's so loyal to the captain?*

CHAPTER 18

CAPTIVE VISITOR

"The only reason you're not all dead men is because of Shark Scar's greed," BlackHeart's chilling words echoed through the ship's crew assembled before him. "We had something he wanted: the real map to the Inca treasures, which are hidden in our hideout on Devil's Rock. The treasures at Devil's Rock belong to us. All of us! Did you want me to give him the map to all the treasures just to save your skins?" A loud murmur went through the crew.

"Silence!" roared BlackHeart. "Shark Scar had us out manned, out gunned, outsmarted, and out of choices. Mr. Token risked his life. For you!"

Jon listened to the captain reprimand his men. He was glad he was not responsible.

A roar of denials and excuses came up from the crew.

"It was foggy ... it was the responsibility of those on watch ..."

"Silence!" BlackHeart shouted again. "There are *no* acceptable excuses for letting a ship sneak up on us, fog or no fog! It is the responsibility of every single crewman of this ship to keep proper lookout for other ships at all times ... especially in a fog where visibility is limited." BlackHeart continued, "The punishment for this offense is a flogging by the quartermaster with the cat o' nines at the least, or hanging from the yards of the mainmast for the betrayal of the officers and crew of this ship. Treason! Do you hear?"

The silence among the crew was deafening.

"I have thought this matter through since its occurrence yesterday and have decided not to punish the responsible parties for this single incident, only because there are far too many of you who are guilty of this defiance. But let there be no mistake," BlackHeart paused as he looked directly into the eyes of every crewmember, including Jon's, "such infractions will *not* be permitted to pass without proper punishment in the future. Do I make myself perfectly clear?"

A murmur and sigh of relief went through the crowd of men as the nods and "Aye, aye," and "Yes, Captain," came up from amongst them.

"Are there any nays among you?" the captain asked fearlessly.

Not a sound was heard, except the slap of the waves as the ship cut her way through them, and the roar of the ocean.

"Dismissed!" BlackHeart shouted. Jon stepped aside as the captain stomped past him through his cabin door and slammed it shut.

"Carry on. Back to work, you swabs!" yelled Curly.

Later in the day, Jon was leaving the galley after the midday meal when he heard the same strange whimpering sounds coming from down the dark corridor. He looked back into the galley and saw that Cook was occupied preparing the nighttime meal, singing happily.

He's busy and won't notice this time, thought Jon as he walked down the corridor toward the door bolted from the outside. The floor boards creaked beneath his feet, and cold air rushed out from under the door, causing the candle flame in a nearby lantern to flicker, almost going out. Jon was suddenly afraid. If the flame went out, he would be here in the dark, alone, with whatever waited inside the room.

Then the sounds started again: a whining and a loud knocking noise. The sounds were coming from inside the room, just like before. *Is it a kitten?* wondered Jon. *And why is it locked in this room?* His curiosity overcame his fear as he reached up, slid the bolt back, and opened the door a crack to look in.

Suddenly, the door was yanked open. Standing before Jon was the sailor who had been groggy and carried below by Skull and Spider the day they had sailed. The wind was blowing through an open porthole window as the swaying of the ship knocked the loose, unlatched window back and forth against the wall.

The dirty sailor smelled of urine and sweat and looked at Jon with a crazy, frightened expression. Then he started laughing weirdly and pointing his finger at Jon as he fell backward onto the cot in a sitting position. "Bang, bang!" he said, "You're dead!" Then he rolled onto his side and brought his knees up under his chin.

"Don't leave me in this cave with the rats and the bats!" he yelled hysterically, covering his face with his long, reddish hair and his hands. Slowly, his hands slid off his face, exposing his wild, gray-blue eyes. He smiled, showing his teeth, and then he whispered loudly, "Marooned ... no food ... left to die ... didn't die ... ate rats." He grinned again, looking up at Jon. Jon had never seen such light gray eyes. The gray iris almost blended into the white of each eye, making the dilated, black pupils incredibly prominent. "*Red Dragon* ... gold, lots of gold ... emeralds ... brilliant green emeralds ... Spanish galleon *Anatole* ... sunken ... shallow waters." He frowned again, whispering mistily as if seeing a mirage. "Marooned, left to die.

"I'll show ye where, Captain!" exclaimed the sailor, jumping up and grabbing hold of Jon's arm. Jon tried to pull away but the sailor only tightened his grip, pushing Jon against the wall. "I'm the navigator of the *Red Dragon*. I speak Mandarin ... lived my life in Singapore ... happy, very happy ... singing songs, beautiful songs, hymns. Parents were missionaries."

The sailor now had one hand on Jon's throat, his thumb under one ear and his fingers splayed across Jon's throat to the other ear, almost choking him. In his other hand, he held Jon's arm in a death grip. Beads of perspiration broke out across Jon's forehead, and fear spread through him like burning fire as he struggled to free himself from the grip of the crazed sailor.

"I know these waters, Captain ... I know where ... twenty-five degrees north, eighty-five degrees west ... no food, marooned, left to die." The sailor relaxed his grip momentarily and Jon broke free, tripping over a chamber and spilling its contents of urine and excrement all over his feet. "Marooned ... *marooned!*" the sailor yelled, his eyes nervously jerking side to side as Jon darted for the door with the wild sailor grabbing at him.

Jon jumped out into the corridor and yanked the door shut, quickly sliding the bolt across, locking the door. He was panting, his heart pounding in his chest as the cursing sailor slammed his fists violently against the other side of the door. Jon turned to see the captain standing right behind him, his hooded green eyes almost black.

"Well, Jon, when will you learn to follow orders?" BlackHeart said in quiet, menacing anger. "I have told you not to wander about the ship!" He grabbed Jon roughly by the arm. "I think maybe you have too much free time. Come with me!" Jon's teeth were chattering as the captain forcefully walked him to the galley, his feet barely touching the deck.

"Find something for Jon to do," BlackHeart said to Cook as he shoved Jon into the galley. "He needs work to keep him out of trouble."

"Oui, I will give it to him," Cook said cheerfully. "Thank you, cap-i-tan! I can use zee help of Jon and his young legs." BlackHeart turned abruptly and stalked back up the steps to the main deck, two at a time.

Turning to Jon, Cook said, "Now, Jon, first you will wash with zee dishes there, and then after, you may dry them, as well. Oui'? Yes?"

"Oui', yes!" said Jon and he smiled at Cook, who smiled back and patted Jon on the shoulder.

"Well? Hop to it! Go, go!" Cook said, motioning toward the dishes.

Jon finished the dishes and asked Cook what else he had for him to do. That's when Cook grabbed a lantern and a metal bucket and took Jon below the decks for the first time.

Though there were lanterns lit below, the passageways seemed darker than those of the decks above. The lower they went, the more Jon could feel the rocking of the ship and hear the creaking of the timbers of the ship's hull and braces. The smell was moldy, sour, and that of animal feces. Stacks and stacks of burlap bags containing flour, grain, rice, and feed lined the walls of the ship's hull. Finally, they reached the many animals that were crowded together in small separate pens: chickens with a roost covered with chicken wire, about twenty goats, fifty pigs, three calves, and rats, rats, and more rats!

Jon hated the squealing and skittering of the rats and kept looking down and about him, to see if they were getting on him or near him.

"You will ignore zee rats," Cook said, unconcerned. "They will not harm you if you do not sit very still for too long. But they are becoming too many, so I will ask Gituku to tell his men to make some of zee rats absent from zee ship.

"Now, Jon," said Cook, pulling up a short stool, "you shall milk a goat in zis manner."

Jon had milked a cow, but never a goat. After watching for a minute, Jon tried his hand at milking the goat. "This would be easier if she would stand still," Jon said as he picked up his overturned stool and started again. Cook laughed and rolled his eyes as he watched the goat squirm this way and that.

He showed Jon how to add rum to water that had sat stagnant in the storage barrels. This would distill it and remove the sour taste, making it safe to drink. This water was called grog, Cook said. He told Jon that four times a day, Jon was to fill all the buckets on the main deck with grog and the bread buckets with hard, flat biscuits, similar to thick cookies but without the sugar, for the crew to nibble on between meals to stave off hunger and fatigue. And later, Jon learned how to feed the animals and collect the eggs, with the cackling hens flapping their wings and pecking Jon on the back of his neck.

"You are very much like a bull in zee china shop, but you shall learn," said Cook. Then he showed Jon how to secure the door to the coop.

"You must be most careful, Jon, to secure the pens. If the animals get out, we could lose them to the sea and have no food," cautioned Cook. "Zee captain would not like it, even a tiny bit."

"I understand," said Jon, remembering the captain's anger that morning. Cook left Jon to his work and went back up to the galley.

Jon had returned to the galley several times, first with buckets of goat's milk and then with fresh eggs in the bucket. When he had finished all that the cook wanted done, he wandered back down the stairway that led to the deck where the animals were, but stopped on the deck just above. He walked through the short corridor that opened into a very long open room with cannon on both sides.

It was a dimly lit, wide room that spanned the entire width of the ship and held ten cannon. A walkway down the middle separated the bronze cannon, five on each side of the ship, with a closed wooden window, or port, in front of each cannon. The cannon rested on slide rails, allowing some recoil movement when the guns were fired and to carry them forward when the port was open and backward, when the cannon were not in use.

"Harrumph!" said someone near one of the ports. Jon walked toward the last cannon and saw a man sitting in the shadows. He could not see the man's head, but the man's wet, scarred chest shone as he moved forward, and Jon saw the face of the man they called Skull.

Chapter 19

Skull

"My name is Jon," he said, and bravely held out his trembling hand to the scarred, bald-headed sailor.

"Skull," said the sailor sharply as he shook Jon's hand with the single downward jerk of his hand and immediately went back to polishing the cannon.

"Are you the master gunner?" asked Jon.

"That's me," Skull said boringly.

Jon's instincts said, "Run," but he was intrigued by the tall man. "I could help you clean the cannon, i-if you want," he said timidly. Jon had helped Pappy polish the brass fittings and rails on the *Carousel* many times.

"Do you want to clean the iron or polish the brass tampons and ramrods?" asked Skull.

"I clean brass really well," answered Jon.

"Grab a rag and polish then," Skull said, pointing to the polish and the rags.

Jon picked up a rag and started to polish the brass on the cannon next to the one Skull was working on.

"You'd best remove your shirt or it'll be black as my hands," Skull said, exposing soot-blackened hands. Jon nodded as he removed his shirt and laid it on one of the cannon.

"Take it off the cannon," Skull said sharply. "Never put anything on top of cannon. Put it in that corner."

Jon put his shirt in the corner and sat down at the cannon. "Have you been on the *Black Opal* long?" he asked.

"Six years," replied Skull.

"Where do you come from?" asked Jon.

"The colonies," replied Skull as he moved to the other side of the cannon and sat down with his back to Jon. Skull's back was very muscular, even though it was marred by many deep scars.

"I'm from the colonies, too," said Jon, trying to remember the history and geography of the late sixteen hundreds. "Where in the colonies?"

"New York," replied Skull as he turned with a slight grin, thinking about home.

The conversation continued, mostly with Jon asking questions, lots of questions.

"How did you meet Captain BlackHeart?" asked Jon

Skull told Jon that he had come to Port Royal to prove to his wealthy family that he could make a grand life for himself without them, living in the tropical islands. He hated the harsh, frigid winters of the Northeast. His father was a publisher, and Skull had wanted no part of the "ink and binding," as he put it.

He said he had put out to sea the first time on a merchant ship. The work had been grueling, and the crew tough and mean-spirited. He left the merchant ship for a schooner owned by a privateer. That's when he learned about the men who worked for the British governor of the West Indies, Port Royal, and other islands in the Caribbean.

Most of the privateers were Englishmen, some very wealthy noblemen from England. Others were from the colonies or elsewhere. They traded and bartered with people in the island ports, South and Central America, and Mexico, and even directly with pirates, for stolen goods. Nothing was off limits, even people: slaves, hostages for ransom.

"Were there slaves on Cap'n BlackHeart's ship?" asked Jon.

"Never! BlackHeart says captains who enslave others have no heart, not even a black one," said Skull. Pirate ships were democratic, Skull told Jon. The crew could vote to put anyone off the ship or put them to death. They could vote one captain out and a new one to take his place. Pirate's code! In that instance, the former captain was usually killed or marooned on an island, he told Jon.

Just like the sailor, Jon thought, and a shiver passed over him.

"You didn't tell me where you met Captain BlackHeart," Jon reminded Skull.

Skull frowned and looked away, trying to decide whether or not he wanted to tell this young boy the gruesome story. Jon looked at the many scars on Skull's head and the small patch of braided blond hair that hung from one side, and waited for Skull's response.

Finally, Skull spoke.

I had just joined the crew of the Accord, *which was Captain Brighton's ship. We sailed for Devil's Rock, where the two captains had planned a meeting at their hideout. That's when I met Captain BlackHeart. The two captains shared the hideout; now it belongs only to BlackHeart and the crew of the* Black Opal.

Captain Brighton was a free spirit; he didn't like living by rules. He was British and knew BlackHeart. They were all friends in England: Captain BlackHeart, Captain Brighton, and Mr. Token—he was their don at Oxford.

We were sitting in the hideout among the vast treasure of the two captains when Captain Brighton threw out the idea of going to the Island of the Lost Treasures. Many lost treasures lie there, it is said, but it is death to any who try to go into that island. Captain BlackHeart immediately said no and tried to persuade Captain Brighton not to go to the island. But the crew of the Accord *was revved up, and our captain willing. So we went, with gold in our eyes.*

Captain BlackHeart and the crew of the Black Opal *followed behind, unbeknown to us.*

It was late afternoon when we entered the bay at Lost Treasures. We rowed quietly to shore and crossed the narrow beach to a clump of trees just outside the main forest of the island. That should have been our first clue to leave the wretched island immediately. Instead, our crew thought it amusing that shrunken heads mounted high on spikes peered down at us, as if deliberately placed there to scare us away from the island.

We continued into the forest, with only the twilight sounds of birds and small predators seeking an evening meal piercing the air. Farther into the forest there were more shrunken heads, their facial features twisted with agonizing expressions of pure torture. We began to hear rhythmic drums off in the distance.

The forest became darker as we progressed, maybe from the sinking of the sun and the dense foliage overhead. The sounds of the drums grew louder and more hostile, pulsating in my head. Although each of us looked at the other with trepidation, no one was willing to admit his innermost fright to the other for fear of ridicule.

Suddenly, the natives came at us from everywhere! Anywhere! The horrors that took place on that island that night are such that I will not recount them even to myself. It is something I have locked in my innermost mind, lest it come out to haunt me still. I was scalped by the natives that night and hung by my feet from a tree and left to die. The pain of it all ...

beyond belief!

Captain BlackHeart and some of this crew—Spider, Curly, others—cut me down and carried me to their ship. They had followed us onto that perilous island.

I can only say to you that Captain BlackHeart saved my life. The legend is that the natives of that island want no visitors. The legend is true—no visitors. I was young and followed my captain and the crewmen of my ship.

After they brought me here, days stretched into weeks as I recovered. I would awake at night to see Captain BlackHeart sitting in a chair, or asleep, with his head lying on the foot of my bed. At first his head was bandaged, but sometime during the time I was recovering, his bandage went away. He got the scar on his forehead that night saving me. Eventually I healed. The others with me that night were not so fortunate. Most of our ship's crew, including Captain Brighton, perished that night.

Guidry told me that our ship, the Accord, *was sunk in the small bay of the island that night by BlackHeart, who was angry and distraught over the loss of his close friend and the loss of our crew. Ninety-seven men! The few crewmembers who had been left on watch aboard the* Accord *were the only other survivors of our crew. They were brought aboard BlackHeart's ship before the sinking. Guidry was one of them.*

Skull looked pointedly into Jon's eyes. "Cap'n BlackHeart can be a tough, unbending man, but as long as I am alive, no harm will come to him. He could have left me to die that night, but he didn't," Skull said finally.

There was a noise in the corridor and the captain burst in.

"Jon!" the captain snapped loudly. "I told you not to be wandering about this ship." BlackHeart stood, hands braced on his hips, towering over Jon.

"Uh-h," Jon stuttered, "Cook was finished with me so I came in here. Have I left something undone in your cabin, sir?" asked Jon.

Ignoring the question, BlackHeart said angrily, "Don't you know how to count the bells even yet? Do we need to fire cannon as a reminder? Where is my dinner?" roared the captain as he looked around at the four clean cannon, their brass shining. Then he looked back at Jon's shirtless and black-smudged chest and hands and at the grin on Skull's face.

"Your dinner?" asked Jon. Then he jumped to a standing position, dropping the polishing rag on the deck. "I'm sorry, Captain, sir!" he said as he grabbed his shirt and ran for the corridor. "Right away, Captain," he said, jerking on his shirt and running for the galley. *In trouble again!* he thought as he peered over his shoulder to see if the captain was following behind him.

He was.

Chapter 20

The Silver Clue

Grammy had spent the last few days at the docks, selling cakes, bread, and muffins, and collecting information. She now knew that Jon was aboard the *Black Opal*, probably held captive. The ship, she was told, was commanded by the notorious and conniving Captain BlackHeart.

The little folded, fried fruit pies Grammy taught Mary to make were such a success at the docks that George hired two new helpers for the baking so that Mary could cook the pies in a pan without burning them.

Today when Grammy, still posing as Gramm, arrived at the docks with her cart of baked goodies and fried apricot and key lime pies, there was a large green ship anchored next to the *Red Dragon* in the bay. "*Shark*" the name on the bow read. The skull of a great white shark, teeth and all, was mounted directly under the bowsprit. As men came off the skiffs from the *Shark*, they made a beeline for Gramm's cart and the delicious baked goods.

Gramm had returned from the bakery twice more, the cart filled with more cakes and pies, when the heavily guarded skiff bearing Captain Shark Scar, dressed in all his colorful finery, came ashore. He strode arrogantly with long steps toward the cart, and Gramm got the shock that most people got upon seeing Shark Scar for the first time.

Having been an emergency room nurse before marrying Pappy and during the time Pappy worked at NASA, she was accustomed to seeing horrible injuries. She had learned to look beyond injuries of the face and straight into people's eyes so as not to embarrass them. As Shark Scar approached the cart, Gramm did not turn away but looked him straight in the eyes. "Cakes, pies?"

"Harrumph!" said Shark Scar, clearing his throat. "What be that?" he asked, pointing to the fried pies.

"Fresh key lime pies and apricot pies," replied Gramm. "Which one do you want?"

"Both!" replied Shark Scar as he reached into his purple long coat for coins.

"Six pieces of eight," said Gramm, hand outstretched.

"Expensive, ain't they?" asked Shark Scar.

"Yes ... good, too!" replied Gramm.

A smile quirked in the corners of Shark Scar's lips as he waited for Gramm to back off his price. Gramm stared him in the eye and did not back down. Gramm reasoned that the sailors had not quibbled over the price, so why should this captain. He knew he had won the debate when Shark Scar handed over the six pieces of eight, took a pie in each hand, and bit down into one.

Shark Scar shut his eyes, and the expression on his face was one of sheer delight. He crammed the rest of the first pie into his mouth and bit into the second one, smiling and nodding his head in approval. "Bring the knapsacks," he told a heavily armed crewman, who motioned to three others. They came forward with sacks.

"I'll take th' lot of it!" he exclaimed. "How much?"

Gramm stood there shocked. "Well, uh, uh," he stammered as he tried to figure out how much for the cartful of goodies.

"I'll give ye five gold doubloons," said Shark Scar, looking around impatiently. "Make up your mind, boy!"

"More than enough," Gramm said, surprised at the huge amount Shark Scar was offering. *Why, that's $600 in modern money,* thought Gramm. *Money means nothing to him.*

Shark Scar handed Gramm the five doubloons and motioned to his men to take the cartful of baked goods. "Put them aboard!" he directed. "We'll be back tonight for another cartful at th' same price, boy. And don't cheat me, ye hear?"

"No, sir ... I mean ... yes, sir!" stammered Gramm.

Shark Scar roared with laughter and stalked away arrogantly, his big boots echoing loudly across the wooden planks of the dock. "I'll be at The Three Crowns," he shouted over his shoulder. His men were left behind to hassle with the knapsacks full of baked goods, muskets, cutlasses, and the like.

The sun was going down when Captain Shark Scar and his men got back to the dock from town. Gramm had sold three more carts of baked goods on the docks since the big sale to the captain this morning. Although

Gramm had not wanted any of the gold, Mary and George insisted on splitting it. They had kept the first five doubloons that morning and instructed Gramm to keep the five doubloons from the last delivery to the captain.

It was dusk when Gramm got back to town and put up the cart for the night. He walked down the street, breathing in the clean salt air. The strong breeze blew away most of the rank street smells usually present.

As he passed the gentlemen's haberdashery, his eyes fell upon something in the window that made his heart beat fast. There in the window of the store next to a "For Sale" sign lay the shiny stainless steel Transformer!

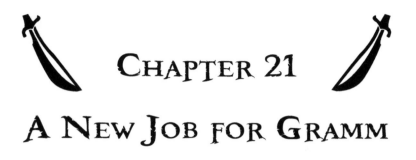

CHAPTER 21

A NEW JOB FOR GRAMM

G rammy rushed inside the haberdashery, talking so fast that the shop owner asked her to slow down. She calmed herself and decided she should not tell the shop owner too much, so she just said, "What is that object in the window?"

"Oh, I don't rightly know," he said. "The captain who traded it to me said it was a goldfinder. But I couldn't make it work, and he couldn't either. I traded for it anyway, because the captain bought three very expensive coats, he did, and two hats with real ostrich plumes on them. A very fancy dresser, he is. *'Only the best for me,'* the captain said."

"How much do you want for the, uh, goldfinder?" asked Grammy.

"What do you think it's worth?" asked the shopkeeper.

"Would this cover the cost?" asked Grammy, pulling out one gold doubloon.

"My, my ... yes!" said the shopkeeper, smiling. "The captain who bought the coats paid with gold doubloons, too—a knapsack full of them."

"What was his name?" asked Grammy.

"Why, Captain Shark Scar from the ship named *Shark*. A horribly scarred man, he is, but nice enough. It is said that once he was attacked by a shark in the water and survived to tell about it. Had his head right in the shark's mouth, he did. Scary tale, huh?"

"Yes ... scary tale," Grammy said as she opened the door to leave.

"Come again, boy. Sometimes I get some really interesting things in trade for clothes, I do. Might need some expensive clothes like these for yourself someday. Oh, I forgot. You paid too much for that goldfinder rubbish. Your change, boy," he said as he handed Grammy a handful of various coins.

Outside, Grammy headed to the outskirts of town. She opened the flip-lid of the Transformer and punched in her codes; no response. She tried the codes again and again; no response. The screen was black—not even a flicker of light. *It doesn't work*, she thought sadly as she put it in her pocket.

Captain Shark Scar knows where Jon is, thought Grammy as she looked at the Transformer. *Looks like I'll have to get on a ship in order to find BlackHeart and Jon. Shark Scar's ship would be best because he's had contact with Jon, or else he wouldn't have had the Transformer. But how can I get aboard? And how much longer can I keep up this charade as a young man without being found out?* Before she went back to the bakeshop, Grammy stopped by McIver's and used the coins given her by the storekeeper for some more clothes, and shoes like the ones George had bought for her. The stone streets were certainly hard on shoes. She had almost worn out the first pair.

The next morning, Gramm told Mary and George that he wanted to sail as a cook aboard one of the ships, and George remarked that all young men wanted to sail. They took the news well and said they'd try to help him.

It was sunrise by the time he got to the docks with his cart. A new ship had docked: the *Scorpion*. The skiffs coming into port from the *Scorpion* were overloaded with sailors. Gramm was sold out of baked goods in fifteen minutes and headed back for more. Some sailors followed behind him and bought cakes directly from the bakeshop.

When he got back to the dock with his double load of baked cakes and fried pies, there was a line of about thirty sailors waiting for him. He sold out immediately and returned to the bakeshop.

He was reloading his cart at the bakeshop when Captain Shark Scar walked up.

"Morning, boy! I come for me pies. The sailors at the dock said ye was running outta goods. Where's the little lady what makes the pies?" he asked.

"Good morning, sir. I'll get her," Gramm said as he went into the kitchen. Mary came out wiping her hands on her apron. George was close behind her.

"I'll take all the pies and little cakes ye has!" Shark Scar said as he bit down into an apricot pie he had picked up from a stack of pies on the countertop. "And more when ye gets 'em made today. Ye can deliver 'em to me ship at midday and the rest at six o'clock tonight. I'll keep me quartermaster at the dock for ye. How much for the lot?"

"George," Mary said turning, "how much?" George did some figuring on a paper, told Shark Scar the price, and they shook hands.

"Too bad ye can't come a' sailing with me. Don't have a cook right now, but soon's I finds me one, we're sailing!" said Shark Scar.

"Uh, I can cook ... really good!" said Gramm, almost shouting. "And I would really like to sail on such a fine ship as the *Shark*!"

"Eh?" said Shark Scar, looking at Gramm with interest. "Ye can cook? Can ye cook these here pies, boy?"

"He taught Mary how to make the pies, and other things, too," said George proudly. "He's a very good cook—good worker, too."

"Harrumph!" Shark Scar cleared his throat. "How old ye be, boy?"

"Uh, twenty, sir!" Gramm said quickly, cringing inside and wondering if this ridiculous sham would work. Shark Scar thought for a minute and then nodded.

"It be settled, then. We sails tonight!" laughed Shark Scar.

"Not so fast," said George. "Gramm is no ordinary cook. He's special. What do you pay?"

"Why ahh, harrumph! Didn't pay me last cook much. Worked for me till he took ill and had to be put down ... I mean, put down off the ship, that is," Shark Scar corrected himself so as not to raise suspicion about the death of his last cook. "What be fair to the boy?"

"No less than what he makes here selling baked goods on the docks," said George with the nod of his head toward Gramm.

"And a room to myself, like I have here at the bakeshop," Gramm said quickly.

"Write it down on paper," said Shark Scar, and George did. He handed the paper to Shark Scar, who looked at it, cocked his crooked eyebrow, and looked over at Gramm. Then he looked back at the pies, picked up another one, and took a bite. The yellow juice of the mango pie ran out of the corner of his red mouth and onto his chin.

"Hard bargain, all right ... for a tyro," he said, shoving in the last bite of pie. "Done!" He put the crumpled paper in his pocket. "We sails tonight, Gramm. Be at the dock at six o'clock. Don't be late. And don't forget me pies!" He paid George for all the baked goods he had ordered and left. Mary cried when she looked at the large pile of gold doubloons heaped on the counter.

Later, George helped Gramm to the dock with a duffle bag containing his meager belongings, and the baskets full of baked goods and pies for Shark Scar. Gramm thanked George again for all that he and Mary had done for him. Then George thanked Gramm, for Gramm had taught him so much about baking and selling his goods on the docks.

After George left, Grammy sat down beside the tall stack of crates on the dock where George had set the baskets of baked goods, and waited for Shark Scar and his crew to arrive in their skiff.

She looked out over the bay at the large ships anchored offshore. One ship in particular caught her eye.

It was a huge red ship, maybe three hundred feet long, with five masts. It was shaped like a long bowl, with the bow and stern pitched higher than the rest of the ship. Twenty or thirty brightly colored flags of all sizes, shapes, and lengths hung from a line that stretched from bow to stern. Red seemed to be the color of choice for the long, narrow, pointed flags, while the big square white flags bore Chinese writing and pictures of dragons.

Suddenly, Grammy heard a shuffling noise and voices on the other side of the crates. One of the voices sounded like Captain Shark Scar's.

"I agree with ye that BlackHeart is the thief o' thieves, Sleg, but he's a slick thief. One that requires some proper planning to git rid of," the voice said. The mention of BlackHeart's name had Grammy's attention. She leaned toward the crates and listened.

"Ye have a plan, do ye, Shark Scar?" asked Sleg.

"Dying is not punishment enough for BlackHeart!" Shark Scar replied. "I plan to keep him alive until *I'm* ready for him to depart this foul sea," Shark Scar oozed. "And whatever torture I makes for BlackHeart goes double for his new sidekick.

"Jon, BlackHeart calls 'em," Shark Scar said with contempt. "A snip of a boy what acts as his cabin boy and what made a fool of ole Shark Scar in front of me crew, with that no-good goldfinder of his."

"But first, Shark Scar, we have to *find* BlackHeart! That bilge rat could be anywhere on the Caribbean a' living it up in grand style with me two thousand-d-duh gold doubloons," seethed Sleg, his anger smoldering beneath the surface of his falsely calm face. "Now I'm tired of waiting. Plot us a plan, and make it good!"

"See that Chinese junk, the *Red Dragon?*" said Shark Scar, pointing to the huge Chinese ship anchored in the bay. "It be all over Port Royal that they found a sunken Spanish galleon, loaded with gold. Those Chinese are a' spending gold coins like they was pieces o' eight. A sailor that understands Chinese sez they came here for more diving equipment. Can't find none, though, cause it seems that the crew o' the *Black Opal* done bought it all up," said Shark Scar. "Ten doubloons sez we'll find BlackHeart at that sunken galleon."

"I'm in. Now, your plan. *Tell me!*" pleaded Sleg.

"I'll draw a map showing ye where we'll meet," Shark Scar said as they walked out toward the water and out of Grammy's hearing range.

Grammy stood up abruptly. *When they catch BlackHeart, they're planning on hurting Jon, too!* she thought frantically. She quickly walked away from the crates and the two captains so they wouldn't know she had overheard them talking. She watched Shark Scar pull out a piece paper, lay it on the top of a crate, and draw something. *Probably a map to the sunken galleon,* she thought.

Shark Scar and Sleg talked a few more minutes before Shark Scar turned and saw Gramm standing on the dock. He motioned for the boy, Gramm, to come to him, and Gramm picked up his duffle and walked toward the two men. Sleg walked away, his peg leg scraping across the deck as he put the paper into his coat pocket. He nodded as Gramm passed him, heading toward Shark Scar.

Sleg yelled back to Shark Scar, "Me crew will need four or five days in port afore we leaves to join ye." Shark Scar nodded and waved, signaling that he had heard Sleg.

Gramm and Captain Shark Scar boarded his skiff, with his men carrying the baked goods aboard. As they rowed toward the *Shark*, Gramm told him they would need special provisions for the making of the fried pies and cakes. Shark Scar told him to make a list and he would send his quartermaster back for them as soon as they reached the ship.

As the skiff passed close to the bow of the monstrous red ship, Gramm looked up at the giant fire-breathing gold dragon with long black horns that decorated the entire front bow of the ship, or junk, as the Chinese called it. The name on the side of the junk was in gold Chinese writing.

"Means, *Red Dragon*," explained Shark Scar. "That dragon's long horns could gore a hole clean through a man," Shark Scar said in a whisper, his eyes looking through narrow slits. Gramm shuddered. Shark Scar burst into mocking laughter, punching Gramm on the shoulder.

They rowed farther, passing under the bowsprit of Captain Shark Scar's ship, the *Shark*. Gramm grimaced at the sight of the frightening skull of a great white shark that decorated its bow. Close up, he could see the brown and rust color of the jagged, sharp teeth that rested in four rows in the lower jawbone. A shiver passed through him as he turned his head away from the gruesome sight. Shark Scar looked at him through squinted eyes as an eerie, grotesque smile appeared on his face.

True to his word, Captain Shark Scar gave Grammy a private room. It was a cabin in the guest quarters of the ship, far away from the swinging hammocks and the noise coming from the crew's quarters. If she could keep to herself, she might be able to keep up the pretense of being a boy until she could find Jon. She had no plan for anything after that. She would just have to pray for the best. But right now, finding Jon was all she could think about.

She looked out over the sea as the ship sailed from port. The city of Port Royal was now only a purple line on the horizon of the sparkling blue sea. She watched the setting sun in the turquoise sky, with wisps of pink and orange clouds, and wondered if Jon was watching the same sunset from the deck of the *Black Opal*. Or was he being held prisoner, being tortured by the wicked and devious Captain BlackHeart?

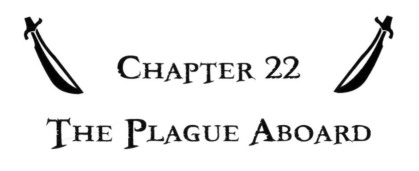

CHAPTER 22

THE PLAGUE ABOARD

Grammy had been on Shark Scar's ship for two days when she began to notice that some of the crewmen had skin problems. She had noticed a red rash on a few men the first day but thought nothing of it at the time.

Most of the sailors wore pants to the knees without shoes. This morning, her eyes fell upon some blue and black bruises on the calves of one man, and bulging veins on another. *Have they been beaten?* she wondered. Then as more men came into the galley, she noticed others with similar rashes and bruises. They were all young men; she wondered what could be the problem. Most were eating well, particularly her fried pies at breakfast. She and her kitchen helper had prepared over one hundred apple pies this morning. She had run out of key limes and apricots her first morning aboard the *Shark*.

Her plan of posing as the boy Gramm was working, with no one the wiser. When Gramm asked if the men were enjoying their food, some of the crewmen looked surprised. "No one usually cares," several of them had remarked. Most just nodded; some smiled, exposing very red and purple gums. One had red, bleeding gums.

"How long have your gums been bleeding?" Gramm asked the sailor.

He quickly covered his mouth with his hand. His eyes darted back and forth, first at the crewmen at his table and then toward the door that led from the crew's quarters. Fear was in his eyes.

"Harrumph, uh, didn't the cap'n tell ye, Gramm?" asked his shipmate. "We has the plague aboard!"

"*What?*" asked Gramm in shock, looking around the table at the others, thinking he was joking.

"We was surprised to get a new cook aboard, us a' having the plague and all. Our last cook, he, uh, died at sea two months ago with the plague. We buried him at sea, with some more crewmen. Mole, he's the quartermaster, he read the scripters. The cap'n shot two more crewmen hisself that same day, 'to keep them from spreading the plague,' he said. He tossed 'em overboard hisself. No scripters. Then the next day, the cap'n left a bunch of men with the plague on an island. There be maybe twenty men or so that he marooned on that island," said a sailor with thinning hair.

Another mate spoke up, "The men had got sickly and couldn't work. The cap'n said we couldn't have no freeloaders laying around the decks of the *Shark*. Deserted them, he did. He left them on that island with two muskets—no shot for the muskets, though. Cap'n was afraid they'd shoot him in the back when we was leaving and take the ship, and they woulda, too! Told them he would bury some shots in the sand on the beach when he left the island. But he didn't. I was there; I saw it! Jest laughed, the cap'n did. Then he sez to the rest of us crewmen, 'Into the boat, ye swab-swill! We'll save the shot for more important shootin'. They won't be a' needing it. If the wolves don't get 'em, the rats will. They'll be maggot meat in a week!'" The sailor sat staring out into the room as if in a daze.

"Do ye have anymore o' them pies? Feels good to me mouth, they do," the first sailor said, now content to know that his shipmates would not tell anyone that he had a bleeding mouth. "Me name's Pug."

Gramm frowned. "Yeh, sure, Pug. I'll get the pies," she said, walking back to the kitchen. She took a tray with the last of the pies and some morning cakes back out to the table. She had not noticed that all the men wore long-sleeved shirts. Six scaly, red hands reached for the pies as Gramm returned to the kitchen.

Plague? Men dying onboard? Marooning sick men? Shooting and tossing men overboard? What is going on here? she wondered. "I'll have to think about all this," she whispered to herself.

Yes, indeed, she thought as she lay in her cabin on the narrow, smelly cot, her head resting on her duffle bag, the cleanest thing in her cabin. *Out of the frying pan and into the fire! What am I doing here?*

Then she remembered: *Searching for my grandson.*

CHAPTER 23

IN DAVY'S GRIP

"Scurvy, Captain Shark Scar! Scurvy!" said Gramm forcefully. "It is not the plague!"

"If it be no plague, then how be it that me whole crew be in Davy's grip? All of 'em is sick!" Shark Scar shouted at Gramm. "Heard of whole ships o'sailors a dying like this. 'Floating Death,' they calls it. Sunk one o' them ships meself, I did! Put six cannonballs right in the middle of it and watched it fold in half and sink with all them living dead men aboard."

Gramm shivered, eyes shut, at the mere thought of it, and then turned back to the captain's desk.

"Better get used to unseemly happenings, Gramm, if you're gonna sail on this ship," Shark Scar scoffed and laughed sinisterly.

"Your crew doesn't have to die, captain. They have a disease called scurvy, and it *is* curable," Gramm insisted. "It's their diet, and it is common among seamen who don't eat properly. It will only take a few days to see an amazing difference! You'll see, sir. We just need to stop at some islands where there are citrus fruit and vegetables. We need limes and lemons. Quickly!"

The captain shook his head no.

"Captain, please, sir. We *can* rid the ship of this disease!" Gramm argued, slapping his hand down on the captain's desk in frustration.

"*Avast!* Don't you disrespect me!" roared Shark Scar, immediately jumping to his feet, leaning over and looking Gramm straight in the eyes. He drew his pistol and laid it noisily on the desk.

"I-I'm sorry, Captain. I meant no disrespect," Gramm said fearfully. "I just wanted you to understand that while this is a dreadful thing for the ship's crew to suffer, it is a problem that we can fix."

"If they goes to Davy Jone's locker, then they goes! We don't have time to be a lollin' in the warm breezes of the islands, picking fruit!" Shark Scar growled. "I done had Mole bring the proper food for a ship's crew onboard before we sailed. And it warn't no lemuns and limes. That's not food for workin' men! We won't be stopping and plundering around for more food when we got a shipful already. And that's the final word of it."

"You have the disease yourself, captain," Gramm said fearlessly.

"What!" yelled Shark Scar, jumping to his feet again.

"Your red and purple bleeding gums, sir," said Gramm sharply. "How long have you had the bleeding in your mouth? Are you bleeding anywhere else? Are you bruised? Do your joints ache?" The questions came pouring out of Gramm's mouth all at once.

"Git outta here, ye scrawny dried-up tyro, before I has ye dancing the *hempen jig* off the mizzens!" yelled Shark Scar, his pistol cocked and pointed straight at Gramm.

Grammy ran out the door toward the ship's galley as fast as her legs could carry her.

Later, Quartermaster Mole came into the galley. He was a small, puny-looking man with thin, scraggly blondish-gray hair. His face was wrinkled and withered from too much sun, bad health, or both. His light blue seaman's coat hung loosely from his shoulders and still bore last month's, or last year's, dirt and stains. His right sleeve had what looked like green paint smudged across the cuff.

Same color paint on his sleeve as the ship's hull, Grammy thought as she stared at the green smudge. *No telling how long it's been there.*

"What do ye want from the islands?" he asked quietly.

"Do you have the disease?" Gramm asked.

"Yes," admitted Mole, lifting his sleeves to reveal black and blue spots on his arms. "I ain't told the cap'n yet, but he told me about what ye said to him about his mouth a' bleeding and his joints a' being sore. He's scared, he is. Wanted me to ask ye about what we needs do."

Gramm nodded. "It will take a week or so to improve the health of the crewmen on the *Shark*. We need to stop at an island or islands where we can gather citrus fruit: lemons and limes. And we need fresh vegetables, particularly the green ones."

"We'll plot a course then," said Mole. "The navigator will know what islands be best. And, Gramm, better ye be a' telling me what ye needs, and not the cap'n. I knows the cap'n better than anybody. He gets riled easy, especially now. Stopping at these islands will delay us from reaching that sunken galleon o' gold and the conniving BlackHeart what owes him. Cap'n don't know how to wait for nothing, not even for sick men to heal. If Cap'n weren't sick and scared hisself, we wouldn't be goin' to no islands."

Mole continued as Gramm listened intently. "Cap'n plans a rendezvous with that sea devil BlackHeart, to git even for BlackHeart's thieving. We almost blowed him outta the water last time we saw him. Cap'n will do it next time, for sure. When that's done, we has another rendezvous with another sea devil, worse than BlackHeart. Cap'n Sleg's his name. BlackHeart be conniving, but Sleg's nothing but mean and sour on the world. Not very smart, Cap'n Sleg—just mean. Devil's own playmate, he is, particularly when he has a partner to rely on for wits. And he's found the master for his dirty games in Shark Scar.

"Like I sez to ye in the first," said Mole, "be a' telling me what ye needs, Gramm, if ye places any value on your life, cause Shark Scar's foul temper will make short of it. Understand what it be I sez to ye, boy?"

Gramm nodded, and Mole hobbled out of the galley.

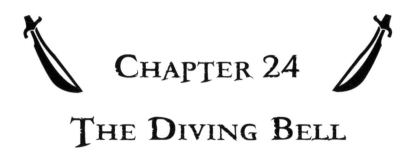

CHAPTER 24

THE DIVING BELL

Jon's curiosity was at its peak when six members of the crew brought up from the hold a huge, bell-shaped object made of lead with a glass window on one side. The bell was set on the deck between the mainmast and the starboard side railing.

Six large tar-covered barrels, with ropes attached to each one, sat near the bell. Jon asked Gituku why all the strange equipment was there.

"Captain dive in water. Galleon and treasure below," he grinned.

"Squawk! Treasure!" repeated Pyrate. "Mine, all mine! Pirate's code!" Pyrate flew to Jon's shoulder, and Jon stroked his red chest with the back of his forefinger. He turned at the sound of the captain's loud boots on the deck behind him.

The captain was wearing skin-tight pants. No shirt. "A perfect day for diving. The sea is as calm as it gets. No breakfast this morning, Jon. I won't eat until the diving is finished today," he said hurriedly and sat down on a stack of ropes. He motioned to Jon to help him off with his boots.

"Aye, aye, Captain," Jon replied as he tugged at one boot.

"Ready, Guidry?" asked BlackHeart. With a nod of his head, Guidry gave a signal and the large bell was hoisted up by the massive winch above. Guided by the crew, it was lowered to the water's surface below. The bell was received by four crewmen in the water, who steadied it as it gently touched the water's surface. Heavy weights were then attached all around the bottom of the bell, and the bell began to submerge. By lowering the bell in this manner, the bell stayed level, with a bubble of air trapped inside.

The captain and Spider went down Jacobs's ladder, a ladder made of woven rope, to the longboat waiting below. The six wooden casks with ropes attached were lowered to the longboat. From there, the airtight, tar-covered wooden casks filled with fresh air would be lowered one at time down to the ocean floor.

This air-filled bell, which hung from the winch attached to a wooden windlass on the ship, was suspended under the water just above the ocean floor. A tar-covered leather hose was attached to one of the air-filled barrels. Another hose was stretched from the barrel of fresh air up into the bell. This enabled the fresh air to flow from the barrel through the leather hose and into the air filled diving bell.

Each diver attached his long breathing hose to fittings up inside the bell. In this manner, fresh air was provided to the diver through his long hose, enabling him to look for the treasure several feet away from the bell. If the diver felt a need for more air, he could also climb up into the air-filled bell and sit in the leather seats that were affixed inside the bell for that purpose.

The diving bell was a new idea, and the captain had brought it from England. Before this bell was invented, men could not dive below twenty feet because the water pressure could burst their lungs. No other treasure-seekers in the Caribbean had a diving bell, although some knew of BlackHeart's Bell, as they called it, and that he had removed some sunken Inca treasures using it.

The captain and Spider put on their tar-covered leather suits, which were then sealed at the wrist bands with tar. With their round leather helmets sealed at the shoulders, the two divers then dropped backward off the longboat into the water, spears in hand.

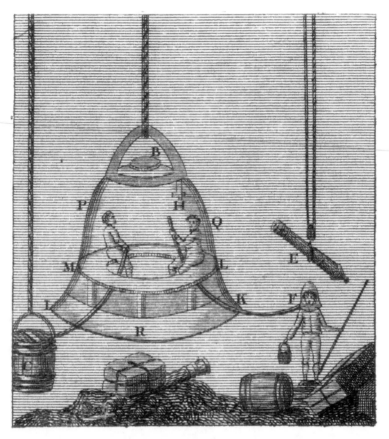

The Diving Bell

CHAPTER 25

PAY DIRT IN THE DEEP BLUE

✖

BlackHeart watched the ripples at the surface of the clear water overhead as he descended down, down, down.

The wreckage lay just beneath them, exactly where the lunatic sailor had said it would be. *He must have been a brilliant navigator,* thought BlackHeart. *Wonder why they threw him off the* Red Dragon? *We'll never know now. Poor devil, he's as crazy as a laughing, diving loon.*

The deeper they descended, the murkier the water became. But after a few minutes, their eyes became accustomed to the dim lighting and they could see quite well.

They had passed eight fathoms when BlackHeart's foot touched the jagged, top edge of the stern of the great Spanish galleon. It was covered in slick green moss and

seaweed. BlackHeart motioned for Spider to bring the
air blower over. Spider swam to BlackHeart and tugged
twice on the long hose that led to the air blower in the
longboat above. Using a manual pump with hand cranks,
the crew pumped air through this hose to the divers
below.

As Spider tugged, bubbles immediately came out
of the hose. He aimed the air-spraying hose at the galleon and blasted the seaweed away from the hull. With
some of the moss and seaweed gone, the carvings on the
back of the ship became visible. Several carved cherubs
surrounded two more prominent cherubs, which held a
coat of arms. In the center, an inscription in Spanish read
"Anatole."

A school of angel fish passed over the wreckage as
the two divers moved farther along the jagged sides of
the ship's hull. A small octopus skittered away when
they approached an area littered with debris and several
piles of large, dark green tubes. BlackHeart and Spider
stopped dead in the water and looked at each other and
then looked back at the moss-covered sight.

The cannon of the Anatole*!* thought BlackHeart. He
pointed toward them, and Spider nodded. They moved
closer, blowing away some of the sludge and moss. *Copper
cannon*, BlackHeart thought as he pointed to the muzzle
of the cannon Spider had cleaned. Spider nodded, and
they moved forward about forty feet. BlackHeart held
out his arm toward Spider and they stopped abruptly. A
long, dark pole lay in the sand.

The mainmast, thought BlackHeart, pointing to the
length of the pole. Spider nodded his understanding

of BlackHeart's motions. *The main hold must be somewhere near here,* thought BlackHeart. He swam toward his left; nothing but sand and coral. He jerked around when he felt something brush the back of his arm hard.

Sharks! BlackHeart thought as he brought his spear up, ready to defend himself. It was only Spider, motioning for him to move toward the right. He followed Spider to the spot where Spider had blown off the top of what looked like a door. It was covered by a big wooden boulder. *Probably part of one of the masts,* thought BlackHeart. They pushed against the long boulder, but it wouldn't budge.

As BlackHeart turned away, he saw the gold edge of something protruding out of the sand. He reached down and pulled on the gold object, and it came free. It was a gold cup about eight inches tall with the head and face of a South American native. He pointed down to where the gold goblet had laid. Nodding, Spider blew away about six inches of sand before he noticed that gold coins were flying with the sand.

BlackHeart grabbed his arm, and he turned the hose away, tugging on the hose to stop the flow of air from the longboat above. When the sand settled somewhat, there were about fifty to a hundred gold coins laying there in the sand. BlackHeart pointed up, and Spider nodded. They both grabbed a handful of the gold coins and swam to the surface.

When they reached the crew in the longboat, BlackHeart dropped the coins onto the deck of the longboat.

A loud cheer erupted from the ship above as those looking on saw the glitter of the gold as it hit the deck.

"We'll rest for a spell," BlackHeart told the crew as they climbed aboard the longboat. "Then, we'll need four of you to go back with us. I think we've found the mother lode!"

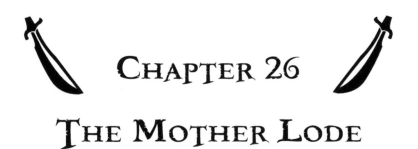

CHAPTER 26

THE MOTHER LODE

BlackHeart and Spider returned to the water with four crewmen equipped in the same diving gear. With the aid of the four men, they moved the wooden boulder off the door. The men stood by as two of the crewmen pried against the rusted iron hinges of the door. When the door was freed, they all moved the door aside.

There was no question about it. By the sight of the gold that shined in the low light of the water, they knew they had found the mother lode. All the men surfaced to the top of water carrying pieces of gold, which they dropped into the longboat.

Another cheer went up from those watching from the decks of the *Black Opal*.

After they had rested a while, the captain and Spider went back down to take another look at what lay in the exposed hold of the Spanish galleon. After a brief visual inventory of what existed, they both surfaced.

BlackHeart gave instructions to Spider and the crew in the longboat. The captain removed his suit, and one of the other crewmen put it on. The diving crew sealed the suit against water leakage with tar, and the crewman and Spider dropped into the water.

The captain then boarded the ship and gave detailed instructions to the deck crew. That being done, he turned to his excited cabin boy.

"I'll take that breakfast now, Jon," he said with a smile, and Jon ran to the galley.

By the time the captain had finished his breakfast and dressed, gold coins were being delivered up from the wreckage by the bucketful.

Later in the afternoon, while the diving crew rested and had a light lunch, Spider called BlackHeart down to the longboat. "There's much more, Cappin. Come," Spider whispered. The captain nodded, donned his diving suit, and followed Spider into the water. When they were on the bottom, the captain motioned for Spider to join him inside the diving bell. They swam under the bell's rim and up inside. Sitting in the leather seats, they loosened the bolts to their faceplates, opened them, and took a breath of fresh air that was being pumped in from the longboat above.

Spider told him that he had seen doors to at least three more holds in the galleon wreckage. "Did any of the crew see the doors?" asked BlackHeart.

"No," said Spider. "I was alone in that section, but the doors are exactly like the first, and all in a row."

"It makes sense," BlackHeart said. "It's evident that the ship was brought down by the weight of her treasure in a storm. The *Anatole* was four times the size of the *Black Opal*, so there must be more gold—much more gold. If what we suspect is true, it will be best that the crew not know. We've both seen what happens when a crew gets a lust for gold. It cost me my best friend last time. Captain Brighton was a good man," BlackHeart said sadly. Spider nodded.

"We take a look, Cappin?" Spider asked.

"Yes, we take a look," the captain agreed.

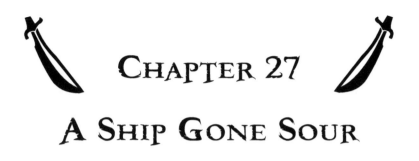

CHAPTER 27

A SHIP GONE SOUR

"You're all a gittin' soft, like babes in the basket! Quit snickering and get back to work, ye swamp-swill!" Shark Scar snarled at the crewmen nearest him on the deck. Shark Scar thought there was far too much happiness going on for very much work to be happening, and said so often.

"But they is getting more work done than ever, cause they feeling good now, Cap'n. Tomorrow we be stopping at another island. This one has pineapples and mangos," said Marley, the boatswain in charge of the ship's maintenance.

"Yum," said a nearby sailor swabbing the deck and sniffing into the ocean air as if to locate a mango nearby.

Marley frowned. "Don't be interrupting me, Snag, when I be talking with the cap'n here," scolded Marley. Turning back to Shark Scar, he continued, "And Gramm said we should get more honey from some hives ashore, cause he needs it for the med'cine he mixes with the limes and gives to the crew in the spoon ever day."

"Gramm promised pineapple pies for dessert tomorrow night after we eat our veg'bles," a sailor climbing down from the riggings said.

"And Gramm said he be cooking mango pies for breakfast the next day," another sailor remarked as he scraped the deck with a holystone.

"Got us over the cursed sickness, Gramm did," remarked Hans, the master gunner on the *Shark*.

Captain Shark Scar walked toward his cabin, a grimace on his face. "Gramm this ... and Gramm that," grumbled Shark Scar in a sarcastic voice as he slammed the door of his cabin, closing out the droning singing from the crew outside. "Sea dogs! All of 'em. Not worth the slobber from me mouth." He sat looking out the window of his cabin. His eyes darkened with scorn and contempt. "We need to be finding BlackHeart!" he said anxiously. His feet shuffled nervously against the wood floor of his cabin.

"Next thing ye knows, Gramm'll be running the ship instead o' ole Shark Scar."

Then he bolted upright in his chair. His eyes and nostrils glared with rage and his mind snapped to attention. "Didja hear what ye jest said to yesself, Shark Scar!" Then he leaned back in his chair at his desk, eyes shut, thinking.

The crew's feeling good, now that the plague or scurvy or whatever t'was be gone. The crew's making Gramm a hero, leading his troops home from victory, as it were. And they're all getting soft to boot! Before I brought Gramm onboard, they wouldn't have dared talk to me like they just did on deck. They acts like I was one of them, instead o' the great Cap'n Shark

Scar that I be. He groaned in self pity. Then he sat up arrogantly.

Pretty soon, they're going to balk at raiding some good-for-nothing sea captain's ship and marooning his crew to get the booty due us as the fearless pirate crew of the Shark *that we are! And then they're going to use the pirate's code to replace ole* Shark *Scar with that waif of a boy, Gramm, as the new cap'n of the* Shark*!*

"Aaarrrghh!" he cried out. He jerked himself up from his desk and angrily stalked over to the windows, pacing back and forth, thinking.

He yanked his cutlass out of his waist belt, nicking his hand in the process. He threw the cutlass across his cabin, breaking a window pane. Then he plopped his dirty, tar-stained boot right in the middle of his new turquoise velvet coat, which lay on his bunk. He leaned his elbow on his knee, his foot still propped on the velvet coat, while blood from his nicked hand trickled onto his new white lace shirt laying next to the coat.

"What to do, what to do," he wailed quietly. He couldn't just kill the scrawny boy outright. He had brought Gramm onboard as the ship's new cook, telling all the crew how great he was, cooking all those good pies and such. The crew would never stand for it now, and he knew it. Likely as not they'd throw *him* overboard with the potato peels and dead rats before they'd let him hurt the person who had saved their lives. They owed Gramm. He owed Gramm, too, but that didn't matter to the arrogant, self-important Shark Scar, captain of the mighty ship, *Shark*!

What did matter was that he had to get rid of Gramm and all those lemons and limes before the whole ship went sour, and before the whole crew went too soft for killing and plundering and looting.

He had to act before the crew used the privilege due each one of them under the pirate's code—the privilege of voting him out as captain of the *Shark* and voting in a new captain—Gramm!

He picked up his cutlass, and in a fit of temper, he rammed it through the top of his new black tricorn hat. Pieces of white ostrich feathers sprang up from the hat and slowly floated over the room.

Yes, his mind was made up. He had to get rid of Gramm.

CHAPTER 28

A HUNDRED CHESTS OF GOLD

Jon had painted over a hundred small wooden chests with each crewman's name or his mark. Each one of them had filled his chest with gold coins and placed it in the ship's hold. Jon was exhausted and leaned back in a hard wooden chair at the massive table that stood directly behind the captain's desk. He was looking out the back windows to the ocean when the captain came into the cabin.

"You didn't paint your name on a chest, Jon," remarked the captain as he examined the chests. He held out the last chest to Jon. "You're now part of the crew, and as such, entitled to have a share of the treasure we have recovered."

The tears Jon had held back for over two weeks welled up in his eyes and threatened to spill over as he looked up at Captain BlackHeart.

"I ... I don't want a share of the gold, Captain. I just want my life with Pappy and Grammy back," he said in a low voice.

"I think it's time we finished the conversation we started the day you boarded the *Black Opal*," the captain said, pulling out a chair at the table. "Let's start at the beginning. Where do you come from, Jon, and how did you get here?"

Jon cleared his throat and began to talk. The captain did not interrupt. When he was finished, Jon leaned back in his chair, looking down at his hands, which were stained with white paint.

"So, let me see if I understand what you're telling me. The *Carousel* is a *time-travel ship*, did you say?" BlackHeart asked.

"Yes, and I came with my grandmother, Kathryn Sinclair. We were separated when I wandered from the *Carousel* without her and got lost in the forest," replied Jon. "The *Carousel* is about as tall as this ship but does not sail, sir. It is shaped similar to a silo that holds grain or a turret in a castle. It travels through time and air, or space, as we call it, not on water."

"And exactly *where* did you come from?" BlackHeart asked patiently.

"Well, sir, in the time I come from, which is the twenty-first century," answered Jon, "it is called the United States of America. It is the same land you now call the colonies."

"Twenty-first century?" asked BlackHeart, somewhat confused. "But this is the seventeenth century."

"Yes, sir," Jon answered. "We passed through a window in our time, into your time."

"Like Atlantis ..." the captain said pensively. "Except that we are alive; those in Atlantis are dead." Then the captain shook his head quickly, as if to shake off the weirdness of what Jon was telling him.

"How do we find your grandmother?" BlackHeart asked.

"Truthfully, Captain, I don't know," replied Jon. "We could have talked to her with the silver Transformer, except that the crew broke it, and then you gave it to Shark Scar. The last time I saw Grammy, she was in the forest near Port Royal. That was before I got lost."

The captain thought for a long time, and then he spoke. "While I don't understand all that you have told me, I do believe that you would not intentionally lie to me, Jon. I don't know how to change what's happened to you. I only know that you are here in my life, and I am here in yours. And, Jon," the captain said as he opened the door to leave, "that's the way we'll have to live it."

When Jon brought up the captain's dinner on a tray, it was the middle of the fifth watch, or what Jon now knew to be six o'clock in the evening. Dinner was conch chowder, from the conch that lived in the conch shells the diving crew had brought up from the ocean floor near the wreckage. The chowder smelled spicy and good. There was also some sort of flounder from the nearby reefs, speared by the divers. He set it down before the captain on the clean white cloth and was leaving when BlackHeart stopped him.

"Go to the galley, Jon, and bring your dinner here to my table. Tonight, you will eat with me," BlackHeart said.

"Yes, Captain," Jon said, smiling, and headed for the galley in a run. When he returned a few minutes later, he saw the huge diving bell being hoisted aboard. He entered the cabin and set his food on the table by the captain.

"Tell me more about your life before coming here," the captain said.

In the hour that passed as they ate, Jon talked about everything: the farm, school, sports, planes, trains, and cars. The captain was particularly interested in the cars—the "carriages without horses," as Jon explained it. Maybe he related to cars more easily because of his own experience with carriages in England, his home.

Jon also told him about air tanks with compressed air, which could be mounted to the diver's back and were used for scuba diving. He, Grammy, and Pappy had used them while diving among the coral reefs in the Caribbean last year on their vacation. He told BlackHeart about the newest mini-submarines made for underwater research and excavating old shipwrecks. The captain sat mesmerized, listening to Jon.

How can a young boy know so much? wondered BlackHeart as he heard the ship's bell. *Nine o'clock! How can time pass so fast!*

There was a slight vibration in the ship, and the captain knew it was the anchor being hoisted up for sailing. When he and Spider had dived to the wreckage below, they had confirmed that the three holds did indeed contain more gold: gold artifacts, some embellished with jewels, others hand-carved with animals or celestial drawings—and more gold bullion and doubloons. All in all, just the gold that was visible without digging was more than enough to sink a ship the size of the *Black Opal*.

"We will have to talk again another night," BlackHeart said. "After you clean up here tonight, you should get to sleep early. Tomorrow's a big day. This afternoon, we brought up some gold artifacts from the *Anatole*; the storage holds of the *Black Opal* are full. The ship will be heavy and riding low in the water. We can't take the chance of running into a storm or being seen by other pirates. We shall sail immediately for our hideout at Devil's Rock near here, where we'll store these treasures.

"Tonight we will sail in total blackout. That means our white sails will be changed to black ones, for black cannot be seen by others against the sea and the moonless sky tonight. There will be no lanterns. We will have double watch duty from now until tomorrow night when we reach the hideout. Finish your duties and stay in the cabin and out of the way. I'll be on deck most of the night," said Captain BlackHeart.

"And Jon, I don't want you to tell *any* of the crew what you have told me tonight. Some of them are very superstitious and would not understand. Sometimes people behave very strangely when things happen that they don't understand, and I wouldn't want anything unfortunate to happen to you." With that, the captain left the cabin.

CHAPTER 29

DEVIL'S ROCK

Jon awoke early the next morning, before daybreak. He dressed and went out onto the deck. The men were changing over the sails from the black to the white. There was a sober mood among the crew as BlackHeart walked toward Jon.

"I'll take my sleep, now," he said and walked past Jon and toward the cabin.

"Will you want breakfast now, Captain?" Jon asked.

"No," was the simple reply as the cabin door closed.

It was mid-afternoon when they arrived at a cluster of small islands. Most of the islands were no more than jagged rocks jutting up from the sea.

Atop the larger islands grew thatches of weeds, bushes, and scraggly short trees, their roots exposed and wrapping around the smooth rocks. Long, thick, rough vines laced over the crude surfaces and sometimes hung off, with leaves growing at the tips. There were no beaches on any of the islands Jon could see.

To Jon, the area looked desolate and foreboding. He noticed that the captain seemed to be heading the ship toward a particular island among the group, one with two tall rock peaks that were joined together at the base.

"Adjust the sails, Guidry! Jibs, staysails, spanker only!" commanded Captain BlackHeart. Guidry repeated the command, and the sailors rapidly climbed the rigging to take in and secure the wide sails.

The crude edges of the rock base of the island could be seen under the sea's surface as the bright afternoon sun shined deep into the clear waters surrounding the small islands. A very narrow channel ran between the two rocks. There, the water was dark green and deep.

Jon looked up and saw that the two rocks had high ledges that jutted out, almost touching at the top, leaving a space of only a few feet in between them. It was as if they had once been joined at the top, like an arch, and that the center part had broken, separating the two rocks.

The lazy waves broke against the east side of the island, causing the water to swirl gently on the west side, where they were headed. There was no doubt in Jon's mind now. *We're going through the middle of those two craggy rocks!* he thought, his heart pounding. *What if one of these rocks breaks a hole in the ship's hull, here, in this treacherous place?* He wanted to hide his eyes but felt compelled by some unknown force to watch his fate unfold as it would.

They sailed toward the rock entrance, the water swirling and pushing the stern of the ship to one side. BlackHeart adjusted it straight again by turning the wheel. Jon looked back at the helm. The captain and

Spider were both manning the wheel, for any slight lurch of the ship or error in the captain's judgment could mean disaster to the hull below or the masts above.

They passed through the two ledges with no more than three feet of clearance on either side of the masts and yards. The captain knew exactly how to maneuver the big ship through this treacherous gorge. It was obvious he had done it many times before. The ship narrowly missed scraping rock after rock at either the top or bottom as they sailed very slowly through the channel.

Up ahead of the ship, the channel grew wider and wider until they were into a larger body of water, a lagoon, right in the middle of all the rocks. The ship continued into the greenish-black, glass-smooth waters.

Jon breathed a great sigh of relief. His mind could now rest—until they sailed back out. The anchors were quickly dropped, stopping the ship with a hard jolt.

First, the dinghy was lowered to the water. Skull, Spider, and a scouting crew boarded it and rowed toward the shore as the first longboat was lowered. Jon was taken ashore in the longboat with Curly and his men.

Once on land, Curly's men cut a narrow path through the brush with their hatchets and machetes, tossing the pieces of green brush far out to the left and right so that the cut brush would not leave a noticeable path later when it dried.

Jon walked with Curly's men as they snaked their way through the brush, carrying chests of gold artifacts and other treasures from the galleon's wreckage. He rubbed his fingers along the smooth silver surface of the jeweled cross he was carrying. It was only seven or eight inches tall, but it was solid silver and heavy. A cluster of emeralds and pearls encrusted the center of the cross, trickling outward.

They stopped abruptly, and word came back down the line that they had reached the hideout. The men had parted the vines and pulled them to either side, thus clearing a pathway into the cave.

They entered the cave. Lanterns were already lit and positioned all about the large cavern and down some of the dark tunnels that led away. The treasures they carried were piled high in a mound near the entrance. Each man dug through the stack of gold and silver, taking some artifact, gold bar with special markings, string of pearls, or such that appeared to belong to him alone. Treasuring it, he would take it to a certain place in the cave that appeared to be his own personal hiding spot.

Guidry called out to Jon.

"I'll be taking the cross from ye, lad. It belongs to me," he said. "Thank ye for taking good care of it."

"It's a beautiful cross, Guidry," Jon said as he handed it to him.

"A true statement, lad," Guidry replied. "That it 'tis!"

The captain arrived with crewmen bearing large crates. They pried open the tops of the crates and began removing the small gold-filled chests bearing the crewmen's names or mark, which Jon had painted at the site of the sunken galleon. Each man took his chest and deposited it with the rest of his plunder in the cave.

Jon sat in awe of the glittering sight before him. Chests of gold! Silver goblets encrusted with stones, beautiful crosses of all descriptions, some encrusted with jewels, some not. There were pearl necklaces, gold bars, and coins in heaps, silver and bronze statues. Jon had never seen the like of it.

There was a commotion at the cave entrance as several crewmen struggled with the big diving bell, bringing it to a resting place near the cave entrance. Other crewmen brought the barrels for fresh air and set them near the bell.

When the chests had been unloaded by the men and placed appropriately, Mr. Token asked the captain if he was ready to go. The captain nodded.

"To the ship, men! There will be plenty of time to sit and admire your treasures soon enough," BlackHeart said.

They pulled the vines back across the cave's entrance and brushed over the sand near it with tree twigs, covering their tracks. They rowed back to the ship rather quietly, most of them deep in their own thoughts.

After boarding the *Black Opal*, they raised and secured only the dinghy. Two long, fat ropes had been secured to the bow of the *Black Opal*. One rope was thrown to the mate in each of the two longboats. Once the lines were secured to the boats, the oarsmen rowed the boats out in front of the ship. As they rowed, the huge ship began to swing around in the middle of the lagoon, heading toward the gorge where they had entered.

When the longboats were safely stored aboard the *Black Opal*, they sailed back through the passageway in the same manner in which they had entered. For some reason, Jon was not quite as frightened as when they had sailed in. Maybe it was because he now trusted the abilities and judgment of BlackHeart and Spider.

The Caribbean was glistening in the late afternoon sun as Jon heard the captain say to Spider, "Plot a course to Tortuga. We shall lighten our load by selling all the diving equipment we purchased in Port Royal. The crew of the *Red Dragon* will be ready buyers, and at a tremendous price!

"Double rum for all the crew!" shouted BlackHeart.

A loud cheer went up from the crew.

CHAPTER 30

THE HURRICANE

Jon could see the approaching gray clouds stretching like a wall across the sea. There was no end in either direction. At first the wispy, wide bands of clouds had been white. Then they had grayed with showers of rain, interspersed with sunshine. Now the solid dark gray clouds were ominous, lurking behind the ship like a shroud.

Spider had plotted a new course hours earlier. They were now tacking north by northwest toward an island with a small bay that Spider said was near. He said it was big enough to shelter them from the storm—he thought.

"Aye, this storm will be a bad one," Guidry said as he watched the approaching storm. "Hurricane, me thinks, Cap'n!" BlackHeart agreed.

"Top sails down! Quickly! Adjust all sails according-ly, Guidry!" bellowed BlackHeart.

"Aye, aye, Cap'n! Tops'ls down! Double time!" shout-ed Guidry to the sail crew, who were climbing up the rigging as fast as their legs could go.

"Curly! Batten all hatches! Move everything loose to the decks below!" BlackHeart shouted.

"Aye, aye, Cap'n!" responded Curly, who then shouted to his crew, "Make ready for storm, ye blokes!"

The captain ordered Skull and the gunners to secure the cannon and powder kegs. Gituku and Cook were ordered below to tie down the animals so they wouldn't fall or panic and break legs.

"Spider, I need you here to help man the wheel," BlackHeart said.

"Aye, aye, Cappin. I think we be close to the island but I can't see through rain," Spider replied.

"Quickly now! She'll hit us hard bloody well soon! Heave! Heave! Heave!" Guidry shouted to his crew, who were pulling on the ropes of the sails.

"Move it along, swabs!" Curly shouted at two men lifting a heavy deck trunk and others who were carrying stacks of ropes and nets to the decks below.

The captain manned the wheel, with Spider directing the crew as they worked feverishly to ready the ship for the massive storm.

Jon stood watching the crew and felt very useless. He knew nothing about what was to be done in such situations as these. The captain saw that Jon was swaying, shifting his feet this way and that, in an effort to stand upright as the ship dipped and dived through the increasingly rough waves. Each time the ship plummeted from a large wave, seawater splashed high into the air and washed over the decks, causing some crewmen to lose their footing and slide to the side-rail walls of the ship.

"Spider, man the wheel while I take Jon inside and show him how to ready my cabin before the storm hits us full," shouted the captain.

The rain was coming down harder now, hitting Jon's face like tiny sharp pellets as the winds howled and whistled through the ship's tight rigging. The remaining sails slapped and popped as the wind gusted. Loose ropes and rigging lines pummeled the deck like long whips until they were secured. Turning to Skull, who had returned from below, BlackHeart said, "Bring up the linen cloth to wrap the china!" Skull nodded and handed a stack of fishnets to a sailor, instructing him to take them down and help Gituku and Cook with the animals. Then he headed below deck.

BlackHeart took Jon inside his cabin, and Skull came in with a tall stack of square, fine linen cloth. The captain was showing Jon just how he wanted his china and goblets wrapped and where to pack them, when Gituku came into the cabin carrying Pyrate. He held the bird with both its wings pressed tightly to its sides so it could not flap them or fly.

"Foul wind blowing! Batten the hatches! Move it, blokes! Move it, swabs!" squawked Pyrate.

"Pyrate no like storm, Cap'n—go wild outside! Better in cabin ... no?" Gituku asked.

"Better in cabin—yes!" replied the captain. "Keep him chained to his perch, Jon, or he'll be gone with the next wind." Jon understood and nodded, taking Pyrate to his perch.

"Animals below deck whining loudly but covered with fishnets and tied down, Cap'n," reported Gituku.

"Good!" replied BlackHeart as he opened the door. They both left Jon to his work ... and worry.

Jon put the black hood over Pyrate's head as he had watched the captain do many times, and Pyrate immediately began to calm down. He looked past the perch to the back of the cabin. The twelve glass windows surrounding the back of the captain's cabin provided a half view of all the sea and left no room for imagination. The *Black Opal* was losing the race with the monstrous black storm that was chasing them.

The sea had been rough all day. Jon and the crew had hung themselves over the rails for the last hour, relieving themselves of Cook's bad stew or the sea's bad temper— those who could make it to the rails. Jon was glad that the captain had him doing work inside his cabin instead of out on the decks where the smell was nauseous and worse than putrid.

He held up a crystal goblet, admiring its sparkle, and then wrapped it securely in a linen cloth. The captain was proud of his Bavarian crystal goblets and his French china. Jon had used them to serve him dinner on the nights that the captain wanted to put on his burgundy velvet dressing coat, sip his brandy, and read from one of the books in his wall library or write in his journal. Today, he would pack the crystal and china in the captain's long chests.

The door opened, and Spider rushed in, going directly to the lanterns mounted on the cabin walls, where he snuffed the flames, putting the cabin immediately into a dim twilight.

"Ye'll have t'do without light from here on, Jon boy," Spider said. "Can't be having no fires to worry aboot!" Then he left. The small bell outside the captain's door continued to ring, like an ominous warning of what was to come.

As the storm drew closer, the swells of the ocean became much higher, lifting the ship to the top of them and then dropping it to the ocean's surface again with a pounding hardness, which caused everything in the cabin to rattle and clatter.

Jon was frightened and said a lot of prayers that this loud creaking and hard pounding and rattling would not cause the ship to break apart. He worried that the high waves would force them down into the depths of the ocean floor, like he had seen in movies.

His thoughts were halted abruptly when two crystal decanters fell to the floor, the smaller one shattering loudly. He quickly took the rest of the crystal out of the cabinets and placed it on the floor. *Safer here until I can get them wrapped,* he thought as he madly rolled each one in linen and packed it in a chest.

The ship creaked and groaned as the bolts strained to hold it together. The rain came in sheets, very hard, then no rain at all, then sheets of hard rain again, as water poured over the decks of the ship.

"Man overboard!" shouted someone loudly. The phrase echoed throughout the ship's deck from crewman to crewman.

Jon opened the door and ran to the entrance of the quarterdeck. He held onto the brass handrail fastened to the wall, straining to see through the rain and wind as the little bell above his head rang loudly in his ear.

There! Jon thought, *I see him!* The sailor's head was bobbing in the rolling swells of the sea. Several crewmen threw life lines to the man, again and again, as the sea tossed him around like a ball sloshing in a child's bathwater. He appeared here and then there in the rough waves. And then—not at all!

"We've lost him!" a crewman shouted just as a tremendous wave hit the *Black Opal*'s side, almost turning the ship over. The wave deposited its innards of octopus, stingrays, fish, and the lost crewman down hard on the deck of the ship. The drowning sailor coughed and spit as he struggled to clear his lungs of the seawater. He was shivering and crying as two men carried him below.

Jon returned to his work with more respect for his captain, who was keeping him safe from the spectacle he had just witnessed. He pulled some of the goblets out of the wooden chest and wrapped them better, making sure they would not break. He wanted the captain to be proud of his work tomorrow—if there was a tomorrow.

Jon had removed all the things loose on the captain's desk and shelves and packed them away. With the crystal and china wrapped and stored, he now had nothing more to do but watch the storm from the windows, and worry and pray. He thought about his home at Three Forks, and Grammy and Pappy. He wished they were here to help protect him, or to reassure him that everything would be okay. He could not remember a time when they were not near.

But they're not *here! I'm here, alone,* he thought sadly. *I wonder where they are. Maybe they're at Three Forks with Trek.* He huddled into the pillow on his bed, wrapping himself in warm thoughts of home, far away from this frightening sea. *But I guess I'm glad they're not in this bad storm, too.*

Jon had no idea that Grammy was not far from him on another pirate ship, living through the same treacherous hurricane and fearing the worst.

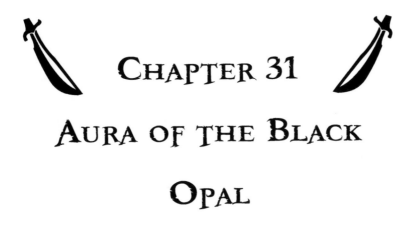

CHAPTER 31

AURA OF THE BLACK

OPAL

The loud shouting of the crew outside on the decks jolted Jon back to the present. He could not contain his curiosity and quickly opened the door and ran to the quarterdeck entrance. His eyes opened wide, and a loud gasp escaped his throat as he clung to the wet brass rail near the cabin.

The crew was dealing with the absolute *insides* of the ocean right there on the deck of the ship. They were throwing back mountains of fish—squid, small sharks, flounder, jellyfish, and even starfish—over the railings as fast as they could.

Suddenly, the crewmen seemed to be panicked by some long, slithering, snakelike creatures that were being tossed from the high waves onto the ship's deck.

One by one, they were backing away from the sea creatures as if they were poisonous.

"Keep the eels off the deck!" BlackHeart bellowed in disgust at the fearful crew. When the men did not respond to BlackHeart's command, he came running forward with a long gaff. He speared the snakelike creatures one at a time and threw them, wriggling and slapping their tails, overboard.

"It not be the eels they worrying aboot, Cappin," said Spider in an eerie, foreboding voice that Jon could hear clearly through the howling wind. Spider's eyes looked fearful as he scanned the heavens and then the waves, finally focusing back on the captain. "They's afraid the sea serpent coming up next!"

The captain looked at Spider threateningly as the rain streamed down both their faces, plastering their long hair to their heads.

"How many times must I tell you?" BlackHeart said angrily. "There is no sea serpent out here!"

"You don't know that, Cappin!" Spider said boldly.

"For the sake of all of us, muster some courage, Spider!" pleaded BlackHeart. "I need you!"

"The crew, they's afraid the *curse* below be a' calling to the serpent! The *curse* be angry now, Cappin! Look at this storm! It takes a curse to make a storm like this one, Cappin!" said Spider fearfully. "And we out in it!"

Jon didn't know what Spider and the crew were afraid of, but he knew it must be bad to strike fear in the faces of this crew, and that was not comforting. No, not comforting at all!

Suddenly, the ship began to swirl in a circle like loose hands on a clock, paying no heed to the straight howling blow of the winds. Then it stopped swirling just as suddenly. The ship floated in the middle of a calm pool of emerald green water, as if there were no storm raging around them. The pool seemed to radiate outward from the ship into the dark blackish-green waters that surrounded it. A misty oval dome covered the calm waters where the ship sat, while on the outside, the violent storm raged on. A light tinkling sound like that of hundreds of tiny bells replaced the howling sound of the wind.

Jon wanted to turn and run back into the cabin, but somehow, his feet just didn't obey his mind. He stood spellbound, looking at the frightened crew and the aura that surrounded the ship. He felt a warm, gentle breeze blowing and a sense of peace settle over him as the panicked crew backed away from the railings of the ship, some running down the stairs to the decks below. *Am I dying*, he wondered. *Is this what it feels like to die?*

The ship was illuminated now with a pink glow, and the tops of the masts were crimson, as were the sails.

The colors—I've seen them before. The ring, that's it. It's as if we're sitting in the middle of the ring, the captain's black opal ring! thought Jon, as he looked at the helm where the captain stood. The captain's black opal ring was illuminated, giving off a brilliant beam that thrust upward, forming the bubble that now covered the ship like a dome, a dome that ended where the calm waters met the turbulent, churning waves.

Gradually the aura of light diminished and the bells grew fainter. The waters began to roll with high waves again, but the mysterious pink color continued to enshroud the ship. Captain BlackHeart was the first to break the spell.

"Get back on those ropes! Keep those sails furled!" commanded BlackHeart from the wheel as the crew stood frozen, just looking at each other, as if any movement might bring some ominous sea creature out from the depths of the sea.

"The curse! The curse!" they yelled.

"Nothing will hurt you!" BlackHeart shouted frantically as rain poured down on the disbelieving crew. The men stood unmoving on the deck.

Jon watched as the lower sail on the mainmast came loose from its mooring on one side and began to flap in the wind, its mooring rope lashing through the air like a long snake. The crew stood dazed and paid it no regard. Suddenly, Jon knew what he must do.

He ran down onto the main deck and jumped high in the air, grabbing the rope of the sail. The sail snapped and whipped in the wind as it pulled him upward, like a kite, tossing him in the wind. Suddenly, he felt two hands grab hold of his ankles. It was Captain BlackHeart! He pulled Jon down onto the deck, and together they heaved, pulling on the rope of the sail, against the strong wind. They had just gotten it under control and looped around a large deck cleat when the rope on the other side of the sail came loose and the captain jumped high into the air, grabbing it. The tinkling sound from the little bells grew louder.

Jon turned to look at the wheel, expecting to see Spider. Instead, he saw the captain manning the wheel. *But how can this be?* he wondered, looking up at Captain

BlackHeart pulling on the ropes next to him. *How can the captain be in two places at once?*

When they had the sail secured, he watched as the captain standing next to him suddenly became transparent, like a ghost of water vapor, slowly disappearing as it blended into the water flowing across the deck of the ship. The tinkling sound from the little bells grew a little quieter but did not disappear.

"Are you just going to stand there and let this fearless boy save your hides by himself?" BlackHeart shouted from the helm. "Take this wheel, Spider!" Spider shook his head as if to ward off sleep or some spell, and took the wheel. The captain came down onto the main deck, where Jon stood.

"Clear the decks of this debris of fish!" BlackHeart shouted at the men. The crew immediately jumped, as if awakened by some force, and began to move, responding to the captain's orders.

"Land ahoy!" shouted Guidry from the center of the deck as everyone turned to see a large mass of land looming directly ahead of them.

The Black Opal in the Hurricane

CHAPTER 32

ABANDON SHIP

Straight ahead of the *Black Opal* was the entrance into a bay of the island. As they entered it, they could immediately feel the sea begin to calm. The island's high land mass was standing between them and the powerful winds of the storm. It would give the ship some shelter from these monstrous hurricane winds. "Drop anchor!" shouted Guidry as several men ran for the stairs below to turn the big cog that lowered the main anchor. "Drop the side anchors!"

The tinkling bells continued to ring, and the waters that surrounded the *Black Opal* remained calm as the seas beyond raged violently.

"Secure all sails!" commanded the captain sharply. "Prepare to abandon ship!"

"Prepare to abandon ship!" repeated Guidry, and the commands echoed through the crewmen of the *Black Opal*.

"Mr. Token. To the helm!" yelled BlackHeart, and Mr. Token came running to the helm. "Bring up all weapons from the hold and pass them to the men."

"Aye, aye, Captain," replied Mr. Token. He headed to the hold, calling some men to help him.

Jon stood wide-eyed, his mouth ajar, when Mr. Token opened the chests they had brought up from the hold and started passing out the weapons. The men eagerly grabbed for the weapons, flashing cutlasses, hatchets, muskets, pistols, and swords. They would need weapons; they didn't know what hostilities might await on an unknown island.

"Lower the longboats! Lower dinghy," shouted Curly.

The men were ushered into the longboats and dinghy by Guidry and Curly. When each boat was full of men, they shoved off for the shore, with Skull manning one longboat and Spider in the other.

As the men were deposited at the shoreline, the oarsmen rowed the three boats back to the ship for another load. BlackHeart took Jon into his boat. The incredibly calm waters surrounding the ship enabled them to evacuate the *Black Opal* very quickly.

When the last longboat was pulled from the water and onto the beach, the tinkling bells stopped abruptly. The wind picked up and the sea worsened as the *Black Opal* began to pitch in the rough waves.

Jon watched as the pink glow became a fine point of light that submerged into the captain's black opal ring, putting the ring and the ship in total darkness.

"What do ye make of this strangeness, Cappin? Ye think it be coming from the *curse?*" Spider asked, moving close to BlackHeart and Jon.

"No!" snapped BlackHeart. "You *saw* it coming from my black opal ring, Spider. I was with Captain Brighton on a long intriguing voyage when I ..." BlackHeart hesitated, "when I obtained this ring. I was told then that the black opal in the ring had mysterious powers that reveal themselves during times of aquatic violence. Once before, I was shielded from disaster in a violent storm when lightning struck the carriage in which I rode, turning it into an inferno. I escaped without injury, as did the driver and coachmen. There was an aura of pink light, and I heard the bells then." BlackHeart looked straight at Spider.

"The black opal ring has never caused harm. It is not a curse, Spider," said the captain, a little irritated. "If you cause the crew to think it so, then we will all be cursed by *their* actions, and *yours*, not by those of the ring."

As long as Spider has sailed with me, he should know I would not tell him there was no curse if, indeed, it were not true! BlackHeart thought. By now, he was clearly angry with Spider. He shook his head and said sharply, "Get out of my sight! Go with Skull; find a place for us to ride out this storm!"

Skull lit some lanterns and brought one to BlackHeart before he headed into the woods with Spider and others to look for shelter.

Jon watched the high, frothy waves as they came ashore from out of the black night. The shrieking wind was increasing, blowing the surf high and pitching the waves hard against the tall rocks that formed a barrier for the beach where they stood.

The lad has courage, I'll give him that—at least as much as any crewman and more than most! thought BlackHeart. He admired that. It reminded him of himself during the earlier days of his youth.

The three boats had been pulled up to the edge of the woods and turned over with the bottoms upward. They had been packed with sand around the sides to prevent the wind from blowing them away or setting them free in the surf. The crew then tied each boat to a tree.

Jon trembled as he stood with the captain on the beach. His mind was jumbled with unanswered questions. What had happened out there? Did the crew see what he had seen or had they been in a daze? Did the men have reason for their fears or were they just superstitious as the captain had said?

BlackHeart looked down at Jon and knew that Jon's trembling was caused by fear, a fear of the unknown. He spoke quietly, "I know you're afraid, Jon. I spoke the truth to Spider; the black opal ring is not cursed. You'll have to trust me."

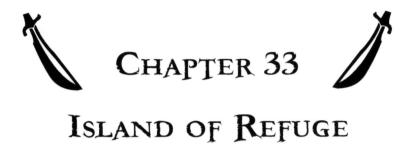

CHAPTER 33

ISLAND OF REFUGE

When lightning would strike, Jon could faintly see the *Black Opal* rising and falling in the waters of the small bay as it took a beating from the powerful waves and the howling wind.

Before they had abandoned ship, the crew had dropped all three anchors and secured the ship with somewhat loose lines to give it some freedom of movement in the bay. The ship was turned straight into the wind, exposing the stern and port side to the shore. As the hurricane continued ashore, the winds would change their direction. The loose lines would allow the ship to move with it, always facing into the wind, thus preventing it from being swamped and sinking.

"Cappin? We found a cave on this side of the island. Skull and Curly are leading the men there now. It be big and safe. I'll take you when you're ready," Spider said. There was a hint of apology in his voice. He knew the captain was disappointed in him for his lack of courage.

"I'm ready now, Spider. There's nothing more I can do here. The ship seems to be riding the waves well, although the storm is worsening. Come on, Jon, let's go," replied BlackHeart.

Specs of sand peppered the back of Jon's neck and legs, and his rope sandals filled with gritty, wet silt and seaweed as they ran from the beach. They made their way a short distance up the side of a hill and into the cave as the tops of the trees continued to toss and whip in the wind.

The crew had gathered the driest wood they could find and brought it just inside the entrance of the cave, where they made a small campfire. It was smoky and crackled as it burned off the moisture, but it gave light and warmth. Jon sat down, wet and chilled. He leaned against a large rock in the cave, watching the flickering flames from the second fire the crew had made inside the cave, while the winds howled and whistled outside. It was not long until he was asleep.

Jon awoke to Skull's whispering to the captain, who had lain down near Jon.

"There are men from another ship on the other side of the island, Cap'n," Skull was whispering. "I don't know how many, but some are officers. Their captain may be among them. They were off to themselves, talking. Pirates, I think, but I'm not sure." Jon sat straight up, wide-eyed.

Several of the men roused up. "We have visitors," the captain told them in a low voice. "Keep the crew piped down, Curly." Curly nodded.

The captain, Spider, and a few men followed Skull through the brush and over the hill to the other side. It was raining, but the winds were calmer and the moon shone through the clouds from time to time, lighting the way.

"The eye of the storm," BlackHeart remarked quietly.

They crouched down near the campfire the intruders had built and listened as the men talked. It didn't take long for BlackHeart to know that they were indeed pirates.

"Shark Scar!" he whispered. "Let's go back to the cave."

When they were a safe distance away, the captain reminded his men that the eye of the storm would soon pass over them and that the winds of the hurricane would be back with a vengeance, this time from the opposite direction, pounding them hard.

"It's obvious that Shark Scar doesn't know we're here," BlackHeart said. "We can't take the ship back into this wind. Shark Scar is in the same situation. To sail now is suicide! We'll have to face them here on the island, but we'll be ready for them. When we have our little trap prepared, we'll let them know we're here—and they'll come to us!"

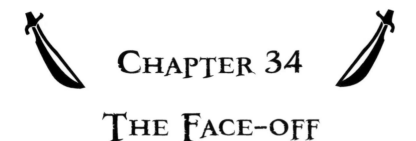

CHAPTER 34

THE FACE-OFF

When they reached the cave, the moon shone brightly through the clouds. BlackHeart, Skull, and Spider walked back and forth in the clearing in front of the cave, examining and measuring. Then Spider went into the cave and came back with six crewmen. The seven men went to the shoreline, where they had turned the dinghy and longboats upside down and secured them to trees to prevent wind damage and keep them from floating away. They turned one of the longboats over and rowed it to the *Black Opal*. Minutes later, they were back, with six barrels of gun powder.

By now, all the crew knew Shark Scar was on the other side of the island and each knew his part in BlackHeart's plan. They busied themselves outside. They had just enough time to finish their preparations before the winds and rain started again, forcing them back into the cave.

"The other side of the storm," Captain BlackHeart explained to Jon. "Best get some sleep, lad, while we wait it out." Jon did as the captain said.

As the storm abated, the men were back out in front of the cave, adding the finishing touch: gun powder.

It was now first light of dawn, and the clouds were beginning to break up.

"Come with me, Jon," BlackHeart said, ushering Jon out of the cave. As they passed, Jon saw a campfire with two skinned rabbits roasting on a twig spit. He smiled.

"Not for us, Jon—for Captain Shark Scar," said the captain. He led Jon toward the beach where *Black Opal* crewmen waited. Skull and a few other crewmen came out of the cave and headed toward the other side of the island, where Shark Scar and his men camped.

Soon Spider, Skull, and the crewmen returned. "Here they come," said Skull as they hurried past the men tending the rabbits roasting on the spit and into the cave. BlackHeart's men in the cave were making loud merriment while BlackHeart and rest of the crew hid in the brush, away from the cave. The scene was set; the trap was laid.

There was a rustle in the brush, and the backs of Shark Scar's men could be seen as they left the cave campsite. They had followed Skull, Spider, and the crewmen back to the cave, and now they were going back to report to Shark Scar what they had seen: BlackHeart's men camped in the cave.

"They've taken the bait," Skull grinned when he and the rest of the men from the cave joined BlackHeart. The unattended rabbits continued to roast to a crisp as the *Black Opal* crew waited, hidden in the brush.

"Let's make sure they know we're here!" BlackHeart said as he lifted his two pistols and fired them both into the air, one right after the other.

"That ought to do it!" laughed Skull. "Curly and his men are circling along the beach to pick up any stragglers from Shark Scar's campsite," Skull informed BlackHeart. The captain nodded his approval. They didn't have to wait long until several of Shark Scar's men arrived.

As Shark Scar's men assembled quietly in front of the cave, Shark Scar came up from the rear and gave a signal. They all stormed the cave in force, cutlasses in one hand, pistols and muskets drawn. Shark Scar held a pistol in each hand as he trailed at a safe distance.

A few minutes later, Shark Scar's men came out of the cave just as the sun broke through the clouds, shining brightly on the entrance. They began to cover their eyes, shielding themselves from the sun's brightness as they came out of the dark cave.

Shark Scar came shoving through the middle of them, his wide-brimmed hat drooping on both sides and his new, wet, turquoise coat sagging well past his knees, all smudged with mud and slosh from the storm. He was holding two pistols down at his sides.

"Where's that squirmy weevil, BlackHeart?" snarled Shark Scar.

"Right here!" snapped BlackHeart.

Shark Scar jerked his arms up to his sides, both pistols pointing outward. He looked side to side, but could not see where the voice had come from.

"Show yourself, ye slimy sea dog, like any honorable pirate should!" he shouted.

"No need to," shouted BlackHeart in his mock pirate brogue. "Ye be at the disadvantage, Shark Scar. Look around ye. See any powder kegs?"

"Wha!" Shark Scar looked startled as he looked around him and saw the powder kegs the *Black Opal* crew had placed near the entrance of the cave and around the clearing. "Devil's teeth!" he swore.

"If ye looks a little closer around you," BlackHeart snarled loudly, "you'll see that me men have placed a fine line o' gunpowder in a circle all around the clearing where ye all stands, me ole friend! One shot from me or me men into them kegs, and ye will all be a visitin' Davy's locker to pick up your new orders! *Drop your weapons! Now!*"

"Why, you bilge rat, I'll ..." Shark Scar started as he looked around him and saw the ring of gunpowder leading to the powder kegs.

"Silence! You'll do exactly what I tell ye to do or you'll be the first to go!" shouted BlackHeart, hidden from view. "Drop your weapons. Now! Don't give me an excuse to do what I'd like to do."

In seething disgust, Shark Scar dropped his pistols as his crew's weapons began falling. *Black Opal* crewmen passed through Shark Scar's crew, collecting the weapons and piling them in a heap outside the circle of gunpowder.

Curly and his men arrived with the remainder of Shark Scar's crewmen all bound together with rope like yesterday's caught fish. They ushered the bound crewmen into the clearing with the others. A scrawny young crewman was brought forward by Gituku and shoved into the lot of Shark Scar's disgruntled, pushing, shoving, and arguing men.

At the sight of the scrawny crewman, Jon lurched forward. He was pulled back by BlackHeart. Jon's instant recognition of the slender youth was not lost on BlackHeart. He eyed both of the boys suspiciously.

They know each other, Jon and this stripling! thought BlackHeart. *But how?*

Jon turned away from Grammy, very obviously trying to cover up the fact that he knew her. She did the same as she stood inside the circle of gunpowder. BlackHeart looked from one boy to the other and then directed his attention back to Shark Scar, who was making some effort to talk to his men. He turned to BlackHeart.

"Well, BlackHeart! Looks like ye makes the best of the ill wind that befalls us both," oozed Shark Scar as he tried to hide his anger. "What d'ye want from me?"

"Better I should be asking ye that question," slurred BlackHeart smugly. "What d'ye want from *me*, since you be the one that comes a calling on me here at my cave on this island, right in the middle o' the high seas. Eh, Cap'n?"

From the distance, BlackHeart could not see the strange quirk working at the corners of Shark Scar's lips as the villain realized that this was his opportunity to rid himself of his current problem: Gramm.

"Well, BlackHeart, at the first I was angry at ye for bamboozling me with the newest map ye give me on your ship, jest like ye bamboozled me before with that other map where the eatin' fishes was hiding out, a' waiting to attack me and my men," Shark Scar said smoothly.

"But let's get back to the latest map ye give me when we met on your ship on the high seas," oozed Shark Scar in a high-pitched voice. "Couldn't find the island that ye drawed on the new map. There wasn't no island there. So, we couldn't look for any treasure on it, ye see, there not being an island to look on. Then, the fancy goldfinder ye give me that you and your conniving cabin boy lied about, it didn't work either. I was mad, all right!

"Then I sez to meself, 'Shark Scar, old friend, Cap'n BlackHeart wouldn't thieve from ye on purpose, would he?' Being the forgiving gentleman sea captain that I am, I gets over with me angry spell, I did," Shark Scar lied.

BlackHeart smirked and waited for Shark Scar to finish with his ridiculous story while the crew of the *Black Opal* kept their guns and muskets pointed at Shark Scar and his men.

"So, BlackHeart, me fellow pirate, let's not ruin our friendship over a few gold doubloons and some mysteriously missing islands. Let's forgive the past. I'll give ye a little peace offering to boot," Shark Scar offered with a smile.

"Peace offering?" BlackHeart asked, almost laughing. He knew something was wrong with this picture but couldn't figure out what twisted plot might be lurking in Shark Scar's devious mind.

"Yes," Shark Scar hissed as he lifted his booted foot to Gramm's back and shoved Gramm, unexpectedly, out of the gunpowder circle toward BlackHeart. Gramm stumbled and fell to the ground. "A *gift* for ye! Me new cook, Gramm. Don't let him being a scrawny kid fool ye none. Sometimes he acts older than death. But Gramm can cook good, he can!"

The faces of Shark Scar's men showed mixed expressions of anger, outrage, and fury toward their captain. What was he doing, giving Gramm, who had saved them all, to this rival pirate? They looked anxiously at each other, grumbling amongst themselves, finally moving forward, some toward Shark Scar in anger and some to shield Gramm.

"Don't take another step!" BlackHeart warned Shark Scar's men, and they stopped in their tracks.

How puzzling, thought BlackHeart. *I've purposely tricked and swindled Shark Scar at every turn. Now he wants to give me one of his crewmen as a gift? Something very strange is going on here. Giving another pirate one of your crew could be handing them over to death! His crew doesn't like it, and it's obvious that Shark Scar doesn't care about this stripling. But why give him to me?* Finally, it dawned on Captain BlackHeart. *Shark Scar wants to get rid of this boy, Gramm, and is using me as a way to do it. I wonder why? If I don't take the boy, Shark Scar will kill him sooner or later!*

BlackHeart felt a tug on his sleeve and glanced down to see Jon standing at his side. Excitement danced in Jon's eyes as he looked up at the captain. BlackHeart returned his eyes to Shark Scar.

"And what does ye want in return?" asked BlackHeart.

"For me and me crew of the *Shark* to leave this island one hour afore the *Black Opal* sails," Shark Scar said smugly. "That's all!"

"No! Tie 'em up, men!" commanded BlackHeart. "All except the stripling, Gramm. He'll go with me." Turning to Curly, he said, "Dig a hole in the wet beach sand where the waves wash in, and bury their weapons."

When Shark Scar and his men were tied securely, BlackHeart, Jon, and Gramm boarded the dinghy with Spider and some oarsmen.

"The ropes will keep 'em busy for a while, Cappin," said Spider.

"And finding and cleaning the wet, muddy guns and muskets will keep them busy for several hours," grinned BlackHeart.

As the oarsmen rowed to the ship, Jon and Gramm sat staring at each other, with an occasional glance at BlackHeart.

Strange! It's obvious that Jon and this young man know each other, but neither has spoken one word to the other, Captain BlackHeart thought as he leaned back against the prow of the dinghy, watching them warily.

Chapter 35

Come Clean

"Spider, why have you lost your trust in me?" BlackHeart asked as the two of them stood by the wooden railing of the ship.

The tall Jamaican ran his long fingers along the smooth wooden top of the ship's railing, thinking.

"I trust ye well enough. Ye be a good man, Cappin, but ye don't know anything aboot curses and the like. You see, Cappin, curses, they not like us ... you know, *human*, I mean. Here on the seas, they is directly from Davy Jones hisself," replied Spider.

"Have you ever been hurt by a 'curse,' as you call it?" asked Captain BlackHeart.

"No, Cappin. But I heard tell aboot lots of people what has!" he said, looking straight at the captain. "From the time ye purchased me on that auction block in Port Royal, I knew ye was a good man. My owner beat my back raw with his whip whilst some men cheered. And then, ye steps up to him on that block and sez, 'How much for this one?' Then, we come onboard the *Black*

Opal and ye sez to me that this ship is freedom. Ye told me that I be a free man from that moment, cause nobody on your ship is property. Not me or nobody else! Ye shares with me, jest the same as ye shares with all the men on this ship."

"Well, Spider, if I didn't like seeing the slave master striping your back with a whip and paid him the price for your freedom, you must know I wouldn't like a curse harming you either. Since no curse has ever come aboard this ship, you have to trust me when I tell you that no curse *will* come aboard. Correct?" asked the captain.

"Correck, Cappin," said Spider without thinking twice. The two of them stood at the railing, looking at each other as Spider thought over what Captain BlackHeart had said. Then he grinned that familiar big Jamaican grin. "Sorry, Cappin," he said.

"Keep up your courage, Spider," the captain said as he gave Spider a pat on the shoulder. "You needed me when you came aboard. I need you now." The captain started to his cabin and then turned back. "Oh, and Spider?"

"Yes, Cappin?" replied Spider.

"Plot a new course for Tortuga and get us underway. We can get there in two or three days. Like I said before, the *Red Dragon* will be in Tortuga looking for diving equipment, and I'd like to sell them the equipment we bought in Port Royal," BlackHeart said. "I may even sell them the diving bell!"

"We not going back for more of that sunken Spanish booty, Cappin?" asked Spider. "The hold in that galleon don't even miss the treasure we took out."

"We all have enough treasure to keep us for the rest of our lives, and our families, as well," said the captain. "Do we need more, Spider?"

"No-o-o, sir, Cappin! We sure don't. And I think I speaks for the crew as well, Cappin," Spider said with another broad smile.

"Tortuga, then!" said BlackHeart.

"Aye, aye, Cappin!" Spider said.

The captain turned toward his cabin and the next problem he had to deal with: Jon and the boy, Gramm.

Jon and Grammy had hugged, cried together, and discussed all that had transpired since they were separated. Now, they sat quietly at the big table in the captain's cabin, waiting for him to come in, just as he had commanded them to do the minute they set foot on the deck.

Jon felt the rough scraping and vibration as the main anchor lifted, and then the jolt and rocking of the ship as the anchor found its secure resting place in the hawse pipe where it would be safe from seaweed and debris.

The door to the cabin burst open, and BlackHeart strode forward, removing his pistol from his sash, his cutlass, and his sword. He dropped them all clattering onto the table where Jon and Grammy sat waiting.

He stood glaring at both of them for a moment and then said in a loud, booming voice, "Talk!"

They both started talking at once, so fast that it was gibberish. The captain raised his hand. "Stop!" he commanded sharply. "You first, Jon," he said.

"Captain, uh-hh, this is Kathryn Sinclair ... my grandmother."

"Your *what!*" BlackHeart exclaimed as he whipped his head around toward Gramm, his green-black eyes glaring sharply at her. "Gramm is a *woman?*"

Neither Jon nor Grammy answered.

The captain couldn't believe what he was hearing. He squinted his eyes and moved his face closer to Grammy's, studying her intently. Then he moved back, batting his eyes, and looked out at the ocean. Then he walked around the table, looking first at Jon and then at Grammy as he thought. When he came around the table the second time, he stopped right in front of Grammy, both his hands braced on his hips and his mouth twisted up into a smirk.

"And what do we do now, Mrs. Sinclair?" he asked loudly as he cocked one eyebrow.

"Just like Alistair when he's angry and perplexed," whispered Grammy, annoyed.

"Did you say something, Mrs. Sinclair?" BlackHeart asked pointedly.

"Nothing of importance, Captain," she replied.

The captain stalked to the door, jerked it open, and yelled, "Curly!"

"Aye, aye, Cap'n," replied Curly, running to the cabin.

"Clear out the storage room up on the poop deck, next to Mr. Token's cabin," BlackHeart commanded.

"But, it be full of new canvas for the sails, Cap'n," argued Curly.

"Well, put 'em somewhere else!" roared BlackHeart. "Immediately! Do you hear?"

"Yes, sir, Cap'n, sir!" replied Curly as he ran down the stairs to the main deck and grabbed two sailors to help him remove the canvas.

The captain paced back and forth, thinking through all that Jon had told him three days ago and all that had happened since. *Jon ought to know his own grandmother,* BlackHeart reasoned. *And she ought to know her own grandson, ridiculous as this story is.* "Talk!" he shouted as he pointed directly at Grammy. "And don't leave out any *minor* details."

In the next few minutes, Kathryn Sinclair explained how she and Jon had been separated in the forest and how she had pretended to be a young man, joining Shark Scar's ship in order to find Jon.

There was a loud knock at the door.

"Enter," BlackHeart shouted.

The door opened and Curly stood there with two sailors. "We cleaned out the storage room on the poop deck. Anything else, Cap'n?"

"Yes. Move my bunk into the empty room," replied the captain.

"Ye be moving to the poop deck, Cap'n?" asked Curly with a look of confusion, and a frown.

"No! Gramm is sleeping there. I am sleeping on the floor in my own cabin, until we reach Tortuga! I'll decide what's to be done by then!"

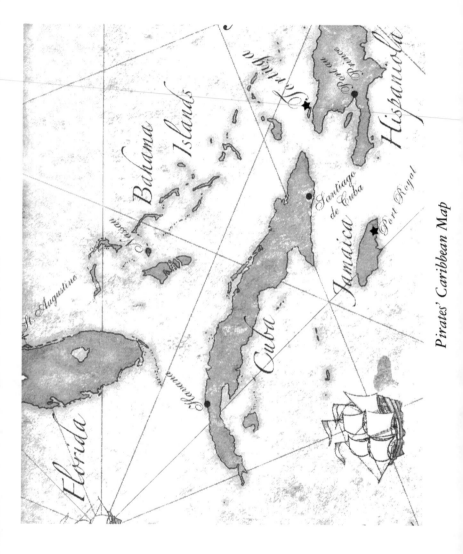

Pirates' Caribbean Map

CHAPTER 36

TORTUGA

J on stood out on the bow of the ship, at the furthermost forward point of the decking as the wind blew his hair backward and the surf sprayed his face with tiny sharp prickles of water. He stuck out his tongue and licked around his lips. The taste was salty and good.

I like being on this ship where people are not always telling me what to do, thought Jon as he stood at the railing, smelling the air's freshness with its special mix of salt, fish, seaweed, and other things growing in the sea. *I have my job, and that's all. Well, maybe I have to do more than my job, like help Cook with the animals or break down the stoves for special cleaning. And, well, maybe I have to polish the captain's tall leather boots or pitch in when there's a hurricane or something. But at least I'm totally free, with nobody yelling at me to do something I don't want to do!*

"Jon!" roared the captain as he strode swiftly forward. "Come away from the bow of the ship. We don't have time to stop the ship and pick you up out of the water in pieces after the ship's rudder passes over you! Do I need to find more work for you to keep you out of trouble?" He grabbed hold of Jon's arm roughly and marched him back to mid-ship. Curly snickered and looked the other way. "Watch from there," he said sharply as he pushed Jon toward the side railing and walked up to the helm.

Well, so much for nobody yelling at me and telling me what to do, thought Jon, looking down at his dripping wet, fish-smelling shirt. *Maybe it's that I know what's expected of me here. As long as I do it, the captain doesn't say anything. And if I don't?* he didn't want to think about that part.

From a distance, Tortuga was an island that looked like a monstrous sea turtle floating in the Caribbean. It lay just north of the great island of Hispaniola.

As they approached the island from the north side, the land was mountainous and extremely rocky. Drawing nearer, Jon could hear the rhythm of the breakers, which sprayed high into the air as the waves beat against the high rocks of the island. Scraggly trees seemed to grow straight out of the rocks, their exposed roots wrapping the rocky surface.

This looks similar to Devil's Rock, thought Jon. He could see no beach, town, or harbor.

"I can't see anything but rocks. Where will we drop anchor?" Jon asked Curly, who was helping his men roll the rigging ropes in the perfect tight circles that were always laying here and there on the deck.

"We makes the turn soon," Curly replied, "to go around to the lowlands on the south side of Tortuga where the harbor and beaches be."

Just as Curly finished speaking, Jon felt the ship lurch sharply and saw that the captain was turning the wheel to go around the big rock island shaped like a turtle.

When the ship was securely anchored, Grammy and Jon were allowed to go into Tortuga together—but not alone. Spider and Skull were assigned to go along to be sure they were safe. After the turmoil Grammy had been through since leaving the *Carousel*, she thought it a little amusing to have bodyguards. After what Jon had been through in Port Royal, he was glad they were along.

Jon and Grammy had heard the captain tell the men yesterday that Gramm was actually a woman—Jon's grammy, in fact. This news had raised the loud, disgruntled response the captain knew it would. By the captain's own rules, the code was no women or children onboard. Not even powder monkeys. The captain hated the idea of children being used on ships as labor and wanted none of it. "Pirate's code," he had always said. And, "Women onboard create confusion and a lack of discipline. Pirate's code," he had told the crew. And now, the captain had broken the code twice, or rather the pirate's code he had set up for the *Black Opal*.

When they went ashore in Tortuga, BlackHeart, Guidry, and Mr. Token had stayed at the docks. They were waiting to talk with the captain of the *Red Dragon* about the diving equipment. Mr. Token's ability to speak Mandarin Chinese would be essential to their negotiations with the Chinese, BlackHeart had said.

Jon, Grammy, Spider, and Skull had stopped at an inn, where they enjoyed a breakfast of fresh eggs, ham, and freshly made morning cakes before continuing into the seaside town.

There are more seamen here than in Port Royal. Not many townspeople, thought Jon. Most were crude-talking men, with wrinkly, weathered skin. Some smoked clay pipes with long stems; some spat sickening-looking, brownish-black globs of wet stuff from their mouths and then wiped their dripping brown slobber on their shirt sleeves. Jon thought he might lose his breakfast any minute and said so. Skull told him that he was being a silly *little* boy, that it was only tobacco. Jon didn't like being called "little boy," but his stomach still retched at the thought of it. Skull grinned; he enjoyed prodding Jon.

Grammy was tired of wearing men's clothing and stopped at a lady's haberdashery. Spider said he would wait for her outside while Skull and Jon went across the brick-laid street into a marine shop.

An hour later, Jon sat proudly on the crude wooden walkway, wearing his new tricorn hat that Skull had bought him and listening to the clopping feet of horses and the rumbling sounds of the carts passing. Skull paced impatiently, wondering when Grammy might be finished in the store. Finally, a bell clanged loudly as it flapped against the door of the shop, and Grammy poked her head out. She was wearing a blue dress and a small straw bonnet with a ribbon pulled under the chin and tied to one side.

"Can you boys help me carry these boxes?" she asked.

"*Boys?*" asked Skull, chuckling as he turned around and saw the smiling owner of the store holding a large stack of boxes. Grammy held another stack, and hat boxes that dangled from ribbon held in each hand. Spider volunteered to take all the boxes to the dinghy and meet them later.

The town was growing more crowded in the late afternoon when the four of them started back toward the ship.

They passed a group of seamen going into a loud, bawdy tavern. The men were dressed in sailor's clothing. As with most in the town, they were dirty, sweaty, and smelling of the sea. But one man in the group stood out from the others. That one wore a dirty, light blue seaman's coat. The hair hanging from under his tricorn was scraggly and grayish. He laughed and patted one of the sailors on the back as they went through the swinging doors of the tavern.

A glimmer of recognition reflected momentarily in Grammy's eyes; but on second look at the man in the blue coat, she dismissed the thought and continued walking.

Gituku was waiting for them at the dock and led them to the longboat.

Jon arrived back onboard the ship just in time to help the crew put the captain's new bed in his cabin and make it up for him. The captain was writing in his journal as he always did at the close of each day, and Jon was putting BlackHeart's dinner on the table, when Grammy knocked at the door.

"Enter!" said BlackHeart.

"Evening, Jon. Captain BlackHeart, may I speak with you?" asked Grammy.

"Please do join us, Mrs. Sinclair," BlackHeart answered as he stood and pulled out a chair for her.

"Captain BlackHeart," Grammy began, "I saw a man in town today, and thought I had just imagined that he looked like Mole, the quartermaster of Captain Shark Scar's ship. The man had on a blue coat like Mole's, and it was dirty and stained like his is, but all the men are dirty and stained here, so I dismissed the idea at the time. Now that I've had time to think about it, I remember seeing a green smudge on the right sleeve of the man's coat. Mole's coat had a similar green smudge in the same place—green paint the same color as the *Shark's* hull. I know the man was Mole, sir, but I didn't recognize any of the men with him."

The captain leaned back in his chair, looking out the back windows of the cabin, thinking.

"See that ship over there? The big brown schooner with two masts?" he asked, pointing to a ship anchored nearby in the harbor. "That's the *Scorpion*. Ship belongs to a captain named Sleg. It anchored there late this afternoon, and the crewmen went ashore. Shark Scar's ship, the *Shark*, is not in the harbor, and there's nowhere else on this island that a ship can dock. How is it, I wonder, that Shark Scar's quartermaster would be ashore with Sleg's crew?" the captain asked himself out loud. "I smell a rat ... maybe two bilge rats!"

"Captain, there's something else," Grammy said. "When I boarded Shark Scar's ship in Port Royal, most of the crew had scurvy, which I helped them cure while I was aboard. Shark Scar was hardened to the needs of the sick men until he found out he had the disease himself. In a conversation I had with Mole about the citrus fruits and vegetables we needed for curing the men of the disease, he told me that Shark Scar had a plan to attack your ship. After you were out of the way, Shark Scar planned a meeting with Captain Sleg somewhere in the Caribbean.

"Before I boarded the *Shark* in Port Royal," Grammy continued, "unknown to Sleg and Shark Scar, I overheard them talking on the dock. Both captains wanted to get even with you, sir. Shark Scar also included doing harm to Jon in his evil plans. They talked of a rendezvous together, and Shark Scar drew Sleg a map of where they would meet. I didn't see the map."

"If you knew back then what you just told me, Mrs. Sinclair, why did you board the *Shark*?" asked the captain.

"I would have done almost anything to find Jon," Grammy replied. "I had information that Jon was with you. And they were looking for you."

"It all fits together," reasoned BlackHeart. "Were you wearing women's clothing today when you passed Mole in Tortuga?"

"Yes, I was," replied Grammy.

"Obviously Mole didn't recognize you in a dress," he said, his voice trailing off. He was now standing at the windows, pensively looking at the *Scorpion* again. Then he turned abruptly.

"Bring your dinner here to my table, Jon," BlackHeart said. "And bring your grandmother's tray, as well. We shall all enjoy this nice dinner of roast duck with oranges prepared by Cook. And afterward, a fine glass of port. Cook can prepare a warm cocoa for you, Jon. He brought fresh chocolate onboard this afternoon from Tortuga.

"While Jon brings up your dinner, I shall excuse myself for a few minutes. Please entertain yourself, Mrs. Sinclair. There are many books in my library. Feel free to borrow from it," BlackHeart said as he opened the door. "I need to speak with Spider and Skull about a matter—a minor detail, of course."

Jon was returning to the main deck with the dinner trays when he noticed that Spider, Skull, and a few men went over the railing of the ship to the longboat below. The captain walked toward him and took one of the trays.

"We delivered the diving equipment to the *Red Dragon* this afternoon, Jon," BlackHeart said as they went into his cabin. "We have no reason to remain here. We shall sail tomorrow with the morning tides."

CHAPTER 37

SECRET HIDING PLACE

After dinner, Jon walked with Grammy to her cabin. They were standing on the poop deck, talking, when Spider and Skull came aboard and went directly into the captain's cabin. Jon waited until their meeting with the captain was finished before returning to the cabin.

"Close the door, Jon, and bolt it. I have something of importance to discuss with you." Jon locked the door as the captain requested.

"Yes, Captain?" he said.

"When we sail tomorrow, we expect to come under attack by one or two ships on the seas," the captain said. "We think we are prepared, but battle against two ships is always treacherous, particularly around some of these rocks. Help me remove the wine goblets from this shelf. I have something I want to show you," BlackHeart said. He and Jon removed all the crystal from the shelf, setting it on the large table.

BlackHeart pulled open one of the drawers of his desk and removed the false bottom in the drawer, thus revealing a small steel instrument that resembled a screwdriver. He removed the instrument—about eight inches long with a round steel tip the size of a small coin. The captain turned the instrument so that the candlelight could shine into the tip and Jon could see inside.

"The inside looks like your seal: the letter B printed backward, encircled by a heart," Jon said in faint whisper.

"Yes," said BlackHeart.

Next BlackHeart used his knife tip to gently pry away the four wooden pegs from the corners of the back panel of the cabinet where the wine goblets had been. He slid the strange instrument into the hole where the peg had been and rotated it gently until it locked into place on top of the embedded metal screw. Then, he removed the screw and handed to Jon.

"Your seal," Jon remarked as he looked at the head of the screw.

When all the screws were removed in like fashion, BlackHeart removed the back panel, revealing a deep hidden compartment.

Inside, Jon saw several scrolls—large maps of some sort—and some small document-type scrolls tied with black ribbon and sealed with BlackHeart's black wax seal. On the other end of the compartment were three small gold chests, all the same size, sitting in a neat row, side by side.

"No one on this ship knows of this compartment, except me, and now you, Jon," BlackHeart said quietly. "This is where I keep all things of utmost secrecy."

So this is where the treasure maps are, thought Jon as his eyes widened at the spectacle before him.

"I only show you because I trust you," BlackHeart said, "and because I could be killed tomorrow. Should something happen to me, you will remove these documents and maps and take them to King William in England. Mr. Token can take you. He knows the king well. Do you understand, Jon?"

"Yes, Captain," Jon replied.

"You will tell *no one* of this compartment. It *must* remain a secret. From hence forward, you—as well as I—will protect my cabin with your life," BlackHeart commanded. "Is that clear?"

"Yes, Captain," Jon replied.

The captain replaced the back panel and the pegs, and returned the screwing device to its place in the desk. Jon replaced all the crystal wine goblets in the shelf and shut the cabinet door.

That night, Jon lay in his bunk wondering, *What was in the gold boxes: jewels, diamonds or emeralds, secret keys? Were those real treasure maps? And were the smaller scrolls letters?* Jon fell asleep fantasizing about what he had seen in the hidden compartment.

CHAPTER 38

AMBUSH

The crew of the *Black Opal* had been well advised by Captain BlackHeart of the new alliance between Captain Shark Scar and Captain Sleg, and of their perceived plan to attack the *Black Opal*. They were on the keenest alert that a pirate could be as they set sail at dawn from Tortuga.

Even without orders from the captain, they all knew from their years of experience with BlackHeart what was expected of them. And they were fully armed in case something unpredictable happened and the *Black Opal* was boarded by the two ruthless pirate crews who sought their destruction.

Last night after talking with Kathryn, BlackHeart had told Spider and Skull what he knew. He had told them to gather a group of men, go into Tortuga, and spread the word in the taverns that the *Black Opal* was sailing at dawn the next morning. Spider and Skull knew Sleg's men by sight. They made sure that several of those men had overheard them discussing their early morning departure. Mole, Shark Scar's quartermaster, was among them. Later that night around midnight, BlackHeart,

Spider, and Skull had watched from the *Black Opal* as the *Scorpion* sailed from its mooring spot.

"That proves it," BlackHeart had told them. "They're planning to attack us. We tricked them into making their move sooner. I'd rather know when we're going to be attacked so we can be prepared for it. They're going to meet Shark Scar now and wait for us somewhere. We'll look over the maps and find the most likely spot for the ambush."

The three of them had agreed that the most likely spot for the attack would be when they came around the island of Tortuga, headed into the north. There, two very rocky small islands sat close together near the island of Tortuga on the left, or the west side. Most of the tall ships leaving the port of Tortuga went through the middle of these two small rock islands because it was the deepest channel. The channel between the first small rock and Tortuga was fraught with the peril of rocks just under the surface of the water. Maneuvering through this side would be most difficult, if not impossible. The *Black Opal* was approaching these two islands now.

"Curly! Man the guns on forward deck! Spider will command those on quarterdeck. I'll man the wheel," BlackHeart shouted.

"Skull! Open ports one, three, and five on each side. More than that will just slow us down."

"Aye, aye!" Skull shouted as he headed down the steps to the cannon bay below.

"Guidry, watch for fires onboard!" BlackHeart commanded.

"Aye, aye, Cap'n" replied Guidry.

Spider had speculated that Sleg and Shark Scar would hide behind each of these two rock islands, which they would have to pass. As the *Black Opal* neared the islands, BlackHeart made a sharp right turn, heading the ship right into the dangerous rocky area between Tortuga and the first small rock island.

Jon and Grammy were tossed this way and that in the captain's cabin as the ship wove its way with precision through the sea of rocks

Just as predicted, there sat the *Shark*, anchored just north of the rock island with all twenty of her cannon ports on the east side, which now faced *Black Opal*, shut! It was obvious that Shark Scar thought BlackHeart would be out of his mind to try to pass through the treacherous rocks on this side. Thus, Shark Scar had all his cannon loaded in the ports on the other side, waiting for BlackHeart to sail between him and Sleg, who waited behind the other rock island.

"Fire one!" shouted Skull. "Fire two!"

The ship sank down into the waves and then pitched high as the loud blasts of the two cannon shook and rattled its timbers. Then the first two cannon on the *Black Opal*'s aft deck responded with ear-popping blasts.

Spider gave the command to the gunners on the quarterdeck, and cannon three and four were fired, just as cannon one and two fired again.

BlackHeart grinned, and the crew cheered as the new chain-cannonballs he had bartered from the Chinese literally ripped the sails of the *Shark* to shreds. Wood flew and fires erupted as the second wave of explosive cannonballs hit the *Shark*. Suddenly, the top of the *Shark*'s

forward mast broke, falling sideways across the railing of
the ship and into the water.

The waves were still pitching fiercely from the fall of
the *Shark*'s mast when BlackHeart turned the wheel of
the *Black Opal* sharply left, passing in front of the *Shark*'s
bow, thus affording the *Black Opal* a perfect shot at the
Scorpion, which lay in wait behind the other island.

The loud blasts of the *Black Opal's* cannon sounded
again. Both chain-cannonballs hit the *Scorpion*, ripping
off the schooner's front mainsail.

The sounds of three quick cannon blasts from the
Scorpion, which were aimed in the direction of the *Shark*
and the *Black Opal*, could be heard as the *Scorpion* initiated its assault against the *Black Opal*. The first wayward
cannonball hit the *Shark*, and a fire erupted on her bow,
as chaos broke out among her crew.

There was a large "splash" as water from the second cannonball washed over the deck of the *Black Opal*.
The cannonball had missed its intended target and hit
the water between the *Shark*'s bow and the *Black Opal's*
portside.

They were not as lucky with the third cannonball
shot from the *Scorpion*: it careened into the deck of the
Black Opal on the forward starboard side. The ship
pitched from side to side; sounds of wood splintering,
crackling timbers, and leaping fires engulfed the deck.
Seawater washed over the top side and into the gaping
hole, causing black smoke to billow as another fire broke
out below deck, thrusting big shafts of flames upward
through the hole.

"We're on fire!" shouted Guidry.

BlackHeart suddenly and forcefully turned the *Black Opal* to the right, directly into the north, and headed her out to sea.

Jon and Grammy sat motionless in the captain's cabin, afraid to move, as smoke seeped under the door.

CHAPTER 39

AN UNLIKELY OBSERVER

Tortuga: May 15, 1692

Watching from a rock high in the mountains on the north side of the island of Tortuga was a man who owed far too much money. He had borrowed all that he could borrow against his worldly possessions in order to travel to Tortuga.

The slender man, dressed in a black seaman's coat, wore high black leather boots with a leather flap that turned down at the knees. His black tricorn hat covered a black scarf that was tied tightly over his head, the ends hanging out from under the hat. A Flintlock pistol was tucked in a leather holster, which was sewn onto his broad, black leather waistband. The metal tip of a cutlass could be seen, the rest hidden by his coat. A tall, daunting figure, to be sure.

As the smoke cleared from the sea battle he had just witnessed, he walked over to a small shanty, which looked like a store of some sort. He approached the merchant who stood in the doorway, still gawking at the three ships below.

"Did'ja sees them, Cap'n?" the burly merchant asked. "Three pirate ships they be, Cap'n, facing off agin' each other! Seen two before—never seen three of 'em fighting, though. Smart cap'n, the one in the black ship be. Caught the other two plumbly off guard, he did. Them two ships what's dead in the water now was a' waiting behind them two rock islands to waylay the black ship."

"I saw the battle," the stranger said sharply.

"Broke the main mast on the green ship, and that brown schooner don't have no main sail, none a' tall. It be laying out yon on the water! See?" he said, pointing to a mass of white canvas that was floating far out to sea. "The other ship, the black brigantine, had a fire aboard but they put it out quickly. They almost over the horizon now. See? Great battle," the merchant laughed heartily, patting his fat belly.

"I said I saw the battle," the stranger said impatiently.

"Oh, uh, yes, so, what was it ye wanted, Cap'n?"

"I want to go down to the harbor," the tall man in black said very pointedly as if talking to a retarded man. "I have things in the mountains I need take with me. I want to buy a wagon and a horse."

"Don't have nary; mayhap the blacksmith know of a cart—no wagon though. Follow me," he said as he spat a huge brown glob into a large can on the tobacco-spattered floor. The stranger held back a gag as he followed the merchant outside into the fresh air. They walked across the dirt road and turned down another, passing by a fenced-in yard with four smelly, sway-backed, scruffy-looking horses.

The merchant explained what the stranger wanted to the blacksmith, and he was helpful; he pointed to the finest he had to offer: a splintered cart with wobbly wooden wheels. From the looks and smell of the cart, it had obviously been hauling horse manure, some still lying in the corners. He hitched the cart to one of the sway-backed horses they had passed on the road.

With a dour face, the stranger flipped him a coin.

"One doubloon! Yes, that will do keenly, Cap'n," the blacksmith said, smiling a completely toothless smile through brown, tobacco-stained lips. The merchant nodded continuously, grinning with another toothless smile, and the man in black knew they would share the *new wealth*.

"Harrumph!" grumbled the stranger as he traveled back into the tall trees of the mountains. *It's obvious that I paid too much for this smelly heap of gag! Never did like to leave money laying on the table. I'll have to check the current value of these coins when I get to the port,* he thought.

The tall man who had paid too much for the horse and cart was Alistair Franklin Sinclair, known to his grandson, Jon, as Pappy.

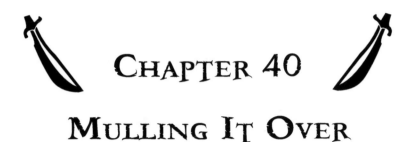

Chapter 40

Mulling It Over

Tortuga: Afternoon of May 15, 1692

Shouting, "Whoa," in any language Alistair knew did not stop the broken-down horse. He pulled back on the reins, which irritated the horse so much that it bucked viciously, causing Alistair to be tossed backward amongst the stinking waste in the cart. Infuriated, he crawled over the front of the jerking cart and onto the bucking horse, sitting on its tired, swayed back. That did the trick. The horse stopped immediately and snorted.

"If I have to use this method to stop this nag every time, it'll take a month to get down to the harbor!" Alistair grumbled as he slid off the horse. The horse snorted again as it gave him a tired, sleepy look.

Taking the new silver Transformer from his pocket, he entered some codes. The red light on the top flashed three times, and the screen lit up. He keyed in more codes, and two green lights, along with a yellow light, began to flash in a pattern across the top of the small Transformer. Suddenly the lights stopped flashing as a bright white light appeared in the air amongst the tall trees and began to grow in size, emitting a blue foglike mist. The mist stayed close to the ground, moving outward in all directions and covering everything in its path, including Alistair's feet, the horse's hooves, and the cart.

Then the white light flashed briefly, followed by a soft popping sound like that of a flashbulb, as the giant *Carousel* appeared in the small clearing. The horse paid no notice.

Alistair keyed another code into the Transformer and the door of the *Carousel* slid open. Emitting a shrill whirring sound, a ramp extended downward from the ship. Alistair went aboard and returned with two large antique wooden trunks. Next he brought down a smaller but heavy wooden chest and a large leather shoulder bag he had bought in Port Royal earlier that morning.

When everything was loaded into the cart, he again activated the Transformer with a set of codes. The red light flashed three times, the screen went black, and the low-hovering blue mist began to pulse as it recorded every molecule of the area. Within forty seconds, the mapping was completed. The mist was abruptly sucked back into the *Carousel,* and the ship slowly disappeared, leaving only a bright light suspended above the place where it had stood. The light lifted higher among the treetops and then above them. A soft popping sound was heard as the white light vanished from view.

That should keep it safe until I return, he thought. The *Carousel* would hover high above the trees there, invisible, until activated again by the Transformer.

Riding in the rickety cart down the hill, Alistair thought about the events that had happened since the

Carousel had reappeared at Three Forks—empty. It had returned the very same day that Kathryn and Jon had left for their travel back in time to Philadelphia.

At first, Alistair had thought his own life would end, for he had no desire to go on without the two people he loved most. Then, after much thought and prayer, he knew he must try to find them.

He had gone into the barn and turned on the *Carousel*'s computer. He selected and saved all the information he could from the original computer in an effort to find out where the *Carousel* had gone awry.

He had spent several days digging into all the computer log files in an attempt to find out how they were corrupted. Nothing! He had checked the switch-over to the second computer that Kathryn had made. Everything looked in order. As he looked over the last group of logs, he found the single phrase "Port Royal, Jamaica."

Finally a clue! he thought. His fingers tapped the computer keys rapidly as he madly sought any clue as to the year in which Jon and Kathryn had been left in Port Royal.

"The year! The year! You dumb heap of computer chips!" he yelled in agony, pounding the console with his fist in frustration. There was a quiet click, a slight whir, and then the sound stopped. It was the *printer*.

Jammed again, he thought in frustration. Then he slowly and suspiciously looked down at the printer that sat below the console. "Jammed? But I haven't pushed Print!"

Then he immediately pulled out the printer, opened it up, and pulled out the piece of jammed paper. He inserted a stack of fresh, flat paper. The printer clicked on, and Alistair grabbed the first piece of paper coming out. It was a map! He laughed until tears ran from his eyes as he held up the vital clue. "Port Royal, Jamaica—May 1, 1692 AD," he shouted. "The same day they left here!"

The printer continued to spit out more copies of the map, and Alistair laughed loudly. *Kathryn never did have patience with that printer. She must have punched the button several times,* he thought. When the printer finally shut off, he held up eleven copies of the same map.

He sat studying the map with the year and date. The icon for the Transformer was shown to be in the Caribbean Sea, near Port Royal. Then he clicked on the Internet. He sought out all the information about Port Royal and the year 1692 that he could find.

He found out that in 1692, Port Royal was noted to be the wickedest city on earth, fraught with pirates, privateers, and a sprinkling of British soldiers trying to keep the peace. He knew instinctively that Kathryn and Jon were not in the hands of the British soldiers. *Pirates,* he thought. *How did the Transformer get in the sea if Kathryn was in the* Carousel? *And how did the* Carousel *arrive back here in the barn, without either Kathryn or Jon aboard? Someone had to input the proper commands for the* Carousel *to come back here. Since the* Carousel *arrived empty, the code had to have come from the Transformer. Kathryn never would have done that; Jon doesn't know how to input that code; so, who did it?*

Are they both captives? he wondered. *Of pirates? Maybe held for ransom? Holding people for ransom was big business in those days.* For the answers to all these questions, he would have to go to Port Royal.

If pirates had anything to do with their disappearances, he knew he would need money—lots of it. But not today's money, yesterday's money—gold! Coins, maybe? Yes, as many as he could find online and from antique coin dealers. And maybe small gold bars, ingots. He would have to check with the gold dealers.

Then his eyes had fallen to a line on the computer screen on the Port Royal page: "Earthquake drops half of Port Royal into Caribbean Sea!" Wildly, he selected the article and read it. Over half of the island of Port Royal had dropped off into the sea and a tidal wave had covered the rest. Thousands were killed or injured: June 7, 1692!

There was not one moment to lose! Even though he had not found the source of the original computer's problem that had trapped Kathryn and Jon in Port Royal in 1692, he had no time to deal with it now. The *Carousel*'s second computer had brought it back safely. He left it connected.

He had driven directly to the bank, where he had drawn out all of their savings. He had mortgaged all their possessions with several banks and converted everything he could to cash, even sold the cars and his truck. Then he had used all the money to buy gold: mostly Spanish doubloons and gold ingots.

This done, he visited a widely advertised antique gun shop, where he purchased some weapons and an antique-looking leather waist belt to hold his new flintlock pistol and the leather sack of shot for the pistol.

Wearing the clothing he had purchased at a costume shop, he packed the weapons, the gold, and a few personal belongings into the two antique wooden trunks with new strong combination locks on them. Three days had now passed since the night he had discovered where and when the *Carousel* had been separated from Kathryn and Jon.

He had arranged for their farm animals and Trek to be fed and cared for and had locked up everything solidly.

It was now May 20. Alistair had only eighteen days in which to find Jon and Kathryn and get them out before the massive earthquake. He sat down at the console of the *Carousel* and entered the place and year: Port Royal, Jamaica, May 20, 1692 AD.

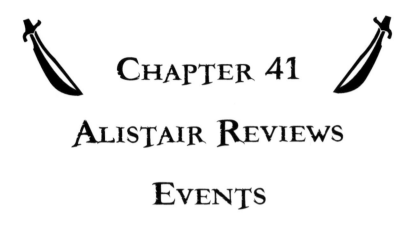

CHAPTER 41

ALISTAIR REVIEWS

EVENTS

As Alistair's cart continued down the road to Tortuga, he thought about his first stop earlier this morning, which had been in Port Royal. He was going over all the events and the information he had gained there to be sure he would not forget any important detail. Each detail, no matter how small, could be significant in finding Kathryn and Jon.

On his early morning arrival in Port Royal, Alistair had purchased a horse and wagon to take his trunks into the city, where he stopped at a men's haberdashery to buy some clothes of that time period for himself. He left his trunks in the wagon in front of the haberdashery's window so he could keep watch over them.

Inside the store, he removed the contents of his pockets to try the fit of a pair of trousers. The owner of the shop saw the *new* silver Transformer Alistair had laid on the small table and said, "I see you have one of those new fancy *goldfinders*, too."

"What?" asked Alistair.

The shop owner pointed to the Transformer and continued, "That goldfinder. A few days ago, I sold a goldfinder similar to that one to a young man named Gramm who works for the bakery down the street. Does it really work—point to gold, I mean? Because the ship captain who traded it to me said it didn't work, and I couldn't make it work, either. Captain Shark Scar said he got the goldfinder from Captain BlackHeart and that a young boy on his ship, the *Black Opal*, could make it work. But neither one of us could make it work."

Alistair's heart beat wildly at the thought that Kathryn and Jon might be right here in Port Royal, but he pretended to be calm as he asked, "Did you say you sold it to a boy?"

"Yes; well, actually a young man, maybe twenty or twenty-five years. He was right anxious to have it," replied the owner.

"Where is the bakery where the boys work?" asked Alistair.

"Oh, not boys, sir—only one boy. He's an older boy, a young man named Gramm. The younger lad I told you about who made the goldfinder work sailed on BlackHeart's ship, the *Black Opal*," replied the owner. "Confusing, isn't it? Now what was the other question you asked, sir?"

"Where is the bakery?" Alistair asked a little impatiently.

"Oh, about three blocks that way," he said and pointed. "Then turn right for about three more. Mary's Bakery it's called."

Alistair put on some of the new clothes and the hat he had just bought. He handed the outlandish costume he had purchased at the costume shop to the shopkeeper. "Put it in the trash," he said.

The owner had just presented him with his boxes of additional clothing when Alistair turned his head toward the shop window. He saw two boys climb aboard his wagon. One of them had a rock in his hand, which he used to pound the lock on one of the trunks. Alistair dropped the boxes and ran out the shop's door. With one swift stride forward, he was onto the side rail of the wagon. He yanked the looter up by the nape of his shirt collar. The ruffian reached into his sock and came back at him with a knife.

That's when Alistair saw them: the shoes! *Those are Kathryn's athletic shoes. Seventeenth-century people don't wear athletic shoes!* Alistair quickly grabbed the looter's wrist. With one powerful thrust, he flung the young man's arm outward, and the knife went flying into the street.

"Owwwh!" yelled the ruffian as he struggled to knock Alistair off the wagon.

"Where did you get those shoes?" Alistair shouted angrily. The young man was shaking with fear and looked to his partner for help. The other freebooter had jumped to the ground and just stood there trembling and saying nothing. "I said, where did you get those shoes?"

"I-I, uh, don't know," he said.

"*Not a good answer!*" roared Alistair as his first blow hit the looter on the right side of his jaw. Alistair yanked him up by the shirt collar to a standing position in the wagon.

"I'll ask again," Alistair sharply barked. "Where did you get those shoes?"

"I-I told you, I don't know!" the ruffian said again.

"You're failing this test!" Alistair exclaimed angrily, twisting the looter's arm behind his back and up between his shoulders.

"I'll tell! I'll tell!" shouted the young thief. "I took them from Gramm, the kid what works at the bakery!"

"That's better," snarled Alistair shoving the ruffian down from the wagon and to his knees on the street below. Alistair jumped down behind him.

"Take them off. Put them in the wagon," Alistair lashed out forcefully. The dirty young bum took off the shoes and did as he was told. "What else did you take from Gramm?"

"This weird compass. Don't work anyway," said the other freeloader as he held out Kathryn's digital compass. Alistair recognized it immediately and drew back his fist at the freeloader. Then he thought better of the idea and reached for the compass. As soon as he took the compass, the first looter jumped up from the street and the two young bums ran as fast as they could to the first alley and darted down it.

Alistair went back into the store and came out with his new clothing and put them into one of the trunks and relocked it. Then he rode down the street toward the bakery as the owner of the haberdashery hung Alistair's old costume in his window with a "For Sale" sign on it.

Alistair talked with Mary and George, who told him about Gramm joining Captain Shark Scar's crew aboard the *Shark*. The haberdashery owner and the ruffians had all thought Kathryn was a young man as well. Alistair had decided not to tell Mary and George that Gramm was not a boy. He didn't know why Kathryn was putting up this pretense, but he suspected it was for her safety. He asked if there was a younger boy with Gramm and was told no.

Next he went to the docks in Port Royal, where he learned that the *Black Opal* had sailed a few days before the *Shark*. A sailor told him that he had seen a young boy board the *Black Opal* with the captain of the ship the afternoon the *Black Opal* sailed. *That would have been the day they got here to Port Royal in the* Carousel. *But how did Jon and Kathryn get separated from each other?* Alistair wondered.

He stopped his wagon on the dock by another sailor who was sitting on a duffle bag near the area where the skiffs and jollyboats were tied. He inquired about the ship, *Black Opal*.

"Bought up all the diving equipment, the crew of the *Black Opal* did. Didn't leave any for the crew of the *Red Dragon*," said the sailor. "Captain BlackHeart must have headed to the site of the sunken galleon that was discovered by the crew of the *Red Dragon*. Chinese said the galleon was their find. They were madder than bees when their hive's disturbed, they were."

"Where is the ship, *Red Dragon*?" asked Alistair as he looked out into the bay.

"The *Red Dragon* sailed for Tortuga several days ago to buy more diving equipment," he replied.

"And the ship named *Shark*?" asked Alistair.

"Oh, the *Shark* sailed before the *Red Dragon*," the sailor replied. "Some said Captain Shark Scar was hunting down the *Black Opal* and would kill its captain this time when he finds him. Uh, that would be Captain BlackHeart, you see. Has a real grudge against BlackHeart, Captain Shark Scar does. It's no secret here around the docks. Captain Sleg dislikes BlackHeart worse than Shark Scar does."

"And who is Captain Sleg?" inquired Alistair.

"Captain of the *Scorpion*. Sleg said that Captain BlackHeart has cheated him one time too many. They's a pair of mean cusses. Saw them both together here on the dock a few days ago. They're concocting something, them two. And I'll wager that it bodes real bad for BlackHeart."

"Did you see a boy board the *Shark*?" asked Alistair.

"Only a scrawny kid of a boy or maybe he was a man—about twenty or so, I'd venture. Uh ... sir?" asked the sailor.

"Yes?" replied Alistair.

"Which ship do you captain?" asked the sailor.

Without thinking, Alistair replied, "The *Carousel*."

"Lookin' to make up a new crew?" the sailor asked hopefully.

"Not just yet," replied Alistair smiling. "But thanks for the information." He handed the sailor one piece of eight as he turned back toward his horse and wagon.

"Thanks, Captain. Thanks a lot! Don't forget me if you need crewmen," yelled the sailor.

The sailor had been a wealth of information. By the time Alistair reached the *Carousel* in the mountains of Port Royal, he knew where he should go.

He loaded his trunks back into the *Carousel* and sat down at the computer console. "Next stop, Tortuga," he had said to himself, as he entered the same date: May 20, 1692, Tortuga.

All that had happened this morning before his arrival here in Tortuga. It was now about 5:00 p.m., and he was nearing the port in the smelly cart pulled by the decrepit horse.

The Caribbean was a bright turquoise as he gazed over it. His eyes focused on a big, red, ornately decorated Chinese junk with a gold dragon decorating the whole bow and stern of the ship.

Though Alistair was fluent in the Mandarin Chinese language from his many years of negotiating contracts with the Chinese for NASA, he would not have to interpret the writing on the bow to know that this was, indeed, the great ship *Red Dragon*.

CHAPTER 42

LORDS AND COMMONS

A listair stopped the rickety cart in front of The Inn of Lords and Commons and headed for the door. A young man wearing a white coat, with red epaulets, and a white gentlemen's hat and gloves came forward from the doorway, "May I assist you, sir?"

"Yes," replied Alistair. "I'm looking to rent a suite of rooms here. Is one available?"

"I'm sure it is, sir. I shall wait here by your, uh, cart with your belongings while you ask," he said with a look of disgust at the putrid-smelling horse and cart.

Alistair grinned. "Thank you," he said and handed him one piece of eight, which is $40 in modern money. "If I take a room here, there will be another piece of eight for you to take these trunks to my rooms and keep watch over my room against intruders."

A big smile crossed the face of the attendant as he put the coin into his pocket. "Yes, sir!" he said. When he turned back to the cart, his smile was replaced with a scowl. He waved his hand in front of his face, fanning away the odor of manure coming from the cart and horse.

A few minutes later, Alistair returned and instructed the attendant as to which room was his. He had chosen the nicest hotel in Tortuga because his trunks containing the gold would be safer there. When all was secure in his rooms, he asked the attendant to bring up hot water for a bath and gave him his smelly clothes for cleaning.

After relaxing for a time in the warm bath, he lay down across the bed and slept. It was dark outside when he awoke.

Dressed in the white linen shirt with the jabot tied at the neck and the new blue gentleman's coat he had bought in Port Royal, he locked his suite door and went downstairs.

There was a lot of activity off the lobby in the adjacent Tavern of the Commons, which was full of loud accordion music, bawdy sailors, and men from the town drinking ale, rum, and the like.

"Excuse me, sir," said the attendant. "We have a more refined gentry's bar across the lobby over there, if you prefer. It is much quieter but more to your taste, sir: The Tavern of the Lords."

Alistair thanked him and walked across to the other bar. It was a quieter, large room with a wooden floor and oriental carpeting. There were several small sitting areas with leather armchairs, and small tables with oil-burning lamps. Across one end of the big room was a long bar, over which hung a large painting of a tall ship on a turbulent ocean.

The long bar with a brass foot railing was crowded with men, so Alistair took his glass of brandy and sat in a large, plush chair in one of the small sitting areas, with his back to two men in seamen's coats. One man was tall, the other short, with a peg leg. Both men had long hair, and Alistair could not see their faces, but he couldn't help overhearing their conversation.

"I got 'em working day and night. We should be ready to sail in a couple of days," said the first man. "We can repair the rest whilst we sail, Sleg."

Sleg? thought Alistair as he raised an eyebrow, leaned back in his chair, and listened intently.

Chapter 43

Plotting Disaster

Sleg leaned forward in his chair. "But, Shark Scar, they can't repair your mast by then, can they?" asked Sleg.

"They can if they want to live!" Shark Scar replied. "The dock master said it would take thirty carpenters and ten sail makers to repair me ship in two days. I give enough money for twice that many men to repair me ship, jest to be sure the job is done quickly. And I give 'em twice the pay! Hence, I has the right to put a hole in 'em if it ain't done on time. And put a hole in 'em, I will. I got no qualms with leaving thirty or forty bodies a floatin' face down in the bay when me ship pulls ahead." He sat grumbling under his breath, his anger working deep within.

"I'd have put a hole in the bellies of that whole crew o' mine if there hadn't been so many of them," Shark Scar said. "And we would have sunk the *Black Opal* this morning if me crew hadn't rebelled against me. They wouldn't fire on BlackHeart cause that good-for-nothing Gramm was aboard the *Black Opal*. I run me whole rotten crew off when we docked today. Didn't keep nary a one of 'em— except Mole, me quartermaster! Despicable swine swill!

I hired meself a whole new crew to sail out with. Had to pay more, but that's all right. These men won't be beholding to Gramm. They won't mutiny against me, and they got the belly for violence. How about the *Scorpion*? Will she be ready for sailing the day after tomorrow?"

"Shark Scar, if ye can get that heap o' splinters that ye calls the *Shark* made into a ship fit for sailing in two days, we can have the *Scorpion* ready to sail by then. We didn't take as much firepower from BlackHeart as the *Shark* did. Only one ruined sail and a hole in the deck."

"Yes, I seen your main sail a takin' leave of your ship and sailing out to sea atop the waves without ye," Shark Scar slurred. He had not forgotten that one of Sleg's own cannonballs had done tremendous damage to his ship, and nobody damaged Shark Scar without incurring his revenge, somewhere, sometime, when they least expected it.

"What's your plan?" asked Sleg excitedly.

Shark Scar told Sleg that he had heard that BlackHeart had sold some diving gear to the captain of the *Red Dragon* and that he would be delivering the diving bell at the site of the sunken Spanish galleon. There, BlackHeart would show the Chinese how to use the diving bell.

"So?" said Sleg impatiently. "Stop dallying. How do we rid ourselves of BlackHeart?"

"I'm a' getting to that part now. He'll be anchored there, and so will the *Red Dragon*. Side by side they'll be, like two peas in a pod." Shark Scar explained that both ships would be at every disadvantage to defend themselves, particularly if he and Sleg stayed out of their firing range by crossing paths forward and astern of the two anchored ships.

"Well, maybe it would work—risky, though," Sleg answered hesitantly, scratching his chin, thinking.

"No risk to it, Sleg!" Shark Scar snarled, obviously annoyed at Sleg's slowness to understand his dicey plan. He continued to explain that they would sail out before dawn, ahead of the *Red Dragon*. Later, they would fall in behind her, keeping a safe distance back, but close enough so as not to lose sight of her. Thus, the *Red Dragon* would lead them to the site of the sunken Spanish galleon—and BlackHeart.

Shark Scar explained that they would wait off in the distance until the diving bell was in the water, and using the *Red Dragon* for cover, they would attack the *Black Opal* first and then the *Red Dragon*, sinking both ships at the site.

"Thusly, the *Black Opal* and her infamous Captain BlackHeart will be sunk, right next to the sunken galleon, six fathoms under the sea! And lying dead beside BlackHeart will be that sniveling cabin boy, Jon, and the spoiler, Gramm, what ruined me crew! It was neat the way I tricked BlackHeart into taking Gramm aboard the *Black Opal*; it makes everything perfect ... almost. I'll rid meself of all three vermin with one well-placed cannon ball," said Shark Scar, gritting his teeth and thinking.

Then, Sleg, ye silly shortsighted fool, thought Shark Scar with a sneer, *I'll deep-six you and the* Scorpion. *That'll be all four of ye out of my life. I'll have the diving bell and the treasure of the Spanish galleon all to meself.* Shark Scar laughed out loud at the very thought of it.

"I don't know ..." said Sleg hesitantly, shaking Shark Scar from his daze. "But, it's the only plan we got and time's wasting away! We needs to finish off BlackHeart and get to Port Royal. My ship's packed full of booty to trade with me partner there. I stopped me another British trading ship, loaded with spices, jewels, and silks. It was bound for the British outpost. If I gets back to Port Royal afore me trading man's ship heads off to England, he'll buy all me plunder. If I'm late getting back, I'll have to store it till his next ship leaves."

"Funny, ain't it," mused Shark Scar, "we hides the goods we takes from the British right under their nose in Port Royal at ole Purdy's what has the storage keeps. That's where I keeps all me plunder: in a storage keep—not in a cave on no island. Purdy guards it for me, cheap enough. Heard tell that BlackHeart has a keep there, too. I decided that's where he hides the Inca treasures, and that's why nobody can find them. Them treasures ain't hid on some island; they's stored at Purdy's, the way I figure it."

As they had talked, the crowd in the tavern thinned out so that only two men stood at the bar.

"Let's get outta here and go drink in the Commons Tavern with the men. It's getting too quiet in here. That man a sittin' behind us is asleep, it's so quiet," Shark Scar said, referring to Alistair, who was pretending to nod off to sleep in his chair.

When they left, Alistair immediately headed to the docks and the Chinese skiff with the ornate canopy on top. He spoke briefly in the Mandarin language with the sailor tending the craft. Then he got into the skiff, which immediately shoved off and headed toward the *Red Dragon*.

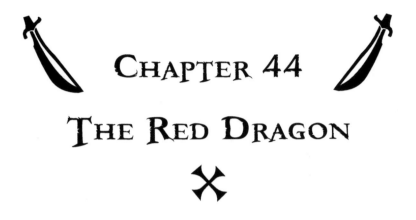

CHAPTER 44

THE RED DRAGON

Alistair had waited patiently for well over an hour aboard the *Red Dragon*. Knowing that Kathryn and Jon were both aboard the *Black Opal* made his decision to board the *Red Dragon* easy—he would now be chasing one ship instead of two. Finally a large gong on the deck sounded, signaling the arrival of the emperor's emissary and Chum Lee, captain of the *Red Dragon*.

The emissary was followed by several of his family members, who were sailing with him on the ship. Unlike British and American customs, the Chinese often took family and sometimes friends on voyages of diplomacy, treasure-seeking, and even pirating. He sat in the ornate chair that rested on a platform about two feet higher than the deck, and his entourage stood behind him. Chum Lee stood to his right.

Alistair had bowed in the customary way of the Chinese. Speaking in the emissary's language, Mandarin Chinese, Alistair introduced himself. He told the emissary what he knew about the plans of Sleg and Shark Scar and that their plans included an attack on the *Red Dragon*, as well as the *Black Opal,* when the diving bell was being delivered at sea. He then told the emissary that his wife and grandson were aboard the *Black Opal*, and that he wished to buy passage on the *Red Dragon* as far as the *Black Opal*. There, he wished to join his family aboard Captain BlackHeart's ship.

The emissary looked through squinted, cunning eyes at Alistair as he studied him in depth. Alistair Sinclair appeared to him to be a learned man, one who spoke fluent Mandarin and knew the ways of the Chinese. The emissary decided that such a man would not come aboard a Chinese junk alone and speak a lie. Death would come too swiftly for such a man, and this man standing before him knew that fact.

"Protected passage on our ship will not be cheap," said the emissary, "and payment will be in gold."

"I am prepared," said Alistair. After a few moments of haggling, Chinese style, they agreed on a price. Once they agreed, the emissary stood, and he and Alistair bowed toward each other, sealing their agreement. The emissary sat back down.

"These two captains," the emissary started, and then he leaned toward Chum Lee and consulted briefly. Then he resumed, "Sleg and Shark Scar, I believe you called them. They are foolish to think that because they see no other Chinese ships in this port or back in Port Royal that we travel the high seas alone. I sail as an envoy of the emperor. Although we have over four hundred men and fifty cannon on this ship for our protection, we would never sail without escort ships. You, Mr. Sinclair, do know this. Is it not so?"

"I do," replied Alistair. *Four escorts, maybe six*, he thought.

"Then these two foolish captains will soon learn, as well," said the emissary. "Captain BlackHeart and his quartermaster, Mr. Token, also know the ways of the Chinese. He has sold us all the diving equipment of the *Black Opal* and has gifted to me the diving bell. We have it all aboard this ship. The diving bell will save us the loss of many men when we retrieve all the treasures of the sunken Spanish galleon, *Anatole.*

"In trade for the diving bell, I have gifted Captain BlackHeart that part of the treasure that he has removed from the galleon. That treasure is ours!" shouted the emissary. His eyes narrowed to slits, but his facial expression did not change. "Captain BlackHeart assures me that very little of the precious treasure trove has been removed by him. It will take weeks to remove it all. My emperor will agree that I have made a good trade with Captain BlackHeart. But there is no agreement with the other two captains of which you speak!

"We will be prepared for these ships, the *Shark* and the *Scorpion*," the emissary continued, "on the high seas, where the smartest and strongest is in command. Should they escape, we will find them eventually. We have our ways of finding those we seek, and we are in no hurry."

The emissary bent close and spoke to Chum Lee, who cut his eyes to where several men in black clothing stood waiting. The men, armed with curved swords and other Chinese weapons, came forward without any verbal command and stood near Alistair. "These men will accompany you to the inn. You will return with them here tonight, with your belongings. You will stay onboard this ship until we deliver you to your destination, the *Black Opal*."

The emissary stood, and the loud gong signaled that the meeting was ended. The emissary left, followed by the men of his entourage first, and then the women dressed in kimonos. The children ended the procession.

It was well after midnight when Alistair and the six men in black went to the Inn of Lords and Commons. In the privacy of his room, Alistair put the gold to pay for his passage on the Chinese junk into his leather shoulder bag and locked the rest in his trunks.

When they returned to the *Red Dragon*, the emissary was waiting on the main deck with Chum Lee. Alistair bowed his head forward, straightened, and held the leather bag out to the emissary, who motioned toward Chum Lee, who took the bag.

"The payment in gold for my passage is in the bag, as we agreed," said Alistair. Chum Lee looked inside the leather bag and then at the emissary, and nodded. The emissary leaned back in his chair, a sinister smile on his face. He watched as the men carried Alistair's two trunks and escorted him toward his cabin.

Alistair understood that until they reached the *Black Opal*, he would reside aboard the *Red Dragon*.

Will I be the honored guest ... or the shackled prisoner? he wondered.

CHAPTER 45

PATCH UP

The *Black Opal* moved slowly through the passage with only the aft sail. All the other sails were furled and secured against the yards. The threatening storm cast dark shadows across the tall rocks and crevices, causing the rocks to appear even more ominous than they were, if that could be so.

The noise of the crashing sea waves breaking against the rocks brought beads of sweat to Kathryn's brow as she stood on deck, watching the captain maneuver the tall ship through the rocks to the pirate's hideout in Devil's Rock. It was so quiet, you could hear every creak and groan of the tall ship.

Captain BlackHeart had said they would rest and patch up the *Black Opal* in the lagoon at their hideout.

"Don't worry, Grammy. Captain BlackHeart knows exactly what he's doing. He's done it for years. The weather makes no difference to him," Jon said as he moved close and squeezed her hand to comfort her.

Suddenly, there was a jolt. The loud cracking sound of breaking timber took the attention of all aboard upward to a broken yard on the mainmast above. As the ship had moved through the narrow passage in the rough waters, one of the yards had scraped against a protruding rock high above, causing the yard to splinter. The broken piece of yard dangled from one side of the mainmast, held there only by the furled sail and some rigging.

"Watch out!" Curly yelled as he ran toward Grammy and Jon. The hanging piece of yard had ripped the sail and broken free, crashing down to the deck beside her. The ropes attached to the piece of yard fell scattered across the deck, some of them hitting Grammy, Jon, and Curly.

"You could have been killed!" shouted BlackHeart from the helm. "Are they injured?"

"Just some rope burns, Cap'n. They'll be all right," yelled Curly, concealing his own scraped arm from BlackHeart.

"Mrs. Sinclair! Jon! I told you to stay in my cabin for your safety! Go to my cabin and *stay there*. I'll deal with you later, Jon, for disobeying orders!" BlackHeart shouted.

"Pull that sail out of the way, Curly!" shouted the agitated captain.

"Aye, aye, Cap'n," yelled Curly.

Jon and Kathryn went into the captain's cabin. "What will the captain do?" she asked Jon fearfully.

"Usually, punishment is a lashing from the cat," Jon answered with his eyes cast downward. "I saw it once here onboard. The crew was made to watch. One of the sailors had lied to Guidry, blaming someone else for some riggings not being properly tied. The lines had come loose and ripped a sail."

"What is the cat?" Kathryn asked.

"The cat o' nines is a short leather-covered stick with nine lengths of leather attached at the end. It's used for disciplining the crew—and, Grammy, you do understand, *I* am one of the crew now," he said as tears welled up in his eyes. "Mr. Token disciplines the crew on the captain's orders." Jon sat thinking for a few moments. "Didn't they discipline with a cat o' nines on the *Shark*?"

"Discipline?" Grammy sneered. "The way Shark Scar disciplined was to throw the crewman overboard or, according to the crew, maroon the guilty crewman. I didn't see one marooned."

"Did you see one thrown overboard?" Jon asked.

"Fortunately, no. But I did see a lack of caring and a total disregard for human rights," Grammy said. Jon nodded. "Shark Scar is an evil man who enjoys inflicting torment and fear."

The ship had entered the large, calm lagoon inside the rocks and anchored, when the cabin door burst open and the captain strode inside.

"You will keep to your cabin now, Mrs. Sinclair," snapped Captain BlackHeart as he held the door open for her to leave.

"But, Captain, it's my fault. I left the cabin, and Jon went with me. Please don't hurt him!" Grammy pleaded.

"Don't you think you've caused quite enough problems for one day, Mrs. Sinclair?" BlackHeart asked her sharply, his eyes a menacing glare. "Now go to your cabin, as I told you!"

"Do as he says, Grammy. I'll be all right—really I will," Jon said bravely. Grammy left reluctantly, crying.

"Wait outside, Jon," BlackHeart said gruffly, as Curly, Spider, Skull, Guidry, and Mr. Token entered the cabin and sat at the big table behind the captain's desk. BlackHeart shut the door, leaving Jon to wait outside and wonder his fate.

Shortly, the door opened, and the crew, with stern looks on their faces, filed out. Jon entered and stood facing the standing captain, who looked firmly at Jon, his eyes a greenish-black.

"It has been the full vote of the officers of this ship that discipline will be waived in this particular instance, since the lack of following orders jeopardized only your own safety and not that of the ship or its crew," BlackHeart said in a stern voice. "However, I should not have to inform you that you, and your grandmother as well, could have suffered the loss of life or limbs in such an occurrence."

"Yes, sir," Jon said.

"Orders are given for a reason! Whether you understand the reason for the order or agree with the order is not important. You are to follow the rule of the order, because I am in command of this ship. *You are not!* Do I make myself *perfectly clear*, Jon?" BlackHeart asked pointedly.

"Yes, Captain, I understand clearly," Jon said as a wave of relief passed through his whole being.

"Go," said Captain BlackHeart as he looked out the back windows. "Report to Cook for some duties that will keep you out of trouble."

"Aye, aye, Captain," said Jon.

Later toward dusk, the captain sent word down to Jon and Cook, telling them to come up on deck. Kathryn had been released from her cabin and stood by the port side of the ship. Several sailors hauled up their second fishing net of parrotfish from the coral reefs below. They were the most brightly colored fish Jon had ever seen. The snout of the fish was rounded in front, resembling a parrot's head, and the colors and markings were just like those of a parrot. The fish were aqua, bright green, and blue. Bright pink edged their scales and fins. Inside their mouths were big, funny-looking teeth that were rounded and protruded like the beak of a parrot.

"Hey, Pyrate!" Curly yelled, holding up one of the fish toward the parrot. "We might toss ye overboard and adopt a new mascot. This one won't poop on me clean decks!"

"Squawk! New mascot! Poop deck!" squawked Pyrate as everyone laughed.

"Watch the teeth of the fish, Jon," warned Spider. "They teeth be capable of crushing coral rock. They eat plankton living on the coral reefs below."

"Are these fish good to eat?" Jon asked.

"Only if eaten raw," Cook answered excitedly as he grabbed hold of one by the tail. "Properly prepared, as I shall do it, they shall be the delicacies of the kings."

"I've never eaten raw fish," said Jon squeamishly.

"Then tonight, you shall learn what it is that you have been missing," Cook said with a smile as he handed Jon the wriggling two-foot-long parrot fish. "Bring it to the galley."

Jon struggled to hold the slippery fish, but couldn't. The fish flopped on the deck as Cook twisted his mouth into a grimace. Curly laughed and handed him a bucket. Jon and Cook filled the large bucket with parrotfish and took them down to the galley and began to prepare supper. The crew brought in more fish, and more fish. Jon frowned. Cook smiled.

Kathryn joined them in the galley, preparing dinner, as the whole crew worked to repair damages to the ship. Some worked on the newly broken yard at the mainmast. The sail maker, with several sailors assisting, mended the sail that had fallen with the yardarm. The remainder of the crew completed the unfinished repair from the fire on the starboard side, which had been caused when the *Black Opal* was hit by a cannonball the day they had the battle with Shark Scar and Sleg at the two rock islands near Tortuga. The fire had been massive, destroying parts of three decks.

Jon looked up at the crew on the cross-rope ladders that were spread and tied this way and that, so the crew could pull the new timber yard up toward the tall mast. Timbers for ship repair were stored in the aft section, below the deck where the ship's provisions were kept. Jon had seen them when he brought up food and supplies for Cook.

The late afternoon sun came through the thin clouds here and there, splaying its rays on the ship and the sailors up on the rope ladders. Jon snickered to himself as the crew moved the large wooden yardarm to its place, high on the main mast. Against the setting sun it looked as if the ropes were the spokes and cross pieces of a giant spider web and the crew in the riggings were spiders taking a long piece of hard biscuit to the center of their web.

"Tonight everyone shall eat together," Cook had told him—on the decks, in the galley, or wherever. They needed no watches, because everything could be seen from right here on deck by everyone, and no sea captain would dare to venture near these ominous rocks in choppy seas.

Although Jon did not enjoy eating the parrotfish the way the captain and crew did, he did try some of it. He preferred the snapper some crewmen had caught from the far end of the reef. Jon and Cook had made it into a fish stew, which Jon ate heartily.

Guidry brought up his hand accordion and began to play some Irish tunes. Crewmen joined in the singing of old sailors' songs: "The Drunken Sailor" and "Danny Boy." Some danced; others joked and told stories. Kathryn kept Jon near her, telling him he was too young to listen in. Jon hated that. He figured that if he was old enough to stand trial aboard ship, he was old enough to listen, and said so. Grammy figured differently. The captain raised an eyebrow and was silent. Grammy won.

The festive mood continued until a flash of lightning, followed by a loud crack of thunder, put an end to the party. The rain splat big drops down hard on the deck and its partiers as the captain jumped up quickly and ushered Grammy and Jon toward his cabin.

"What's wrong?" Grammy asked as she and Jon hurried with the captain to his cabin.

"Lightning can be very dangerous here amongst these rocks. With our high masts and the metal pulleys on them, we're sitting ducks in the middle of a pond. My cabin is safer, protected by the poop deck above. You will wait in here until someone comes for you," the captain commanded.

After what had happened earlier that day, neither Jon nor Kathryn had any desire to disobey the captain's orders. They watched from the cabin windows as the lightning flashed mightily across the Caribbean sky and torrents of rain poured down for more than an hour. When the rain slacked off, the captain came in and told them that they would be moving ashore to the cave, where it would be safer.

Kathryn and Jon hurried with the captain to the starboard side. A longboat sat below in the water. Spider waited there with some other crewmen and a lantern.

Kathryn looked out into the night. It was the blackest black she had ever seen. "No wonder that they call this Devil's Rock," she whispered.

CHAPTER 46

TREASURE ATTRACTS PERIL

S kull had gone ahead with some men to clear a path to the hideout.

Jon and Kathryn entered the lantern-lit cave of treasure and—*rats*! Shining gold and brilliant jewels glittered brightly against the dark walls of the cave. Spider and the others beat at the rats with clubs, sticks, and branches. The screeching and jumping rats ran rapidly here and there over the treasure, entering crevices and holes in the walls.

Kathryn screamed as some of them jumped on her skirt. She knocked them off and they went scurrying, but not for long.

"Aighhh!" shrieked Kathryn. "They're under my skirt! They're on my legs! Yeoww!"

Spider came running. He jerked her skirt off her and threw it aside. Kathryn stood there wearing her old white cropped pants, which she usually wore under her full skirt. With her loud screaming, the rats had begun to swarm, running in packs everywhere. Jon batted rats off Kathryn's pants and then put his arms around her to calm her as Spider and the crew dealt with the wild rats.

When the crew finally had the rats under control, there were dead rats—and blood—everywhere. Kathryn didn't know where the live ones went, but as long as they weren't near, she didn't care. The blood-spattered crew swept the dead rats into piles, away from the treasure.

With the rats gone for now, Kathryn calmed down, and after a while, she and Jon walked around the cave. She was awed by all the gold, silver, and jewels. There were statues, goblets of silver and gold, and a multitude of beautiful crosses, some jeweled, some not. Jon pointed out the wooden chests he had painted with the crew's names on them. Gold coins and pieces of jewelry were scattered on the floor of the cave.

"Don't go in that part!" Spider said forcefully as he held up his arm to stop their advancement. "That be the Cappin's own private treasure," he said. "And beyond that be the treasures of the now dead Cappin Brighton."

Kathryn looked at Spider curiously.

"He being the other pirate cappin what shared our cave with us. Brighton be dead now. He was a friend of Cappin BlackHeart," Spider explained.

She looked at the treasures beyond Spider, where she saw jeweled monarch's scepters and crowns. One crown bore the name Anne in large emeralds across the front. She told Jon it must have been a gift intended for Queen Anne because she remembered that Anne was the previous queen of England, before the present king.

Captain BlackHeart entered the cave and came to where Jon and Kathryn stood admiring his treasure trove. Jon was looking at a particular small gold statue that looked like an eagle and a man combined into one.

"Would you like see the Aztec eagle warrior, Jon?" the captain asked.

"Oh, yes!" exclaimed Jon. "So there really is an Aztec eagle warrior."

"It's heavy," the captain said as he picked up the gold treasure and put it into Jon's hands. Jon quickly squatted to the rock floor and set it down so he could look at it. He rubbed his fingers over the smooth satin finish and the feathers on the arms and legs of the warrior.

"It is thought by the Aztecs," explained the captain, "that two eagles carry the sun to the sky each morning and away to a resting place each night. The eagle adornment on the warrior represents the mighty eagle's strength and protection of the Aztec warriors."

"What is that?" asked Kathryn as she walked past the large bronze bell.

"The diving bell," said BlackHeart. "Jon can explain it to you when you get back aboard the *Black Opal*. The squall has passed through and it's safe to return to the ship."

Spider held out Kathryn's skirt. "It be free of the rats now, Mrs. Sinclair." Kathryn shook her head.

"Leave it here! I need no reminders," she said sharply.

Once onboard, Jon went to his cot in the niche of the captain's cabin, and Kathryn went up to her cabin. But she didn't sleep. She tossed and turned until the wee hours of the morning, hearing every half hour of ship's bells as they clanged, marking the time. Finally, she got up and walked out on the poop deck. The air was fresh and clean-smelling after the rain. A light ocean breeze blew through her hair.

Jon has grown up in the short time he's been on BlackHeart's ship, she thought.

Jon's hair had grown longer; he had pulled it back into a short ponytail, tied by a thin length of leather, like that of the sailors on the ship. The stripped navy and white T-shirts and white cotton knee breeches of the crew were quite similar to his own styles at home. His hand-made rope sandals, made by the sail maker onboard, were like his favorite brown leather ones. His light brown hair was now sun-streaked, and his suntanned skin just made his eyes appear bluer, like the Caribbean waters.

Kathryn had watched one day as Guidry instructed Jon in the use of a flintlock pistol. Jon had learned quickly, firing round after round of shot off into the air above the open sea.

I wish Alistair could see him. Oh, I don't know what's to become of us now. We may never see Alistair or Three Forks again. Our life may never be as it was. She let out a heavy sigh as she watched the moon glisten across the ripples of the lagoon.

Two voices below interrupted her thoughts. She moved close to the railing, which overlooked the quarterdeck. It was Captain BlackHeart and Spider.

"The diving bell and all the diving gear is secured in the hold, Cappin," said Spider.

"Very well," BlackHeart said. "We will sail at first light in the morning. I need the daylight to navigate through the rocks heading out. Plot a course for the sunken Spanish galleon so we can deliver the diving bell to the Chinese. It should only take a few hours to show them how to use it. If they arrive on time, as they said, we should be on our way to New Providence by late afternoon of the same day."

Spider nodded and walked toward the crew's quarters. The captain walked toward his cabin on the quarterdeck, pretending not to notice the figure who had been listening from the shadows of the poop deck above.

New Providence? thought Kathryn. *We could spend our lives sailing these islands—with pirates! I'll ask the captain to let us off the ship when we dock in New Providence. I know it's in the Bahamas. From there we can get passage to the colonies. My mind's made up. If Jon and I have to live out our lives in the seventeenth century, I'd rather it be in the colonies, where we would be safer and have a decent life. If Captain BlackHeart won't let us off the* Black Opal *willingly, well, then, I don't know how we'll do it, but we will get off this ship!*

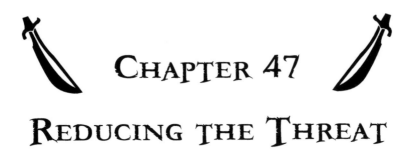

CHAPTER 47

REDUCING THE THREAT

Alistair looked through his spyglass toward the narrow strip of purple that edged the top of the blue Caribbean waters. Sure enough, there were two small specks of black on the horizon: the *Shark* and the *Scorpion*.

He collapsed the brass spyglass and attached it to his belt.

"Yes, they sail behind us," said the emissary, who had quietly crept up close behind him. "Just as you said they would."

"How long will it take to reach the site of the sunken galleon?" asked Alistair, changing the subject abruptly. He didn't like or trust sneaky people; and the emissary was definitely a sneak.

"We should be there after sunrise tomorrow," replied the emissary. "Until then, you will be my guest. Come, we shall partake of food."

The food served him was highly seasoned with Szechwan peppers and had small pieces of what looked like chicken, but he wasn't sure. He had seen no chickens about, not even when the emissary proudly showed off the farm animals aboard, which mostly consisted of goats and swine. He knew that some of the older generations of Chinese had very strange diets. Pappy chose to eat the tofu, which was made from soybean curd. He didn't like tofu, but he knew what it was—maybe. By drinking a lot of tea, he found that he was not as hungry.

The time passed without incident, the two ships still little specks on the horizon. Alistair had been treated kindly, as a guest, in the Chinese tradition. But his senses told him to beware, even though everything appeared to be in order.

He slept uncomfortably through the night, his ears peeled for sounds and his eyes opening often, checking for the presence of others in his room. No one entered his room. Alistair knew that he was being watched. Sometimes he would catch a glimpse of the men in black, or Chum Lee ... always sharpening some instrument of death and watching him through squinted eyes.

On his third day aboard the *Red Dragon*, Alistair was again strolling on deck when the emissary noiselessly appeared, standing behind him. His voice startled Alistair. "We will anchor the *Red Dragon* soon near the *Black Opal*. It is anchored up ahead, just off our bow. Come, I will show you."

He led the way up the steep stairs to the high bow of the ship, where the golden dragon's neck and head crowned the bowsprit.

"You see it there," he said as he moved aside for Alistair to step to the railing next to the dragon's head. Alistair could see the tall, black Brigantine ahead, the same ship he had seen fighting Sleg and Shark Scar off the island of Tortuga on the day he had arrived there in the *Carousel*. He looked around the horizon and toward the *Red Dragon*'s stern.

"There is no need for you to look for the other two ships, the *Shark* and the *Scorpion*," said the emissary. "They no longer exist. If you will look, you will see that they have been replaced by four sloops with red sails, which are stationed around this ship in each direction. Those sloops are Chinese escort ships."

"But," Alistair started, "I heard no guns firing during the night."

"The two ships were boarded by Chum Lee and the men from our sloops. Once the treasures were removed and the crews silenced, holes were chopped through the hulls of both ships. The *Shark* and the *Scorpion* and all aboard, including the two captains, disappeared into the sea rather quickly—and quietly," he said.

A quiet shiver passed through Alistair as he thought about the brutality of these pirates. Emissary status or not, these were indeed true pirates, with no regard for life—only treasure.

CHAPTER 48

DIAMONDS AND EMERALDS

From the moment the *Red Dragon* dropped anchor about one hundred yards from the *Black Opal*, Alistair had searched the railings of the tall brigantine for *two* boys. He found none.

Then, he spotted a woman in a blue dress and a straw bonnet standing near an entrance door on the poop deck. He adjusted the lens and saw that it was Kathryn. *She's shed her disguise as the boy, Gramm*, he thought. *But where is Jon?*

He looked down at the Chinese skiff manned by six oarsmen, which was now making its way back to the *Red Dragon,* with three men from the *Black Opal* aboard. He turned and walked downstairs toward the emissary, who was sitting in his chair.

The three men from the *Black Opal* came onto the main deck from a stairway nearby. The first, a very tall black man with a bushy black beard, was followed by a shorter, gray-haired man in a black morning coat, wearing a broad-styled top hat. They waited on either side of the stairway for the third, a tall man with braided black hair tucked neatly under his tricorn hat. He wore an elaborate captain's black coat cut to the knees, with brass buttons; gold epaulets accentuated his broad shoulders. His tricorn hat was trimmed with gold and adorned with a black ostrich plume. *This man obviously is Captain BlackHeart,* thought Alistair. *All three men are fully armed; but if they make one false move, that won't be enough.*

The men bowed toward the emissary, who greeted them, speaking in Mandarin. The short gray-haired man returned the greeting in Mandarin and reminded the emissary that he alone spoke Mandarin. Therefore, he would speak for Captain BlackHeart and Spider, his navigator. The emissary nodded. Because he too understood Mandarin, Alistair was able to follow the conversation between the emissary and BlackHeart, interpreted by Mr. Token, which went thusly:

"You are here as you said you would be, Captain BlackHeart. Is the diving bell ready for delivery?" asked the emissary.

"It is ready, and I have brought the equipment that is used with the bell, as we agreed," replied BlackHeart. "It will take only two or three hours for your divers to learn how to use the diving bell. Then I shall be on my way."

The emissary smiled and nodded toward Captain BlackHeart as his eyes moved toward Chum Lee, who stood near Alistair.

"There is another matter, Captain," the Emissary said as he pointed his hand toward Alistair. "This man, Mr. Alistair Franklin Sinclair, has purchased passage on the *Red Dragon* to join your ship. He says his wife and grandson are aboard the *Black Opal*."

Captain BlackHeart stiffened in shock as his eyes darted toward Alistair, who tipped his tricorn hat to acknowledge what the emissary had said. BlackHeart eyed Alistair suspiciously. Then he spoke in a low voice, but Mr. Token *did not* interpret what BlackHeart said.

"Mr. Sinclair, you will smile at all times, as if we are old friends. Your life depends on it; nod your head that you understand."

Alistair nodded and smiled.

"Identify yourself to me. What are your wife and grandson's given names?" BlackHeart continued in English, a language not understood by the emissary and his counselors.

"Kathryn and Jon," replied Alistair pretentiously as he extended his hand. BlackHeart shook his hand and slapped him on the shoulder in greeting, both smiling.

"And what is the name of the ship you captain?" the smiling BlackHeart asked, continuing to quiz Alistair as he studied him intently.

For a brief moment, Alistair looked confused; his expression quickly brightened. "The *Carousel*," he replied.

Having confirmed to his satisfaction that this was indeed Jon's grandfather, BlackHeart spoke briefly with his men. Then, Mr. Token said to the emissary in Mandarin, "Captain BlackHeart has been expecting Mr. Sinclair but did not know he would book passage on the *Red Dragon*. Mr. Sinclair will return with us now to join his family aboard our ship."

"There is a matter of additional monies owed to His Excellency, the emperor, by Mr. Sinclair," the emissary said as Alistair's head jerked abruptly toward the emissary. "I will keep Mr. Sinclair's trunks with all of his belongings, including his weapons and gold, within them, as payment of his debt to the emperor."

"I have paid you the agreed amount!" roared Alistair in Mandarin as Chum Lee moved forward with two of the men in black, who grabbed Alistair's arms.

"A minor detail!" Captain BlackHeart burst out while smiling through gritted teeth. Even though BlackHeart did not understand Mandarin, he understood that Alistair's anger could upset his plans. "Quell your anger, Sinclair!" BlackHeart said quietly through clenched teeth, but loud enough for Alistair to hear. Captain BlackHeart conferred with Mr. Token, who then interpreted to the emissary.

"Captain BlackHeart speaks for himself and for Mr. Sinclair, who now comes under his command, since he will be boarding the *Black Opal*. Your terms, Excellency, are acceptable to both men," Mr. Token said.

Then Mr. Token told the emissary that BlackHeart had another matter of more importance to discuss with him. Mr. Token said that BlackHeart had brought some jewels with him, which he had obtained from a section of the sunken galleon wreckage. This section, Mr. Token explained, was separated from the main *Anatole* wreckage site, where they presently were anchored.

Then BlackHeart spoke as Mr. Token interpreted:

"Emissary, the wreckage of the Spanish galleon, *Anatole*, lies beneath the sea in two parts. The main part of the wreckage, which you have discovered, lies just below us, here at this site where we now sit. But we have discovered another part of the *Anatole* that you have not seen because it is only accessible by using the diving bell.

"We believe this *new find* to be the admiral's quarters. It is located about twenty leagues, or one hundred and twenty miles, from here and lies in much deeper waters—nine or ten fathoms down.

"Before the *Anatole* sank, the hurricane winds had broken off the mizzenmast of the ship. When the mast fell, the admiral's quarters and part of the massive rudder fell with it into the sea, where it now lies. The rest of the galleon sailed intact to this spot where we now sit. Here, the ship was taken down by the hurricane winds because of its vast weight and the lack of the mizzenmast and rudder to stabilize it.

"You have already seen the immense treasure that lies below us, but let me tell you about the treasure hidden in the admiral's quarters, which you have not seen.

"In this part of the wreckage, there are two gold chests full of diamonds and emeralds. These few jewels I will show you came from those chests. The mizzenmast lies firmly across the top of both chests, but one corner of each chest was crushed slightly. These few stones were forced out through small corner openings in those chests."

BlackHeart then stepped forward. Chum Lee stepped between BlackHeart and the emissary. The emissary jumped off the platform and pushed Chum Lee aside. BlackHeart removed a small gold box from his coat pocket and opened it. Inside were many loose, sparkling diamonds, with a few very large emeralds sprinkled in the mix.

Alistair watched as the emissary looked into the small box, his eyes glistening with desire to possess these precious jewels.

BlackHeart started to talk again, in a silky voice, so as not to disturb the greedy thoughts of the emissary. Mr. Token interpreted quietly.

"Additional equipment will be needed if you are to remove these two chests containing the precious jewels. You will need heavy winches, pulleys, and cranks. And I should warn you that you will lose some men diving at this depth, even with the use of the diving bell for air. I have a small crew and could not risk the loss of that many men. A large ship like yours can support the weight of the hoists needed to lift the massive mizzenmast and rudder off the two chests of jewels."

The emissary broke the spell by saying, "The loss of men is no problem for me. Men are dispensable. I have four hundred men on this ship and more on the four sloops of the escort." He reached for the gold box in BlackHeart's hand.

"No! These jewels belong to me!" BlackHeart said firmly as he snapped the lid shut and put the box into his coat pocket. Mr. Token relayed the message in Mandarin.

"I have a map," BlackHeart continued, "which pinpoints the exact location of the *Anatole*'s sunken admiral's quarters to the Nth degree. The map is in Port Royal in a special hiding place. What will you pay for the map to the *Anatole*'s jewels, emissary?"

The emissary put his hand to his mouth, rubbing it as he thought, all the while looking at BlackHeart's hand in his coat pocket, clasped around the box of jewels. He moved the fingers of his other hand, as if he were running his fingers through those very jewels. Suddenly the emissary's eyes brightened and a sneer crept over his face.

"I will trade you the trunks of Mr. Sinclair," the emissary said.

"Not enough! What else will you give?" BlackHeart asked firmly, his hand still on the jewel box concealed in his pocket. It did not escape the notice of its intended party, the emissary, as he continued to look directly at BlackHeart's hand in his pocket on the box of jewels.

"I will leave for Port Royal tonight," the emissary said, "after my divers have practiced with diving bell, to be sure that all is satisfactory. There, I will purchase the heavy winches, pulleys, and cranks for lifting the mizzenmast off the chests of jewels. Then I will meet you aboard your ship there, where I will personally pick up the map. You are to give the map to *no one* except me! For this map, I am willing to pay twenty gold bars. No more! I will bring the gold bars to you when I come aboard the *Black Opal* in Port Royal."

"Show me the gold bars now!" demanded BlackHeart.

When Mr. Token relayed the message, the emissary nodded toward one of his counselors, who then left with two others. A few moments later, they returned carrying the heavy chest that held the bars of gold. BlackHeart picked up one heavy gold bar in each hand, looked them over, and handed them both to Spider.

"We have an agreement. I will take these two with me now, as well as Mr. Sinclair's trunks. We will collect the rest of the gold in Port Royal when you pick up the map," BlackHeart said as he bowed to the emissary. The emissary bowed in return, sealing the agreement. With a nod from the emissary, the men in black released Alistair, who joined BlackHeart and his men. They all walked toward Alistair's trunks, which had been brought from his cabin and now sat on the deck.

"Captain BlackHeart," said the emissary, and Mr. Token interpreted. "I will send two escorts with you—for your safety, of course—until I retrieve the map in Port Royal."

BlackHeart grinned, tipped his hat, and grabbed for one of the trunk handles while Alistair grabbed the other.

When they got down to the floating platform below with Alistair's trunks, BlackHeart's longboat, with eight of his well-armed crewmen, waited. They loaded Alistair's trunks into the longboat, ignoring the Chinese skiff that had brought BlackHeart and his men to the *Red Dragon*.

As they shoved off from the platform, BlackHeart sat in the bow of the longboat, facing the rest of his men and the ship, *Red Dragon*. The emissary watched them through his spyglass as they rowed toward the *Black Opal*, BlackHeart's hand still in his pocket on the box of jewels.

CHAPTER 49

DO TELL

The big brass diving bell sat prominently on deck as BlackHeart's skiff slowly plied the waters toward the tall, black Brigantine. Alistair's eyes searched the top decks for something more important. There was still no sign of Jon; and Kathryn was now gone, as well.

"Captain Shark Scar and his ship, the *Shark*, were destroyed last night by the Chinese in the sloops," Alistair said quietly. "Scuttled."

BlackHeart's mouth twitched as he immediately focused his attention on Alistair, his eyes large and piercing. Then they narrowed to small slits as he eyed Alistair curiously. "Do tell!" he said haughtily as though he had no particular interest in what might have happened to his unrelenting enemy. A wicked grin spread across the faces of the crewmen in the longboat.

"Captain Sleg and his ship, the *Scorpion,* met the same fate," Alistair continued. "A visit to Davy Jones, I believe you call it, right, Captain?"

"Precisely, Sinclair. Well, now ..." said BlackHeart as he leaned comfortably back against the prow of the long-boat, facing Alistair. "That just made our work much lighter! Tell me, how did this happen and how did you come to be on the *Red Dragon?*"

Alistair told BlackHeart about overhearing Shark Scar plotting with Sleg in the tavern, and of his ensuing meeting with the emissary. Then he told BlackHeart of his buying passage on the *Red Dragon* in order to get to his wife and grandson aboard BlackHeart's ship. He did not discuss anything about the *Carousel*, how he got to Tortuga, or why he was not traveling with Kathryn and Jon. He decided it would be best to discuss those topics with the captain privately and let the captain decide what he wanted to tell his men.

"I don't see Mrs. Sinclair or my grandson, Jon," remarked Alistair uneasily.

"Their orders are to stay off the main deck," said the captain curtly, "for their own safety."

"I don't know how to thank you, Captain," said Alistair. "You are giving up a lot for me and my family."

"Thank me? Giving up?" BlackHeart laughed loudly. Then with a sneer, he said, "I don't plan on giving up anything! I'm saving *myself*, Sinclair, and my crew. You just happen to be along."

Then, BlackHeart's expression turned grim. "Surely you didn't believe that cockamamie story about the diamonds and emeralds I just told the emissary and Chum Lee? It was made up! Invented ... to save our necks— for now. Without a reason to keep us alive, the Chinese would blast us out of the water once they had the diving bell in their possession!

"But, I must say, I hadn't planned on their sending two escorts with us," BlackHeart said, rubbing the back of his neck. "I'll have to decide what to do about them later. If the men in the Chinese sloops have scuttled the ships of two of the most notorious pirates in the Caribbean, as you say, then you've witnessed what they're capable of doing. The captains of those two escorts, as they were so eloquently called, will have their orders from the emissary before we sail from this site, and those orders will not include anything about watching out for *our* safety! We'll be sailing as their *hostage*, Sinclair!"

Alistair knew BlackHeart was right.

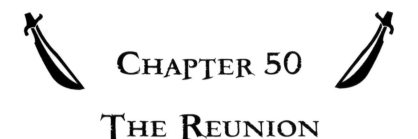

CHAPTER 50

THE REUNION

Captain BlackHeart climbed aboard the *Black Opal*, shouting orders to his crew.

"Curly! Order the support team into the longboat below, the diving crew into the water! Lower the air barrels!"

"Aye, aye, Cap'n!" said Curly. He eyed the stranger with BlackHeart curiously.

"Guidry," BlackHeart continued, "ready the men at the cranks to hoist the diving bell. Spider will dive today and instruct the Chinese about the bell and how to use it."

"Aye, aye, Cap'n," said Guidry.

"Let's get this bell delivered and get out of here!" the captain shouted to the crew. Turning to Alistair, he said, "Follow me, Sinclair."

They entered BlackHeart's cabin, and he asked Alistair to sit at the big table.

"I'm going to ask you to wait here while I explain your presence to Mrs. Sinclair," said Captain BlackHeart.

"Otherwise, I'm afraid the shock of seeing you here will be too great for her." Alistair nodded in approval, and the captain left.

BlackHeart found Kathryn in her cabin on the poop deck and escorted her down the steps to the quarterdeck as he told her that her husband had sailed here on the *Red Dragon* and was now waiting in his cabin. At that news, she bolted from BlackHeart, running toward his cabin.

"What's that all about, Captain?" asked Jon as he came up the stairway from doing his chores in the galley below.

"Come walk with me, Jon. I have a little story to tell you ..." the captain began as he put his hand on Jon's shoulder and they walked toward the stern of the ship. The men were now hoisting the diving bell into the air.

When the captain had explained to Jon about his grandfather's arrival to the extent that he had knowledge, he took him to his cabin and left the family to share private time alone.

Several longboats had been launched from the *Red Dragon* and now surrounded the diving site. Chinese divers and crewmen from the *Black Opal* were in the water and the bell was submerged when the Sinclairs came out on deck. BlackHeart stood leaning at the ship's side rail, watching his men in the water.

"I'm afraid we owe you some explanations, Captain," Alistair said.

"Yes, and I shall be happy to hear them," said the captain, "as soon as we're underway from this site. Until then, I have to be sure nothing goes wrong with the delivery of this bell."

Alistair turned and looked around the deck. The crew of the *Black Opal* looked remarkably different. They were heavily armed, and their hair was being managed in the wind by bandanas tied tightly over their heads. Even the men standing in the riggings, awaiting a command to drop the sails, were armed. Their faces were solemn, their eyes penetrating, their manner coarse. They were no longer a ship's crew; they were pirates.

"Where did you put my trunks? My weapons are in them," Alistair told BlackHeart.

"Show Sinclair to your cabin, Mrs. Sinclair. His trunks are there," BlackHeart said as he headed for his own cabin. A few minutes later, he emerged, his head tightly covered with a black cotton scarf, like a skull cap. The gold earring was still in his ear, but his captain's regalia were gone. In its place were the weapons of a pirate: a strapped holster holding a flintlock pistol slung across his chest, a cutlass hanging from his waist, another flintlock pistol tucked into his black waistband.

"Jon, you and Mrs. Sinclair will wait in my cabin with the door shut," BlackHeart said. "You know where the loaded flintlock is kept." Jon nodded. "Take it. There are two daggers in the crystal cabinet, as well. One dagger is in a sheath. Strap it on. There's a small loaded pistol in my desk drawer. Give it to Kathryn. Use the guns if you have to. You will not come out on deck unless one of us comes for you. I expect trouble. I just don't know when it will come. Do you understand?"

"Yes, Captain," Jon said.

"Go now!" BlackHeart said.

"Aye, aye, Captain," Jon said and ran up the stairs to the quarterdeck where his grandparents stood. Alistair then joined BlackHeart on the main deck, and they were immediately engrossed in plans.

As Jon walked Grammy toward the captain's cabin, he turned and looked across the decks at the crew. Even Cook had shed his white apron and was armed: a saber in one hand, his meat cleaver in the other. Jon knew that Skull and his crew of gunners were already manning the cannon below. He had seen them earlier when he'd come back up from milking the goats.

BlackHeart paced the main deck like a tiger waiting to attack.

Jon and Kathryn went into the captain's cabin and shut the door. There they would wait.

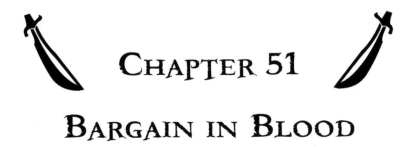

CHAPTER 51

BARGAIN IN BLOOD

"Standby to weigh anchor!" shouted Captain BlackHeart as he stood at the helm.

"Standby to weigh anchor!" yelled Curly down to the men below who stood ready at the capstan to crank up the heavy anchor.

"Standby to drop top sails!" shouted the captain.

"Standby to drop tops'ls!" repeated Guidry to his crew. Eight men immediately mounted the rig ladders, rapidly climbing to the top of the tall masts.

The *Black Opal* began to pull away from the men diving near the Chinese junk. BlackHeart gave the wheel to Spider and joined Alistair at the railing on the main deck.

"There will be another Chinese sloop dropping in behind us soon," said BlackHeart, pointing to the sloop sailing forward off in the distance ahead of the *Black Opal*. "I saw it leave the *Red Dragon* a while ago." He took his spyglass from his belt and surveyed the Chinese junk, looking for the emissary and finally locating him.

"*No!*" shouted BlackHeart.

Alistair quickly pulled his own glass up to his eye and followed the direction of BlackHeart's spyglass to the highest point of the *Red Dragon*, the place where Alistair had stood with the emissary on their arrival at this site.

There, next to the golden dragon's fire-breathing head stood two men and a young boy who looked like ...

"Jon!" shouted Alistair. He ran to the stairs leading to the quarterdeck and took the steps three at a time to the top, with BlackHeart almost running over him.

There in the cabin they found Kathryn lying on the floor, tied and gagged. One of the back windows of cabin had been broken out, and a mallet, covered with sailcloth to quiet its impact, lay on the floor beneath it. There was no sign of Jon.

While Alistair removed the gag and loosened Kathryn's bonds, BlackHeart removed the blood-smudged note that was fastened to his desk with his dagger, taken from the wine cabinet. Three of his wine goblets lay shattered on the floor—three gold doubloons lay atop the shattered glass.

The note read:

"*If ye wants to see Jon alive, ye'll follow the plan ye made with me new partner, the emissary. When we load enough gold from below, we'll meet ye in Port Royal and trade the boy for the map to the Anatole's emeralds and diamonds. No tricks! Or we'll spill the best of Jon's belly on the deck and feed the rest to the sharks!*"

The note was signed, *SHARK SCAR*—in blood!

"They were hiding behind the door and grabbed us when we came in! They cut Jon's hand, and Shark

Scar signed his name with Jon's blood!" Kathryn was screaming hysterically. Alistair put his arms tightly around her and tried to soothe her.

BlackHeart ran out the door, pulled his glass up to his eye, and looked again at the top of the *Red Dragon*. There stood the two men: the emissary with his spyglass to his eye, a man in a big ostrich-plumed hat. "Shark Scar," seethed BlackHeart. A boy, Jon, stood waving bye with a bandage-covered hand.

CHAPTER 52

BRITISH INTERFERENCE

"I thought you said Shark Scar was dead, Sinclair!" BlackHeart shouted as he burst into his cabin.

"Obviously, the emissary lied to me. The *Shark* and the *Scorpion* were both missing from the horizon, replaced by two Chinese sloops this morning," replied Alistair. BlackHeart sat panting at his desk as he tried to control his anger.

"Shark Scar's slick!" BlackHeart snarled as he pounded a fist on his desk. "When the Chinese boarded his ship, he must have made himself a nice little deal with Chum Lee to save his own hide. He let them scuttle the *Shark* and his crew. He couldn't care less about his men—or Sleg and Sleg's men, for that matter. Shark Scar knows Sleg's not so smart or ruthless; he wouldn't hesitate to cut him out! Sleg's dead, I have no doubt of it."

Kathryn stood grieving for Jon as she looked through tear-filled eyes at the Chinese junk, now being left in the distance behind them. "The *Red Dragon* is so big," she said in a low voice.

"Yes," replied BlackHeart, "and we're no match for their guns and their four hundred men."

BlackHeart bent down and picked up one of the gold doubloons from atop the shattered wine goblets, thinking—remembering the time he had made Shark Scar pay for breaking his wine goblets. Kathryn looked at the broken glasses and started crying anew.

"Shark Scar had such an evil look when he threw those coins on the broken glass," she said.

"Check yourself, Mrs. Sinclair. You've travelled with Shark Scar. You know him well. He's after me; Jon just got in the way and gave him an opportunity to get me at the disadvantage. Until the *Red Dragon* reaches Port Royal, Jon will be safe. Even Shark Scar wouldn't harm such a valuable hostage. Take your wife to her cabin, Sinclair, and let me think," said BlackHeart as he began to pace the floor of his cabin. "And, Sinclair, tell Curly I said to send someone in here to repair this window!"

Over two hours had passed when Alistair returned to the captain's cabin. Two crewmen had finished replacing the stiles and glass panes in the window of the cabin as BlackHeart continued to pace. Alistair sat down at the table as the men left, closing the door behind them. Finally, the silence was broken by BlackHeart.

"The emissary is a shrewd, greedy impostor, who aspires to amass fortune and power. But Chum Lee, his captain and henchman, is known to be a barbarian who enjoys violence—the more gruesome, the better. And now Shark Scar is their ally: the devil's own playmates!

"If we have any hope of devising a plan to get Jon back alive, I'll have to know more about the Sinclairs:

where you come from, how you got here. From the beginning, if you please, Sinclair."

Alistair gave BlackHeart a brief account of the *Carousel*'s time-travel capabilities. He related the story of how Jon's father, their only child, had died in a fiery plane crash along with Jon's mother, leaving Jon an orphan and Alistair's ward. He explained that he, Kathryn and Jon had come from the twenty-first century and about computers, which operated everything in that world.

As Alistair talked with BlackHeart, a large man stood sheltered in the alcove outside the cabin door ... listening.

"My son, who worked in a top secret United States government agency, had brought the computers to my farm. They came from a mysterious craft that had crashed in the Mohave Desert of our country. Weston and I hid the computers in an antique carousel that I had stored in a barn on my forty-acre property. Although we suspected it at the time, it was much later that I actually discovered the computers' time-travel capabilities. I tinkered with first one computer, then the other, eventually linking them together.

"Soon afterward, I noticed that when I accessed certain icons, there seemed to be some kind of response, but not one that I could readily identify. All my efforts to engage the responder failed. Then, very late one night I answered a knock at the door. It was at that moment that I learned the source of the magnificent devices. Standing there before me was four ..."

Outside the cabin door, the man pressed his ear tighter against the door to hear. There was a sudden noise as something fell on the lower deck—an oil lamp blown off a holding bracket. The sound frightened the listener and he shrank into a dark corner of the alcove outside the captain's cabin. While the crew busied themselves cleaning up the broken glass and spilled oil below, he slipped away unnoticed.

The noise was not noticed inside the cabin, where Alistair was finishing his brief account. BlackHeart was overwhelmed with Alistair's story, breathing heavily as he paced and listened. Alistair had confirmed all that Jon had told him and more.

"So, they first arrived *after* Weston's death?" BlackHeart asked.

"Yes," Alistair answered.

"And, you think Jon's parents were purposely killed?" he inquired.

"Yes; I just don't know by which of the powers. As I just told you, it could have been either one of the two," Alistair answered.

"Are you in danger?" he asked.

"Not until I can give them what they want and they know I'm not yet able to do that," Alistair answered.

"And I thought the stories of Atlantis and the Blue Caribbean Curse were weird when I first heard the accounts from my friend, Brighton!" BlackHeart chuckled to himself. "I'm beginning to understand things I had thought absurd before." He looked out the cabin window at the sloop with black sails, which was off in the distance behind them.

"The two sloops will remain in place, forward and aft, as we sail around Cuba and until we reach Port Royal.

Or perhaps the Chinese will try to intercept us somewhere in between. In any case, my crew is on keen alert," BlackHeart said.

They were interrupted by a loud knock at the door.

"Enter!" said the captain.

"Begging your pardon, Cap'n. There be two new ships on the horizon off our starboard side. One of them is advancing toward that Chinese sloop off our bow, sir!" said Curly sharply.

"Can you see which flag they sail under?" asked the captain as he grabbed his spyglass and quickly walked to the cabin door.

"No, Cap'n, but they be big ships, sir!" replied Curly.

"We'll have to talk later, Sinclair," the captain said as he walked briskly across the deck to the railing where Mr. Token stood.

"Ship advancing on *Black Opal*, starboard forward!" cried the sailor from high in the crow's nest.

"What do you make of it, Mr. Token?" BlackHeart asked as he peered through his glass.

"I'm not sure. One of the ships is coming this way, rapidly. Notice the high spray of the waves off her bow," Mr. Token responded. The captain stood looking through the glass, adjusting it first one way and then another to get a closer view.

"Try this one," Alistair said, handing BlackHeart his own spyglass. "It's the latest thing and more powerful than yours."

"Powerful is not the word of it!" BlackHeart said excitedly as he peered through the glass. "Those frigates appear to be sitting on the bow of my ship." Turning to Guidry, he yelled, "British frigates! Hoist the British flag!"

"Aye, aye, Cap'n!" answered Guidry.

"Adjust the sails to slow the ship," Blackheart added.

"Slow the ship, Cap'n? With a frigate advancing on us?" asked Guidry, somewhat confused.

"Affirmative. Slow the ship!" replied BlackHeart.

"Aye, aye, Cap'n!" shouted Guidry, shaking his head in confusion as he passed on the commands to the sail crew.

The captain ran to his cabin and scribbled a quick letter. He sealed it with his black wax stamp and put the letter in the pocket of his coat. He returned to the quarterdeck wearing his black captain's coat, his tricorn hat, and a clean white linen shirt.

"You just lost this spyglass, Sinclair. I need it worse than you do," BlackHeart shouted to Alistair as he stopped in the middle of the quarterdeck and fastened his *new* spyglass into the holder of his belt. He stood in an at-ease position, his hands clasped behind his back, as Spider continued to man the wheel of the *Black Opal*.

Off in the distance, one frigate fired on the sloop sailing forward of the *Black Opal*, as the other frigate continued its approach.

"Second frigate almost upon us, Captain," said Mr. Token.

"Curly, make ready to transfer documents!" shouted BlackHeart.

"Aye, aye, Cap'n," shouted Curly as he motioned toward one of his men, who brought him a crossbow. The bolt mounted in the crossbow had a metal tube affixed.

"Give this letter to Curly." BlackHeart took the letter from his coat pocket and handed it to Mr. Token. Curly put the document inside the small metal tube, closed the end with a cap, and waited.

The British frigate had circled around the stern of the *Black Opal* to her port side and was now sailing closely alongside the *Black Opal*.

A group of officers, including the captain of the British vessel, *Triumph*, stood at their starboard railing, facing the *Black Opal*.

"Captain Villeroy, in command of the *Triumph*," shouted the captain of the frigate. "Thought you might need some help with those two Chinese sloops that are escorting you to Davy's locker, BlackHeart!" shouted the captain of the British ship. The officers standing with him laughed heartily.

"I'm glad you assessed my situation so quickly, though I don't know how you did," shouted BlackHeart, who had moved to the port railing.

"It was easy," shouted Captain Villeroy. "Chinese sloops only escort Chinese ships, not brigantines! And you, BlackHeart, sail the only brigantine on the seas. How did you pick up the sloops?"

"They're from the *Red Dragon*," said BlackHeart.

"You're lucky we came along, and lucky to be alive after encountering the emissary, who they erroneously call a diplomat. Where is the *Red Dragon*?" asked Captain Villeroy.

"By now, she's making her way to Port Royal behind us. Sleg is dead. The *Scorpion* and the *Shark* have been sunk in the Caribbean near the straits," shouted BlackHeart.

"How did you manage that?" shouted Villeroy.

"Read this report," shouted BlackHeart. "It's all in there!" BlackHeart motioned for Curly to send the tube containing the report across to the British ship. Curly fired the crossbow, and the bolt sailed through the air to the main deck of the *Triumph*, hitting the sidewall of the forecastle, near where the men stood.

"There's one minor detail," continued BlackHeart. "Shark Scar did not go down with his ship. Somehow, he persuaded Chum Lee not to kill him and is now aboard the *Red Dragon*. He's made an alliance with the emissary. Shark Scar and the *Dragon*'s crew have kidnapped my cabin boy, Jon, who is the grandson of Mr. Sinclair, here," BlackHeart said, motioning toward Alistair. "They're holding Jon hostage aboard the *Red Dragon* and are to meet us in Port Royal, to trade young Jon for my map to some sunken riches."

Villeroy burst into laughter. "How *do* you get yourself into these embarrassing situations, BlackHeart?"

"I need time to work out a plan to get the boy back alive," BlackHeart said, ignoring Villeroy's question and his disturbing laughter. "Can you provide us safe sailing to Port Royal?"

"Affirmative. We'll help clean up your mess," Villeroy said, still laughing heartily. "Take your leave, BlackHeart. After we take care of the sloops, I'll bring the other frigate captain aboard with me to hear your plan. God save King William!"

"God save the king!" replied BlackHeart, and the British ship turned back to face the oncoming sloop.

I understand it all now, thought Alistair. *BlackHeart's alliance with the British captain, the military way he runs a pirate ship. BlackHeart is a privateer working for England!* Loud gunfire from the cannon of the British frigate, *Triumph*, sounded in the background.

Alistair knew that privateers were often men who were commissioned to work undercover for a country to rid it of its enemies. Sometimes those enemies were other warring countries. More often, the enemies were individuals or groups of individuals, such as pirates who raided their merchant vessels, wreaking havoc on their economy.

Privateers were paid well by their government for taking the risks necessary to bring the criminals to justice, or taking justice to the criminals. They were similar to bounty hunters and some were very wealthy, even noblemen who had bought the commission.

As they sailed toward Port Royal, Alistair's thoughts returned to Jon. He could not shake off the dark thought that was haunting him:

Can we rescue Jon and get out of Port Royal before the earthquake of 1692 occurs?

CHAPTER 53

THE PAST REVEALED

Off in the distance, the *Triumph* and her sister British ship returned the barrage of cannon fire coming from the second Chinese sloop as Alistair and BlackHeart sat in the captain's cabin, discussing a plan for Jon's rescue.

"How long have you been a privateer?" Alistair asked him bluntly.

"From the beginning, since my arrival here in the Caribbean," replied BlackHeart. "I came here with British Letters of Marque signed by our monarch, William III of England. The letters are legal commands for the arrest or otherwise demise of several men. Sleg and Shark Scar are among a long list of such men. Most on the list are now dead or have been turned over to British authorities for trial and execution at the gallows."

BlackHeart related that he had recently sent a new list to King William, asking for British Letters of Marque that would enable BlackHeart to go after this new group. Some of the men were privateers who had turned pirate.

Three of the men on the list were in the Crown's employ: traitors. He had not received a reply from the king. "The band of men are led by someone here in the Caribbean, someone in authority, someone very smart—someone able to get information from within the British command posts. I've been working on a plan to flush him out," BlackHeart said.

"Why did you take on such a dangerous job? Was it for wealth?" asked Alistair.

BlackHeart explained that he and his twin brother, George, had been born into British wealth. A few years ago, his father had died, leaving them both titled noblemen and sole heirs to his great fortune.

"Sometimes, having all the necessities of life can get boring. George was happy taking care of the family's business affairs, and they were happy with him doing it. So, I bought a commission in the British Navy and commanded a ship for five years. When I became bored with that, I came here, thinking to do something useful for my country—and maybe, just for the fun of it!" He grinned broadly. "I'm really quite good at this pirating, you know."

"I have no doubt of it," said Alistair with a chuckle.

"But now, Sinclair, if we are to get Jon back alive, it is of utmost importance that we execute my plan to the letter."

BlackHeart made marks on the map of Port Royal, all near the docks. Alistair looked at the map and was seized with panic. The areas marked were those that would drop into the sea immediately when the earthquake occurred.

"There's something crucial I must tell you that will change these rescue plans," Alistair blurted out. BlackHeart's eyes lifted abruptly from the map on his desk and stared directly into Alistair's eyes, waiting.

"A massive earthquake will occur in Port Royal the morning of June 7, dropping more than half the city into the sea. Over four thousand people will die in the rubble or be washed out to sea," Alistair said flatly.

If Alistair had dropped a bomb on the desk, it could not have brought a stronger reaction from BlackHeart, who jumped to his feet, shoving everything from his desk, howling in anger.

"What? Preposterous! It's not possible!" BlackHeart shouted.

"It is possible and *it will* happen!" Alistair shouted back. "It's written in the history books of the twenty-first century. The maps reveal it. You've got to believe me!"

BlackHeart flopped back into his chair, his mind rapidly examining all the details. After doing so, he no longer doubted what he had just heard. Sinclair would *not* lie to him with so much at stake. "Why didn't you tell me before?"

"Because it would have made no difference; Jon was already kidnapped and aboard the *Red Dragon*, headed for Port Royal. I was afraid that if you knew about the earthquake, you might avoid Port Royal and I would never see my grandson alive again," Alistair revealed quietly.

"What?" shouted BlackHeart, again enraged. "You think me such a coward as to shirk away from rescuing a young boy from the clutches of those blood-thirsty blackguards?"

"I only know that I will do whatever is necessary to protect Jon and Kathryn," Alistair replied.

BlackHeart paced back and forth in front of the back windows of his cabin, as was his habit when he was frustrated. "Before Kathryn came aboard, it had been my plan to send Jon to England to stay with my family and complete his schooling. You see, I have no children.

"Then, knowing that Jon had a grandmother," BlackHeart continued, "my second plan was to sail to New Providence and put them both on a boat headed for Charleston in the colonies. I was going to send a letter with my seal to friends who maintain my secret residence there. I own other assets there, as well. Jon and Kathryn could have lived there in safety. I'm not able to go to the colonies at the present time because many there think me a dangerous criminal; I'd be arrested on sight."

Alistair knew that BlackHeart had formed a father-like bond with Jon. And, true enough, BlackHeart was just about Jon's father's age.

BlackHeart began to shuffle his hand among the papers and things he had shoved from his desk in anger. He picked up a small piece of paper, which looked like a calendar. Quickly running his finger across the calendar, he stopped at June 4, 1692.

"Only *three* days left," BlackHeart said solemnly. "The *Dragon* should dock in Port Royal the night of June 6, but most probably the morning of June 7. I need to know more, Sinclair!" BlackHeart was gathering his emotions back under control. "Where's the *Carousel*?"

"In the hills of Tortuga," Alistair replied.

"Can you move the *Carousel* from Tortuga to Port Royal?"

"I'm not sure," Alistair answered as he pondered the thought.

When he had built the new Transformer, Alistair had added newer microchips, but he didn't think that its signal would be powerful enough to reach from Port Royal to Tortuga. He traced his finger along the map to the spot where he had first arrived in Tortuga, the place he left the *Carousel* enshrouded.

"Small hills on the edge of Tortuga," BlackHeart interjected. "Is that where the *Carousel* is?"

"Yes. It's possible that I could reconstruct my Transformer using some of the parts from the original one that Kathryn has. If I could get a more powerful signal," Alistair said, pausing as he thought, "then, from the highest point in these hills ..." He pointed to a spot on the map between Port Royal and Fort Rupert. "Yes, it just might work! This area of Port Royal would also be safe from the earthquake."

"All right! Things are coming together. Now, to work out a few minor details," BlackHeart said. "We can't risk Jon's safety in a sea battle. We have no choice but to take this battle ashore, in Port Royal."

"The *Triumph* arrives," Alistair said, pointing to the approaching frigate.

"It serves us no purpose to reveal the details of our plan to Captain Villeroy. I'm not sure I can trust him, and I don't know the other captain," BlackHeart continued, remembering how Villeroy had found amusement in Jon's capture. "I'll tell him only what's necessary to gain his assistance at sea. He'll escort the *Red Dragon* into Port Royal Harbor and depart, leaving Jon's rescue to us."

As the *Triumph* pulled alongside the *Black Opal*, BlackHeart asked, "What time will the catastrophe occur on Sunday?"

"The earthquake occurs at 11:45 a.m. on June 7, 1692," Alistair said grimly.

CHAPTER 54

THE PLAN

With his part of the plan worked out, Captain Villeroy and the other British captain returned to their frigates, which turned back to await the approach of the *Red Dragon*. They had agreed to escort the ship into Port Royal Harbor.

According to BlackHeart's plan, when the two frigates intercepted the *Red Dragon*, Captain Villeroy would offer the services of the British Crown to the emissary, calling him a notable dignitary. They would provide him with a *royal escort* into Port Royal Harbor, thus ensuring that the *Red Dragon* would arrive at the right place at the appointed time, with Jon onboard.

"In his predictable arrogance, the emissary will delight in such a display of servitude toward him," BlackHeart told the Sinclairs as they sat in his cabin, watching the departure of the frigates.

The agreed time that the *Red Dragon* was to be escorted into Port Royal Harbor would be as soon as possible after sunrise on the morning of June 7.

"The greedy, pompous emissary will not risk having the map to the riches be given to anyone other than himself," BlackHeart told them. "I know he will not play according to plan. He will send Chum Lee and his henchmen ahead to take care of us. When he thinks everything is safe, he will arrive with Jon. We're going to have to turn the plan to our advantage."

BlackHeart told the Sinclairs he would send a letter with his seal to the emissary by longboat as soon as the *Red Dragon* drops anchor. "I'll insist that Jon be brought ashore with the emissary; otherwise, there will be no deal. We'll meet them on this pier." He pointed to a spot on the map that was farther east, but close to the docks

Alistair then told BlackHeart of the sixty-foot tidal wave that would follow the earthquake, washing over the island, wreaking even more devastation and drowning thousands. BlackHeart threw up his hands in frustration.

"You do love to withhold these *minor details* and feed them to me one morsel at a time, don't you, Sinclair?" BlackHeart gritted. "Are you saving some other catastrophe for my dessert?"

"Unfortunately, yes," Alistair said. "All the ships in the harbor will be sunk or severely damaged. So, I suggest that you dock the *Black Opal* farther east in the bay near Fort Rupert, where historical accounts stated that the damage to ships anchored there was slight."

"Any other minor details you'd like to add?" BlackHeart asked, his greenish-black eyes looking up threateningly from the map on his desk.

"No. I think your plan is a good one," Alistair said hesitantly. "However, we will have to execute your timeline exactly in order to get out of Port Royal before the earthquake occurs. There will be no trembling or shaking of the earth. No warning! Once the water starts to seep up into the streets, we will have less than two minutes to be out of the city before Port Royal abruptly sinks into the sea."

CHAPTER 55

CATASTROPHE

Port Royal: June 7, 1692

A listair had reconstructed the Transformer using parts from both the old one and the new. He had carried his trunks of gold into the small hills on the east side of Port Royal, near the road that led to Fort Rupert. The new Transformer had worked, thus transporting the *Carousel* from Tortuga to Port Royal. He had put his gold-filled trunks aboard the *Carousel*, which now sat waiting in the hills, invisible. In the meantime, BlackHeart had reported on events to the Fort Rupert British commander, a man he knew from years of experience that he could trust.

It was 9:00 a.m. when the *Black Opal's* longboat returned to shore. Spider had delivered BlackHeart's letter to the emissary aboard the *Red Dragon*. The late arrival of the Chinese junk was pressing unfavorably on BlackHeart's precise plan for Jon's rescue.

BlackHeart, Alistair, and Kathryn took turns watching through the spyglass from atop a building on the eastern edge of Port Royal as the Chinese loaded two longboats with men, Chum Lee, Shark Scar, the emissary ... and Jon. The boats proceeded to the docks at the center of the city with Jon in the emissary's boat, as BlackHeart's letter had instructed.

"The timing will be tight because of the *Dragon's* late arrival, but if we keep to the plan, you should be out of here well before the earthquake," BlackHeart told Alistair. "I'm sure the emissary wouldn't come ashore with only those men in the longboats for protection. There must be others here. I haven't seen the two Chinese sloops that were escorting the *Red Dragon*."

"From the hills a while ago, I saw the two frigates sail east through the bay and anchor near the *Black Opal* at Fort Rupert; no sloops, though," Alistair reported.

"They didn't arrive yesterday; my men kept vigil around the island," BlackHeart said pensively. "According to Chinese custom, the escorts would have travelled with the emissary to a safe distance of the port before departing. But mark my words: they're here today—somewhere."

"You all know the plan," he said to Skull and approximately fifteen crewmen assembled near him. "Let's go!"

The sun shone brightly and the city was quiet— only a few vendors dotted the streets. BlackHeart and Skull led approximately fifteen men through the city's plaza where two stone soldiers mounted on horseback stood proudly at the entrance of the Building of Justice. BlackHeart had sent Kathryn, with six men for protection, to a safe area beyond the long narrow stretch of land that connected Port Royal to the mainland, not far from Fort Rupert.

Curly and a small band of men were stationed in the outer perimeter, near the road to Fort Rupert. Guidry and a few crewmen took up their posts on the east end of the town as Spider and the remaining crewmen headed into the city, a short distance behind BlackHeart.

The plan was in action.

A short time later, BlackHeart and his men rounded the corner of a narrow street and were met by several Chinese men in black. Instantly, the warriors assumed a crouched attack position, knives drawn. BlackHeart and his men immediately drew their swords.

Suddenly, from a darkened doorway nearby, out stepped a man in a red Chinese silk coat: Shark Scar!

"Did ye think ye had seen the last o' Shark Scar, BlackHeart, ye miserable dog?" Shark Scar snarled loudly. One of Shark Scar's men stepped out from behind him and shouted a command in Mandarin. The Chinese warriors stopped their advancement but continued to crouch tensely, ready to attack.

Shark Scar ranted on, spewing his hate and venom. "I made a deal with the Chinese when they boarded me ship. My crewman here, Schlink, who speaks Mandarin, made them recognize me as the true pirate I am," he boasted with his head held high. "After Schlink told Chum Lee that I could take him to *your* Inca treasures, BlackHeart, we was taken aboard the *Red Dragon* and treated with the respect we deserve. The rest of me grubby crew went down with me ship, me beloved *Shark*!

"Argh! Oh, how I miss me beautiful *Shark*," sobbed Shark Scar, covering his eyes momentarily in grief. Quickly recovering, he pointed a shaky finger at

BlackHeart and shouted arrogantly, "But now I'll have a better ship. I'll be taking the *Black Opal* from ye, you hog swill! You won't need it where you're going!"

"Where's Jon?" BlackHeart shouted angrily, ignoring Shark Scar's remarks.

"Now, now, BlackHeart," Shark Scar scolded. "We was having a nice quiet conversation. *Don't spoil it!*"

"Where's the boy?" BlackHeart gritted out. He pulled his dagger from his boot with his left hand. Holding his sword in his right hand, he slowly began moving forward, his men inching along with him.

"Did ye think I'd follow *your* demands ye put in the letter you sent to the emissary?" mocked Shark Scar. "Or the orders of the emissary, what thinks I'm following *his* plan? Nobody but nobody tells ole Shark Scar how things be done! I do the tellin', don't you see. Now, if ye be kind enough to give me the map to the sunken galleon jewels, please. Don't hold out, BlackHeart! The emissary told me you're holding a map to the jewels for him. I know you have it; give it to me. Now!"

"He's gone mad!" BlackHeart whispered under his breath. "If he's double-crossing the emissary, we'll play along with him." BlackHeart handed over the fake sunken treasure map he had drawn on the ship. Shark Scar grinned; then, his expression darkened.

"And, you, ye blackguard," Shark Scar continued. "I know ye be keeping the Inca treasures hidden at ole Purdy's in your storage keep by the docks. So, be handing over the key to it, as well."

BlackHeart pulled a key from his pocket and handed it over, just as Spider and his men quietly rounded the corner behind Shark Scar and the warriors. Shark Scar grabbed the key and ran. Spider's men engaged the Chinese from the rear as BlackHeart's men advanced upon them from the front.

A shrill evil cackle of a laugh echoed through the streets as Shark Scar and Schlink fled toward the docks.

The skirmish between the men raged for a few minutes but was soon over, leaving some fifteen or twenty bleeding and moaning black-clad figures littering the street. Two of BlackHeart's men were injured, but not severely. All his men circled round BlackHeart, who said, "These obviously were not their elite forces. Forget about Shark Scar and the map; it's not important. Shark Scar wouldn't be this brave if the emissary was close by. The emissary—and Jon, for that matter—is not here. They're back at the city plaza as my letter instructed. We'll backtrack to the city square, which will force them to bring Jon to us there. Spider, go and get Alistair. Bring him and the rest of our men to the Building of Justice in the square. We'll make our stand there as originally planned. Hurry! Time is short!"

As BlackHeart and his men made their way back to the city square, a heavy pounding sound could be heard off in the distance.

They stopped between the two stone horse-mounted soldiers in front of the Building of Justice. BlackHeart's eyes quickly made a sweep of the tops of the buildings and alleys. "Where are they?" he cried out in frustration.

"Right here!" yelled a man in captain's uniform who stepped out from behind a building, followed by the emissary and Chum Lee—holding Jon.

"Villeroy!" BlackHeart's voice echoed against the buildings. Several Chinese warriors stepped out behind the emissary and Villeroy.

"The map!" said the emissary in Mandarin, holding out his hand. Alistair immediately interpreted.

BlackHeart answered, "Not before you hand over the boy."

The emissary said something in Mandarin, and Chum Lee moved forward with Jon. Villeroy lunged, making a grab for Jon, and yanked him from Chum Lee's grasp, putting his knife to Jon's throat. BlackHeart gasped and started to move forward, but withheld himself for fear that any sudden movement might cause the nervous Villeroy to act.

Alistair, Spider, and crewmen came running into the square and stopped dead in their tracks when they saw Jon being held with a knife to his throat.

"Surprised, BlackHeart?" Villeroy asked sarcastically. Not waiting for an answer, he continued, his grip tightening around Jon's middle as the squirming boy howled out in agony. "I've fought against repulsive pirates here for the last six years, all for the Crown. I get only a pittance of what you make, BlackHeart, and I work just as hard—even harder!"

"I suspected you might be the leader of the traitors, Villeroy. Your attitude and indifference to the crimes of the pirates gave you away," BlackHeart answered. "But I can't understand why. You're a captain, moving up the ranks of the king's navy."

"Hah! When I expressed my desire to become a privateer, they laughed in my face," Villeroy continued. "Said those cushy jobs were reserved for the nobles, men like you, BlackHeart. The rich just get richer!"

As he became more agitated, Villeroy was unconsciously easing his grip on Jon. "You think I want to retire on a captain's meager pay, or even an admiral's, with all the gold and riches that pass through the Caribbean? It's lying out there," he gestured toward the sea, "just waiting for those who'll dare to take it. Well, *take it I shall!*" Villeroy said, laughing coarsely.

"Working for the emissary," he continued, "I'm piling up instant wealth just for giving him information and helping a little now and again, like today. Do you hear me, BlackHeart?"

Off in the distance behind them, a bell was chiming from a bell tower, signaling the end of morning prayer services.

"It must be eleven thirty!" shouted Alistair anxiously.

Villeroy started to tighten his grip on Jon, and Jon reacted with a fierce backward kick of his heel, connecting with Villeroy's groin. As Villeroy screamed and bent forward, Jon shoved his elbow sharply into Villeroy's stomach, breaking free of him. Jon ran to Alistair as the Chinese warriors leapt into action against BlackHeart and his men.

Spider thrust his long arm forward in a visual command, and several of his men moved swiftly forward to form a shield around Alistair, who was holding Jon.

"Degollar!" The Spanish battle cry, meaning "to slit their throat," arose from Spider's men as they joined the battle in the square. Skull, wearing a red Jolly Roger tied over his bald head, and his elite fighters jumped straight into the Chinese warriors. True to the phrase "no quarter given," they cut a swath through the very middle of them. The cries and moans of men at war and the clash of metal against metal echoed against the buildings as BlackHeart and his men beat back the warriors, exposing the dreaded Chum Lee to his enemy.

BlackHeart sprang at Chum Lee, engaging him in a fierce battle of swords as first one and then the other took command. Chum Lee was shorter than BlackHeart, but that did not lessen his abilities to be a formidable opponent. His chunky build concealed a powerhouse of well-toned muscles which he unleashed against his opponent. BlackHeart, on the other hand, was no less powerful. His tall, slim body enabled his movement to be as graceful as it was agile. The sword he wielded appeared weightless in his masterful hand—right or left, it seemed to make no difference. The shrill clanging and screeching of their powerful weapons could be heard as the two men matched skill and strength to gain the upper hand. Suddenly, the advantage was struck by Chum Lee as he fiercely flung BlackHeart's sword aside and lunged at him. BlackHeart twirled, thus dodging his intended blow. He jumped onto the base of one of the horsemen statues; and as the ground beneath them began to tremble, BlackHeart pulled his knife from his boot. Chum Lee swung his sword in a wide arc designed to slice through BlackHeart's ankles. BlackHeart jumped high into the air, somersaulting backward to the ground. The slight quake had detached the statue's stone head which then plummeted to the ground beside BlackHeart, knocking him flat on his back in the street. Chum Lee swung around, raising his sword high for a final assault on BlackHeart. He was stopped with his sword-wielding arm stretched in midair as the headless stone statue suddenly unseated itself and toppled forward, crushing Chum Lee under the front hooves of the massive stone soldier's horse.

As BlackHeart jumped to his feet, he realized that the back of his clothes were drenched with water from the street where he had fallen. He looked down and saw a glimmer of light glowing from his black opal ring and heard the faint tinkling of tiny bells.

Chinese warriors began to pour into the square from the west as the pounding sounds from the north, the east, and the south grew louder. Moments later, their source became evident: British red coats appeared from streets all around the square. They marched into the plaza, their feet pounding the dry brick that quickly became puddles of splashing water as they joined the fray with the Chinese warriors.

Villeroy dropped to his knees in front of BlackHeart, crying and begging for mercy. BlackHeart grabbed him up by his hair, holding his flintlock to Villeroy's back, while Skull grabbed hold of the emissary.

"The whole world hates a traitor, Villeroy, especially a sniveling one," BlackHeart gritted out as he shoved Villeroy into the arms of two of his men.

"Look!" shouted Alistair, pointing to the puddles of water beginning to seep into the streets all around the square.

BlackHeart grabbed the emissary from Skull. "This one deserves to go with his men," BlackHeart said and shoved the emissary toward his warriors, who were flee-ing toward the docks with the red coats in hot pursuit. The emissary joined his men, water splashing on both sides of his heavy robe as he ran toward the docks … and into the path of the earthquake.

"Go, Sinclair! Go!" shouted BlackHeart. "We'll take this traitor and go to Fort Rupert, where you told me it would be safe. Run, men! Run!"

Without knowing why they must run, all the crew-men obeyed their captain, who was only steps behind Alistair and Jon.

When they reached Kathryn, Alistair grabbed her arm with his left hand and Jon's arm with his right. They started up the steep hill where the *Carousel* was hidden, invisible to all. BlackHeart and his men continued run-ning up the road that led to Fort Rupert, built high atop the hill overlooking the Caribbean Sea.

Alistair paused on the hill, pulled out the Transformer, and input some codes. The small bright light zipped through the sky, stopping abruptly, suspended above them. He entered command codes, and fine blue smoke crept from the light as the *Carousel* became visible. The ship lowered slowly to the ground nearby, spreading its blue mist around the Sinclairs' feet.

From the hill where they stood, Jon looked down across the city. He watched as the west end of Port Royal, where the main docks, taverns, and storage areas were located, abruptly sank into the sea. It was followed by toppling stone and wooden buildings of the city's entire west end, extending eastward and beyond the heart of the city. Over half the city sank right before his eyes. The high waves produced by the sinking of the land caused boats and ships that had been anchored in the bay to come careening into the city, smashing into stone buildings that remained standing. Ship masts, sails, hulls, anchors, small boats, and all manner of ship debris were deposited atop those buildings that remained standing. The whole of the port's bay now lay atop what remained of the city of Port Royal.

Jon could hear the horrible screaming and moaning of the people who were trapped in the city by smashed building and ship debris. He could hear the cries of those floating in the bay or being pushed out into the sea, some injured, with nothing to grab on to. Those fatal cries and the crashing, thundering sounds of a thriving city turning to instant rubble were being forever etched into his memory. He covered his ears to shut out the sounds, but he couldn't shut out the echo of the people's cries, or what he had seen.

As high waves were forced into the bay, a piece of the bow from the demolished Chinese junk bearing the golden dragon's head came crashing ashore down below the cliff where Jon stood. There atop the head of the great dragon was Shark Scar, his long black hair pasted in strings across his grotesquely disfigured face. He was laying face up, dead! One horn of the giant golden dragon had gored him precisely through his middle, just as he had predicted it could.

Jon's daze was broken by Alistair's shouts. "Look!" he exclaimed, pointing out to sea. The sixty-foot tidal wave Alistair had read about was coming straight at Port Royal. Jon had never seen anything like the monstrous wall of water coming at them. The wave extended as far as he could see in either direction. Riding in the curl of that gigantic wave, near the top, were the two Chinese sloops with red sails. Jon watched as one of the ships reached the top of the sixty-foot wave and teetered there a moment before it came crashing down to sea-level— right on top of the other sloop with red sails.

"Quick! Into the *Carousel*!" shouted Alistair. Kathryn ran up the ramp, but Jon just stood there, captivated by the high wall of water coming, coming ... *coming!*

Alistair grabbed Jon, shoving him up the ramp and into the *Carousel*. Then he ran to the computer console, frantically pressing buttons, pulling levers, entering codes, not waiting for indicators to respond or check points to be verified.

The *Carousel* began to vibrate forcefully. Water began to seep in around the doors in the cabin as the *Carousel* rapidly disappeared.

Epilogue

London, Summer, 2010 AD

They had escaped the tidal wave in Port Royal by mere nanoseconds. Immediately upon his return, Alistair had removed the gold from his trunks and sold it back to the gold dealers. Thanks to Captain BlackHeart, he had been able to pay back every last penny he had borrowed from the banks.

Kathryn had always wanted to see the capital cities of the Baltic Sea, and Alistair had arranged for three cruise tickets to take them there. He had also planned for three sightseeing days in London just prior to their cruise. They had visited many sites, including the British Museum, where they now stood.

"I want to see this one next," said Jon, pointing to an artifact in the booklet Kathryn was holding. It was entitled simply "Aztec Eagle Warrior," with no other information. Alistair pointed out the direction, and they wove their way through the crowds of the museum.

When they reached the exhibit, Jon stared through the glass showcase at the fifteen-inch gold statue, the same one he had held in the cave at Devil's Rock. The statue was that of a warrior wearing what looked like an eagle suit, with its sharp eagle talons poking out around the warrior's knees, and the warrior's face showing through the eagle's open beak. The artifact description card read "Benefactor Unknown"—the same inscription that appeared under the bejeweled crown with Queen Anne's name in emeralds, and under others. But Jon knew the identity of the benefactor. He smiled.

Leaving the museum, Alistair suggested that they have lunch down at the port in Dover, where they would board their cruise ship.

Their cruise ship was docked among the many ships in the port. Alistair tapped Jon on the shoulder and, saying nothing, he pointed in a different direction.

There, anchored at the end of a very long pier, was a tall, black ship with two masts. The ship had white sails that were tied high at the yards.

"It looks just like the *Black Opal*. Can we get a closer look? It's not far down to that pier," Jon said excitedly. Alistair nodded, and Jon was off in a run toward the dock. A sign on the pier stopped him dead in his tracks. Alistair and Kathryn caught up behind him while he read the sign.

Special Bayside Sailing Tours:
Heirloom Historic Ship, Black Opal
For tickets, call:
Colin Black
Tele: 777-5000

"Oh, Pappy, could we go?" asked Jon. Alistair didn't answer, so Jon turned around to see him smiling and holding up three tour tickets.

"I already have tickets," Alistair said. "I bought them from the concierge at the hotel yesterday after seeing an advertising leaflet left in our room by the cleaning staff. We'll have just enough time to sail on the *Black Opal* before we board our cruise ship."

They were greeted aboard the *Black Opal* by the ship's crew, who were dressed in pirate costumes, including guns and cutlasses. A cheer came up from the passengers as the anchor was raised and the ship pulled away from the pier.

The main deck of the *Black Opal* appeared unchanged. Tourists milled about, looking at the cannon on the top decks and the sailing crew climbing high in the yards and dropping the sails. A few tourists went below, where a pirate crewman said there was a galley with food and frozen drinks.

Jon had walked the ship, stem to stern, and was now standing at the railing with the wind blowing through his hair. The salt air tasted good and brought back memories—lots of memories.

He walked up the steps to the quarterdeck and into the captain's cabin, with Alistair and Kathryn following behind. The cabin looked the same, except that a large picture had been added. It was a life-sized painting of Captain BlackHeart in his tricorn hat, wearing his black captain's coat with the gold buttons and his white linen shirt, tied at the neck. He was fully armed, just as Jon remembered. Perched on his shoulder was Pyrate, his red and blue parrot. The inscription under the picture read "Captain Lord Emery Hart Black, known as BlackHeart."

The Sinclairs didn't hear the young man enter the room.

"It's a good likeness, I am told," the man said.

Jon recognized that voice! *Captain BlackHeart!* he thought and whirled around, only to see a young man dressed in a captain's costume just like that of BlackHeart's. He resembled BlackHeart quite remarkably, except that his hair was blond and, of course, he was quite younger.

"You look a lot like Captain BlackHeart. Are you related?" Alistair asked.

"Yes. He was me great uncle from many generations back," the young British man said in a mock pirate's brogue. "Me name's Colin Hart Wentworth Black, but ye may call me Colin!" he offered and bowed in a formal fashion. "And what be your name, lad?"

"Jonathan Alistair Weston Sinclair," Jon returned the bow with a big sweep of his hand and a giggle. "And you, kind sir, may call *me*, Jon!"

The smile abruptly faded from Colin Black's face and he turned toward the door of the cabin. "Enjoy your tour," he called out as he walked across the quarterdeck and down the stairs.

"Abrupt manners," remarked Alistair with a chuckle.

It was an enjoyable tour. The mock pirate crew had hoisted the sails and even dropped the wide sails for a short time, letting them billow out and catch the wind. Even the Jolly Roger flew for a time.

When the tour was finished, Colin Black stood at the exit, handing out leaflets and talking in his pirate's brogue to all the departing passengers. The Sinclairs were the last to leave. Jon stepped up, stretched out his hand to Colin, and they shook hands. Colin removed a letter from his pocket.

"This document was left with the inheritance trust documents of Captain BlackHeart years ago and passed down to me, since I am the current owner of the *Black Opal*. I don't know how he could have known that you would be here during this era of time, but he did, and said as much in other documents. He left explicit instructions regarding this document. I think it is addressed to you, Jon," Colin said as he handed a much-yellowed, antique parchment to Jon.

Jon took the document. The name *Jonathan Alistair Weston Sinclair* was inscribed on the outside of the letter. The letter bore a black wax seal with the letter **B** encircled by a heart.

"The captain's seal," Jon said as he broke the seal. The brittle black wax fell in small pieces to the deck as he unfolded the parchment and began to read aloud.

Hello, Jon—

If you are reading this letter, Jon, I know you are aboard the Black Opal, *for I am leaving this letter as part of my last will and testament to be passed on to the prevailing owner of the ship,* Black Opal.

I have left some of my personal possessions as my legacy to you, Jon. They are kept in the place where I keep all my things of utmost secrecy. The secret compartment is known only to you and me, Jon. I hereby bequeath everything hidden there to you, Jonathan Alistair Weston Sinclair. I have left instructions for you there!

With kindest regards, I remain,
Yours Respectfully,
Captain Lord Emery Hart Black,
Captain BlackHeart

Jon looked up excitedly.

"I don't know how you've done it, but you have seen BlackHeart, haven't you?" asked Colin. Jon did not reply. "According to journals left by the family, when BlackHeart came home the last time in 1696, he made several short trips to Scandinavian countries, Sweden in particular. His solicitor, or lawyer as we call them today, noted that he spent weeks preparing all his legal documents: his will, trusts, bequeaths, etc., including a perpetual care trust for the *Black Opal*. In 1697, he vanished and was never seen again. Certain of his clothes and personal items were missing, and though his family and friends sought to find him, all were unsuccessful," Colin continued.

Jon looked at Kathryn, then at Alistair, and then to Colin, almost pleadingly.

"Where is the secret compartment, Jon? I will take you there," Colin said.

"The captain's cabin," said Jon, and they all headed toward the stairs leading to the quarterdeck.

Once there, Jon retrieved the screwing instrument from the false compartment in the back of the desk and opened the doors to the wall cabinet. He fully expected to see the crystal wine goblets, but instead, the goblets had been replaced with books of all kinds.

Jon hastily pushed all the books off the shelf, revealing only the back panel of the cabinet shelf, with its four wooden pegs. He took his Swiss army knife from his pocket and twisted out the small hinged knife. Using it, he gently removed the four pegs from the corners, revealing the heart-shaped steel screws with the backward letter B. He used the screwing device to remove the screws, and then he removed the back panel.

Inside the secret compartment were several long, yellowed scrolls, and a single small gold box. Lying next to the box was the captain's letter seal and a stick of melted black wax. Jon pulled out the gold box and opened it.

"The captain's black opal ring!" exclaimed Jon as he turned it in his fingers, looking into the brilliant depths of the magnificent stone, with its aqua, pink, red, and turquoise colors. Finally he put it on his forefinger. The ring fit him perfectly.

Next Jon pulled out the long yellowed scrolls of maps, charts, and documents. Kathryn and Colin helped him spread the maps on the captain's desk, reading over first one and then another, with Alistair making historical comments and Colin pointing out sea markings and inscriptions. The charts were antique-looking sea maps with all kinds of depth markings, compass headings, arrows, and island markings. One much-browned map had frayed edges, and Colin commented that it appeared to be ancient; it was obviously only a part of a sea map. There were other similar map parts, but of different colors than this one. Other maps appeared to be the layouts of three separate islands, with definite geographical markings for cities, mountains, and volcanoes.

Then Jon opened the last document: the small scroll containing BlackHeart's seal. He read the document aloud:

Dear Jon,

    Always wear my ring, for it will protect you during all your sea voyages and near all forms of dangerous water.

    And now, I must ask a favor. For the last three years, I have been studying Captain Brighton's journals on his travels and find it imperative that I complete his journey. Certain truths lie there that I am convinced will benefit mankind.

    You once told me about the twenty-first-century diving

    equipment. If I had the concealed air vessel you spoke of, we would be able to dive deep enough to reach the Pinnacle. *According to Brighton's last memoirs, the answers to the dilemma now facing your grandfather, as well as other things of great value, lie hidden there. It is imperative that Alistair come with you.*

    I shall arrive in Crete on May 30, 1699 AD, and I shall expect to see you there. Bring only those people you can trust with your life, for it will be a perilous journey to the greatest treasure on earth!

    Come to me in the Carousel, *Jon. Bring the maps and charts from my hiding place, and bring the diving vessel. Travel with me to ... Atlantis!*

        Respectfully,
        Captain BlackHeart

Jon looked up at Alistair excitedly with a grand smile on his face.

"Now, Jon!" Alistair said, holding up his hand and shaking his head *no*. "First, we're going on that cruise we promised Grammy. "Then ... well ... harrumph ... perhaps we'll discuss it."

"A cruise first—*a minor detail!*" said Colin, his green eyes sparkling with excitement. "Go! Take the cruise. When you come back ... Atlantis!

Alistair pondered the thought momentarily, and Jon's eyes brightened hopefully as he realized that Pappy might be relenting.

Alistair's hesitance was not lost on Colin. Seizing the opportunity, he shouted, "Yes!" and gave Jon the high-five as if it were now a certainty. "I want to go," he said eagerly. "I have a master's degree in archeology. There will be encryptions to decipher. I have studied ancient encryptions in Cairo, Greece, and Paris!"

Alistair looked at Colin skeptically.

"You must take me! Now I know the secret; the *Carousel* is a time-travel vessel, isn't it?" Alistair didn't reply. "Don't worry. Your secret is safe with me," Colin said as he looked from one Sinclair to the other, his gaze stopping on Jon. "Don't you see? It's meant to be. You need me, and you know you can trust me. I'm BlackHeart's ancestor, his family!" Colin almost shouted. "Take me with you! *I know you can!*"

Author

Biography

S ally Copus has been writing stories her entire life.
The former CEO of a large direct marketing firm,
Copus resides in a house built in the 1850s, perched atop
a precipice overlooking the majestic Missouri River, in
historic Lexington, Missouri. Her books are targeted to
children pre-teen to mid-teen, with a captivated audi-
ence that includes her four grandchildren. *BlackHeart's
Legacy* is the first in her *The Odyssey of Jon Sinclair* series.
The second novel in this collection takes her protagonist,
Jon Sinclair, to the Lost City of Atlantis.